REVEL

Also by Maurissa Guibord

WARPED

_c. v_

REVEL

MAURISSA GUIBORD

DELACORTE PRESS

Text copyright © 2012 by Maurissa Guibord
Jacket art copyright © 2012 by Barbara Cole

Delacorte Press is a registered trademark and the colophon is a trademark of Random House, Inc.

Visit us on the Web! randomhouse.com/teens

Educators and librarians, for a variety of teaching tools, visit us at RHTeachersLibrarians.com

Library of Congress Cataloging-in-Publication Data
Guibord, Maurissa.
Revel / Maurissa Guibord. — 1st ed.
p. cm.
Summary: "Looking for her grandmother, seventeen-year-old Delia goes to an isolated island in Maine and discovers a frightening and supernatural world where ancient Greek symbols adorn the buildings and secret ceremonies take place on the beach at night"—Provided by publisher.
ISBN 978-0-385-74187-3 (hc) — ISBN 978-0-375-98734-2 (ebook)
[1. Supernatural—Fiction. 2. Mythology, Greek—Fiction.
3. Islands—Fiction. 4. Maine—Fiction.] I. Title.
PZ7.G938334Re 2013
[Fic]—dc23
2012008028

The text of this book is set in 12-point Granjon.
Book design by Trish Parcell

Printed in the United States of America

10 9 8 7 6 5 4 3 2 1

First Edition

This book is dedicated with love
to my mom and dad,
Rudolph and Emelie Gionet

Man marks the earth with ruin—his control
Stops with the shore.
—LORD BYRON

CHAPTER 1

Maybe I should have known from the beginning to stay away from Trespass Island. The signs were all there, as clear as flashing neon. Like *Don't Eat at Joe's—I Got Salmonella*. I guess I was just too blind to see them.

I stood at the counter of the Portland Ferry Company to get my ticket, pulling my short-sleeved hoodie close against the gusts of cool ocean air that blew through every time the doors swung.

"You can't get there from here," the ticket clerk said. His Maine accent broke *there* in two. *They-ya.*

I blinked, then smiled. "What? Oh. Ha. Good one." I definitely wasn't at my best. I'd just ridden by bus for two days from Garden City, Kansas; I'd slept sitting upright last night next to the Pavarotti of snorers and was seriously undercaffeinated. And I obviously didn't get New England humor.

But the ticket clerk just scowled at me, leaned forward, and fired his words through the circular hole in his window like spitty missiles. "I *said,* you can't *get* there from here."

He actually wasn't joking.

I held up a finger, rummaged in my backpack and took out an old book. *Mysteries of the New England Coast* fell open to a faded map in the center. I slid the book under the ticket window.

"See? This is where I want to go." I pointed to a small blob on the map, squishing down the book a little because the blob was almost hidden in the crack of the spine. "That's Trespass Island, right? Doesn't one of the ferries go there?"

"Nope," the ticket agent said. "Ferry for Saylor Island goes *past* there." He poked a finger on the map. "Doesn't stop at Trespass. That's a private island. Residents only. Hey, watch it."

I'd twisted the book a little, accidentally nudging his Portland Sea Dogs mug, and a spout of coffee splattered his shirt.

"Oh my gosh. I am *so* sorry. Here, take this." I pushed a wad of napkins under the window.

The ticket agent waved away my help and wiped coffee from his name tag, which said *I'm Richard,* meanwhile muttering something under his breath about tourists.

"But people live there," I said. "How do the residents get back and forth?"

The ticket agent eyed me, then shrugged. "Most folks who

live on an island have their own boat. 'Less they're real good swimmers." He snorted.

"Ha ha, right." That was so—not funny again. My laugh sounded distracted, bordering on panicky. "So how do *I* get out there? There must be a mail boat or a water taxi. Something."

The man's smile faded. As if he'd expected me to be miles away by this time, pestering someone else. When I didn't budge from the counter, he said with a touch of impatience, "Folks on Trespass are real private. They don't want tourists poking around. Or treasure hunters." He gave a disparaging jerk of his chin toward the book.

"Oh, I'm not a tourist," I said quickly. "I have family on the island."

Family. That word felt strange. My grandmother was the only family I had left, and I'd never even met her.

"Oh yeah?" The guy looked me up and down. "Your family know you're coming?"

"Well, no, not exactly."

"Huh." The ticket agent chewed on the problem, looking bored. "Guess you're out of luck. Best let 'em know you're here. Make arrangements that way."

He looked past me and seemed disappointed to find that nobody else was in line.

"Okay. Thanks." I took the book, picked up my small suitcase and turned away. There must be a way. I'd find one. After coming all this way, I couldn't go back.

"Wait a minute," the ticket agent called. "You say you've got family out there on Trespass?"

When I looked back, he fidgeted, as if trying to decide something. "I *might* be able to find someone to take you," he said at last, rubbing the bristles on his jaw. "Old fella that comes out for the mail will be coming by. But it's against the rules. And expensive." He licked his lips. "Say . . . three hundred dollars?"

"Three hundred dollars?" It was a crazy amount for a simple boat ride. On the other hand, I had the money. And no other options. Not at the moment, anyway.

I dug into the pocket of my jeans and pulled out a small plastic change purse. The thing was kind of embarrassing, with its gaudy polka dots, but it was secure, and small enough to tuck in a pocket. "I don't have that much in cash. But—" I flipped open the clasp and extracted a misshapen coin. I'd taken five from the safe-deposit box at the First National to fund this trip. There were three left. "I have this." I tapped one of the coins on the counter and slid it forward.

"It's a Spanish gold piece," I told him. He slipped a hand over the coin. "Two escudos or something. It's worth about three hundred and fifty dollars. You can look it up online."

"So it's true," he whispered. He rubbed the coin between two thick fingers.

"What's true?"

"Nothing," he said, pocketing the coin.

"Okay," I said with a shrug. "Can I get a ride?"

"Wait outside." His gaze fixed on the gleaming coin like his eyeballs were magnetized. "Dock seven."

Rolling my small suitcase behind me, I went from the dimness of the ferry terminal into the bright sunshine. Outside, the sounds of clanging bells, horn blasts and screeching gulls filled Portland's harbor. I sat down on a bench and wrinkled my nose. I'd never been this close to the ocean before. Wasn't the sea supposed to smell fresh and tangy? This just . . . smelled. The fishy odor of the dock felt cloying and thick, almost as if the salty air were trying to seep into my skin. A damp, cool breeze blew in from the water and, as if to defy the warm June temperatures, made me shiver.

This was nothing like Kansas. I'd left bright green fields bursting with crops and the smells of warmth and grass and sunshine. Here the vast gray-blue ocean looked cold and bleak. I felt lost already.

At Dock 6 the *Island Mermaid* was boarding. I watched as cars lined up on the lower deck and foot passengers jostled in a ragged line up the ramp. A rowdy group of little kids all wearing red T-shirts emblazoned with *Camp Sunshine* were the last to board, herded by teen counselors.

The campers pounded up the steps to the upper deck of the ferry and immediately rushed to the railing, giggling and poking each other. One curly-haired boy slung himself halfway over the top, seeming to teeter as he pointed down at something in the water. He bounced back down and I let out the breath I hadn't realized I'd been holding. I watched them.

Interesting. Not one of them looked as though they were contemplating a dreadful, watery death. They probably hadn't even seen *Titanic*. I had. Seven times.

With the blare of a horn that made me jump, the *Island Mermaid* pulled away from the dock, leaving a long white trail of churning water.

Just don't think about it. It's not a big deal. It's perfectly safe.

I swiped a coil of hair from my eyes and looked up at a colorful map painted on the wall of the building. Dotted lines crisscrossed the blue expanse of Casco Bay, showing the paths of ferries between the coastal Maine islands. Pushing my glasses up on my nose, I peered at it. There was nothing on the spot where Trespass Island should have been. It was missing.

And there was something else: the few dotted lines that went through that area of the ocean where Trespass *should have been* curved in wide arcs around the spot. Almost as if the ferries went out of their way to avoid it.

Weird.

———

I shifted on the hard bench. The ferry had become a distant white spot on the water. Suddenly it was gone, seeming to vanish in an instant.

A long time ago I bet someone stood on the shore and watched someone they loved sail away. That was the person who came up with the idea of the earth being flat. Because that's exactly what it looked like to me, as if the boat just fell off the edge of the world.

Maybe I should give up and go back to Kansas. Then I wouldn't even have to get near a boat, never mind *in* one.

Water wasn't exactly my element. I could make do just fine with fire, air and earth. Not that I was terrified of it or anything. That had been Mom's thing; she wouldn't go near open water. In fact, I could swim reasonably well. As long as the pool was heated, I had a sturdy flotation device, and I could stand up every few feet.

No, I decided. This was too important. I picked up my backpack and clutched it close to my chest. A measly little thing like the Atlantic wasn't going to keep me from what I'd started to do. I stared out across the water. The islands in view from the dock had names like Peaks, Little Diamond and Cushing and must be only short ferry rides from Portland. Judging by that old map, Trespass Island was much farther away.

And once I got there—what then? If the past few months had taught me anything, it was that I needed to change if I wanted to make a new life here. To fit in, to be more . . . unobtrusive, that was the word for it.

I'd been with three different foster families in the six months since my mother died. The last time I'd seen Mrs. Russell, my caseworker from Social Services, she'd seemed to imply that this was somehow *my* fault.

"Delia, I'm here to help you," Mrs. Russell began, folding her plump hands on top of her desk blotter.

From her careful tone and patient smile, I knew it wasn't going to go well.

"Why didn't you call me to discuss the situation with Linda Derosier?"

"I told you. Linda was smoking. In the car. With a baby in the backseat."

"So you called Child Protective Services." Mrs. Russell frowned and checked her notes. "From a Mobil station."

"Are you saying I should have ignored it?"

Mrs. Russell took a deep breath that looked like part of some Eastern meditative exercise. "No. Not at all. I'm saying you could have handled it differently. You could have talked to me, for instance." She frowned, reading my file. "Oh, you've got asthma, don't you?"

"That's *not* why I called," I said in a low voice. "I can open a window. A baby can't."

Mrs. Russell closed the folder and rubbed her temple. She must have had another of her headaches. I had that effect on her. "Linda says she doesn't think she can handle you. You're a kind-hearted person, Delia, and it's good to be outspoken." She paused. "To a degree. But she doesn't think you're a good fit."

Not a good fit. It was a phrase I'd heard before, and it

made me feel like a pair of grungy hand-me-down shoes. The thing is, nobody ever tells you how to *be* a good fit. They just tell you when you're not one. I clasped my hands tight in my lap and smiled. "That's okay with me. I can take care of myself. There's the money Mom left. I could get a job and—"

"Delia," Mrs. Russell said. "The fact is, until you turn eighteen, the State of Kansas is responsible for your safety."

"But not from secondhand smoke, apparently."

Mrs. Russell pressed her lips together in a very thin smile that said *I don't get paid enough for this.* "I'll need to make some calls to find another placement for you. It may not be local. But we'll do our best to try to keep you in your current school until the end of the year. It's a shame," she added, "that there isn't some family member you could go to."

"Actually," I'd told her, "there is."

———

The hard seat of the bench was getting uncomfortable, and I shifted position.

While I was stuck here, I decided to call Mrs. Russell. Weekly check-ins were part of the conditions for me being allowed to come to the island for the summer.

I got her voice mail and left a message, telling Mrs. Russell that I'd arrived in Portland safe and sound and was on my way to my grandmother's house.

"Excuse me, miss? You was asking about Trespass. That right?"

Startled, I looked up. A figure stood a few feet away, outlined against bright sun. I lifted a hand to shade my eyes and an elderly man came into focus. His upper back was bent into a stoop, and suspenders held up work pants over his concave chest. Beneath a faded Boston Red Sox cap, the man's face was old. The kind of old when wrinkles get so deep they begin to look like actual features—sideways mouths or squinted extra eyes.

"Uh, yes." I straightened up. "Trespass Island. That's where I'm going."

"What's that? Speak up, girlie."

"Yes," I said, and nodded for emphasis.

"Huh," grunted the old man. "Pretty young to be traveling all by yourself, ain't you?"

I glanced down at my jeans and my purple Converse All Stars. And my Snoopy and Woodstock tee, which probably made me look more like twelve than seventeen. "I'm older than I look."

"Me too." He grinned at me, wrinkles making accordion pleats on his face.

Honestly, I didn't see how *that* was possible.

"Beggin' pardon, but I was told you've got family on Trespass." He took off his cap, revealing bristly white hair on a spotted scalp. "Who are your people?"

He watched me expectantly, his baseball cap folded between his hands. *My people?* The expression seemed sort of old-fashioned. And sweet.

"My grandmother lives there. Marianne McGovern."

"Who?"

"Marianne McGovern!" I shouted.

"Pipe down!" snapped the old man, waving his knobby sticklike arms. "Want the whole Eastern Seaboard to know your beeswax?"

I glanced around the nearly empty dock. There didn't seem to be anyone nearby who'd have a consuming interest in my beeswax, but I shook my head.

The old man tottered closer, peering at me. "Then you're Helen McGovern's girl? Course I should have known it. Just look at you. You're the spittin' image of your ma. Like a little china doll." He stuck out a hand. "The name's Ben Deare. Pleased to meet you, miss."

"Delia." I smiled and shook his hand. *China doll.* I knew he meant it as a compliment, but the expression always bothered me. As if I had little rosy circles painted on my cheeks and those creepy, flip-open eyes. And maybe bloomers. But I *did* look a lot like my mom: petite build, blue eyes and blond hair that curled up like crazy in the damp.

My grip on the backpack tightened. "My mom died a few months ago."

The old man's shoulders slumped and he put a withered hand out and rested it on my shoulder. "I'm sorry. Real sorry, miss."

So many people had said that to me that a quiet thank-you and change of topic had become smooth automatic responses; I didn't really like people feeling sorry for me. It just reminded me of everything all over again. But something in Ben Deare's face was different. My throat didn't have that raw, closed-off feeling.

"You knew my mom?"

"Know her? Pshaw. When she was seven, I taught Helen McGovern how to tie a gill net so fine you could catch a fog in it. Taught her how to whistle too," he said, grinning wide and gap-toothed.

His blue eyes narrowed on me appraisingly. "So. You want to go to Trespass."

"I wanted to take a ferry but they said there wasn't one."

Ben Deare's head bobbed. "That's right. None of 'em can take you. It ain't allowed."

"But I paid that man," I argued.

He shook his head. "He should have known better, the fool. Nope. You can't go to Trespass." But his blue eyes gleamed beneath scraggly eyebrows and flicked back and forth over my features. As if memorizing the details of my face, to recall later.

"You live there, don't you?" I asked. "Why can't you take me?"

When he didn't answer, I cranked up the volume. "I *said,* why can't you—"

"There ain't no use in shouting at me!" he hollered. He

cast his eyes down, then fixed his cap firmly on his head. "Miss Delia, I'm awful sorry but you can't go there."

"Look," I said, taking a deep breath. "Mr. Deare. I'm going to get out there and see my grandmother. " As I spoke, a desperate, stupid idea occurred to me, and I added, "I'll buy my own boat if I have to and sail there." I was so close; I wasn't going to let rules or politeness keep me back now. Of course, I had no idea how to sail a boat or how much a boat cost, or even the slightest desire to get *into* a boat. But he didn't know that.

"It's a free country," I said, raising my chin. Mrs. Cronus, my eighth-grade civics teacher, would have been proud of my basic grasp of the Constitution. "I can go where I want."

"Well, that ain't *exactly* true. Nope, not exactly."

"Which part?"

"Ayuh." The old man peered at me and let out a wheezy chuckle. "But I do like your gumption. Sound just like your mother too. You just don't know what you're asking." He looked out at the water for a long moment, his flinty blue eyes roving back and forth. Trying to judge the weather, maybe, though the sky looked perfectly clear to me.

"You've a right to go and see your people, I suppose," he said grudgingly. He reached into a sagging pocket. "But it's not you or me that'll have to decide. Here."

His gnarled hand placed what looked like five white sticks into my palm.

"Throw the knuckles."

"Excuse me?"

"When an important decision's to be made, I strew them fingers," he said with a solemn nod.

Fingers? With horror I realized what I thought were sticks were actually pieces of bone with irregular, yellowed surfaces and knobby ends.

"Gah!" My hand shook and the bones dropped to the ground, clattering and bouncing before coming to a stop. The old man crouched to inspect them.

After a second he slapped a knee. "Clear enough," he said. He scooped them up and returned them to a pocket, then straightened. Or as near to straight as he was able. "I'll take you to Trespass. And you can call me Ben."

With that he whirled off and strode down the dock, leaving me to grab my belongings and scramble after him. I caught words here and there as he muttered to himself:

"Miss Delia McGovern, harrumph. Spittin' image. Buy a boat. Harrumph . . . Devil to pay . . . the hands."

I couldn't make any sense of it. And the resemblance to one of Popeye's monologues was kind of scary.

We passed boat after boat tied to the dock: from fishing boats stacked with lobster traps to tall-masted sailboats whose glossy cabins were studded with electronic equipment and antennas. At the very end of the dock, the old man stopped. I stared down a rusty metal incline and felt my stomach contract. A dilapidated wooden sailboat floated below. Barely. Rope, plastic buckets and fishing poles littered the floor of the boat. Peeling paint nearly obscured the name on the side: *Belores.* A frayed piece of rope was fastened to a barnacle-encrusted timber of the dock. The boat looked like a mangy dog left on the curb, tugging at its leash.

"We're going in that?" I said, staring. "Isn't it kind of . . . small?" He would probably take it as an insult if I used some of the other words that came immediately to mind: *filthy, leaky, death trap,* etc.

"Got to be small to get through the Hands," replied Ben. He'd already hopped nimbly into the boat. When I didn't nimbly follow, he said, "The reef around Trespass. We call it the Hundred Hands." He squinted up. "You ain't one of them queasy types, are you?"

"No. No, of course not. This is great."

I inched down the wobbling ramp, the small suitcase bumping behind me, stepped in, teetered for a second and plopped down heavily. The orange life vest Ben handed me smelled musty, but I slipped it on and tied each of the three straps tight.

"Don't you need one?" I asked.

"Nah. I just keep that one in case the Coast Guard wants to make a stink about their rules. Couldn't drown if I wanted to."

I must have given him an odd look. "I was born with a caul," he explained as he fired a battered black motor to life. "A birth membrane over my head. It's a good omen for a sailor—I'll never die in the sea."

The smell of gasoline fumes and salt air filled my nose, and a puddle of water sloshed over my feet as we chugged out of the harbor. I held myself rigidly in the middle of the boat's hard bench seat. I clutched my backpack on my lap with one hand and held tightly to the side with the other. The inside of the wooden rail had been scratched and carved with pairs of letters.

"What are all the letters for?" I asked.

The old man gave me a wry smile. "The initials of all my old sailing mates from years past. Just an old man's fancy."

This was crazy. I'd just hopped into a boat that looked about as seaworthy as a bobbing coffin. With a complete stranger who carried old finger bones in his pocket and doodled on his boat.

But for some reason I wasn't afraid of Ben Deare. There was something comforting about the odd little man. He moved like a little brown spider, handling the ropes and wheels and cranks of the boat as if they were extensions of his own limbs. "What did you see in those bones, anyway?" I asked him.

"Portents. Things in your future."

"What things?"

He looked me in the eye from beneath his scraggly brows. "A monster," he said solemnly.

He was teasing me. Or maybe this was some kind of weird fortune-telling act he performed for tourists. "Really?" I said with a smile. "Only one?"

He frowned, seeming to consider the question carefully. "No," he answered at last.

I'd had about enough of this. "Okay, right. How long will it take to get there?" I asked in a small, tight voice.

"Never know," he answered with a shrug. My face must have shown my confusion, because he added, "I mean . . . maybe an hour." He reached up and resettled his cap. "Maybe less if the winds favor us."

As I stared down at the water racing alongside the boat, an hour seemed like a long time. The churning noise of the motor sounded like a noisy washing machine, and the air whipped my curly hair every which way. I closed my eyes and tried to get used to the swaying, dipping movement. I *was* the queasy type. Definitely.

Shouldn't have been a surprise, I guess. I'd never been out in a boat before.

"Open your eyes, miss," said Ben as he pulled a rope taut. "Look where you're going. It'll pass."

The old man shut off the motor. Now the only sounds were the slap of wind against the huge canvas sails overhead and the splash of water. The air had changed; it had turned cooler and had lost the fishy smell of the harbor—the scent was clean and fresh.

I tried to follow Ben's advice and kept my eyes trained on the edge of water that blended with blue sky ahead. After a while my stomach felt better.

"How many people live on Trespass?" I asked.

"Oh, 'bout twelve hundred folks live there. Give or take," he answered.

I spoke up to ask Ben a few more questions, but the old man didn't seem to hear me. Or maybe he just wasn't interested in talking; he was completely focused on the task of sailing, his eyes scanning the horizon. That was fine. The less talk, the fewer questions he could ask me. As the *Belores* sailed I felt myself relax. Fatigue crept up and made my head droop, cushioned by the bulky life preserver.

"Almost there. May get a bit rough here." Ben's voice jolted me awake.

I opened my eyes and let out a gasp of surprise.

White fog surrounded us.

"What's happening? Are we lost?"

"*Pshaw.* Lost," answered Ben with derision. He leaned forward and his grizzled features popped into view. "There's always a bit of fog here."

A bit of fog? Dense mist swirled around my face in thick swaths, cool and wet as fingers stroking my cheek. I shivered.

Ben Deare reached down and rapped his knuckles against the bottom of the boat.

As soon as he did this, the fog parted. It was as if a giant hand had reached down and pulled aside a white curtain. The *Belores* floated into blue skies and sunlight.

Blinking against the glare of sun, I held a hand up to shade my eyes and gulped in a breath. Ahead loomed the shape of an island. Gray rock topped with a fringe of evergreen. The silhouette was a craggy face emerging from the water.

The crashing noise of surf became louder as water lapped up the side of the small boat. The *Belores* lurched up and over waves. On impulse I leaned over the side and looked down at the water's rippling surface. Tentatively I dipped my hand in. The cold was a shock against my skin, but it felt good. Like icy silk, rippling through my fingers.

Beneath the water something cold and slick touched me.

It grabbed my hand.

I screamed and yanked back as a long black form streaked beneath the surface. The boat rocked hard and I toppled, hitting my shoulder against the opposite side.

"Wh-what *was* that?" I screeched, scrambling to right myself.

"Keep your hands out of the water," Ben called, his voice gruff.

He was leaning over the front. I heard him mutter indistinct words and he tossed a handful of what looked like dried leaves overboard that scattered and sank beneath the surface.

"There's something under the boat! Something grabbed me!"

Ben didn't turn, only shook his head. "Just seaweed, miss. We're past the reef now. Just got your hand tangled in it as we passed over. Best to just sit still, here in the middle."

"Right. No problem," I whispered, wiping my cold, wet

hand on my jeans. I was too shaken to take my eyes from the water. I wanted out of this boat. Out of this ocean. I was totally ready to admit this had been a mistake, probably my biggest to date. But it was too late to turn back now; we were approaching Trespass Island.

CHAPTER 2

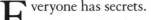

Everyone has secrets.

My whole life my mother had never told me where she was born, or anything about my family. It was as if we had emerged together, she and I, from some shadowy past, without a connection to anything. The only things I knew were that she'd left home at sixteen when she was pregnant with me and that afterward she and my grandmother had never spoken again. She'd told me my grandmother was a reclusive, "eccentric" woman who wanted nothing to do with us. And neither did my father. In fact, I only knew my grandmother's name because it was the one I'd been given for my middle name; I was Delia Marianne McGovern.

It may seem strange, but I never really resented this secret or wondered very much about it. I liked my school and my friends. Even my part-time job was fun; I got riding time in exchange for helping out at Chamberlain Stables, cleaning stalls and brushing horses. Plenty of other people had single parents. It was no big deal.

I guess I was just happy.

But then my mother got sick, and one night the secret slipped away from her.

Mom had breast cancer and it had spread. Metastases, the doctor called them. She showed me the CAT scan of my mother's brain where the tissue had been riddled with what looked like pale white bullets.

She'd been at home at the end, in her own bed, which was just as she wanted it. So exhausted and in pain that when she'd finally allowed the hospice nurse to apply a morphine patch, she'd sunk into a deep sleep for nearly thirty-six hours. When it seemed like her body had come to some semblance of rest, she'd begun to talk. She'd whispered, giggled and rambled. Sometimes she seemed to hear my voice and sometimes she didn't. It was like she was in a world of her own.

———

"I want to go back," Mom whispered, her eyes staring up at nothing.

The hospice nurse had just finished getting her settled into bed and had gone for the night. "To the recliner?" I asked. She didn't respond. "Janice just left," I told her. "But I can help you if you want." I pulled back the satin-edged blanket and put my hand beneath her to lift her upright. The soft flannel nightgown hung on her tiny frame, and I could feel the jut of her shoulder blades and ribs beneath the fabric. It felt like I held a ghost.

"No," she moaned, pulling away from me with surprising strength. Her eyes were closed and the pool of light from her bedside lamp highlighted violet shadows under her eyes and hollows beneath her cheekbones. "The compass spins from north to south."

"What?"

Her eyes opened very wide; their blue irises looked pale and watery. "I want to go home," she whispered. Her voice was so plaintive she sounded like a little girl. "To Trespass."

She wasn't making any sense. "Tell me where you want to go," I urged.

"No." She closed her eyes and drew her arms tight around her chest. "Don't let them take the baby."

Those were the last words I heard her say.

Mom died in December. It may sound strange to say this, but I think she had a good death. She wasn't in pain and she wasn't alone. But she was still gone. For a while I forgot all about her words. Grief made me slow and lazy. I hardly wanted to bathe, never mind go to school, learn stuff and make decisions about my life.

But later her words came back to me, haunted me, in a way. I had to find out what they meant.

As I stepped onto the dock of Trespass Island, my legs wobbled, searching for gravity. I was so focused on keeping my balance as I scrambled out of the boat that I hardly looked around. When I did straighten, I let out a little gasp.

It was so . . . pretty. We stood on a long wooden pier that wrapped an L-shaped arm around a group of six or seven boats in a little inlet. Steps wound up a steep slope from the dock. Above, green canopies of pine trees sheltered a row of small clapboard houses facing the sea. Their window boxes spilled over with bright scarlet and yellow flowers that fluttered in the breeze.

I turned to look at where we'd come from. Past the calm of Trespass Island's harbor, it was just blue water as far as I could see. I squinted. There was a break in the smooth surface out there: an irregular ridge of small waves looked like it circled the whole island. What was it Ben Deare had called the reef? Oh yeah. The Hundred Hands.

Remembering the black thing beneath the boat, I suppressed a shudder. Seaweed? Yeah, right. Seaweed didn't *swim*. Ben Deare probably just didn't want to scare me. Maybe there were sharks out there.

"The village is just up the hill there," said Ben. "But best if you stay here on the dock for now. First I've got to deliver this." He held up a small cardboard box labeled with Priority Mail stickers and the words *Fragile—Medical Supplies*.

"Won't take but a minute. And then we'll see what's to be done with you. Stay here."

The wiry old man made his way up the flight of railroad-tie steps and disappeared.

What's to be done with me? I would be glad when people realized *I* should be the one to decide what was to be done with me.

High overhead a single seagull wheeled, making a lonely, harsh cry of *"Scree-scree."* There didn't seem to be anyone else around, and I paced the dock, my steps creaking on the worn gray planks. I stopped and listened. Weird noises came from under the dock as water sloshed against the supports.

There was a symbol burned into the wood on one of the timbers. It looked like a pitchfork. There were others too; swirling designs that I didn't recognize marked every upright post of the dock. There was that strange sound again, from beneath me.

I walked to the edge and peered down. Strands of seaweed undulated in water so clear I could see the rocks and sand at the bottom as if through a green glass lens. Tiny fish no bigger than my pinkie darted in and out of the shadows. Something made a gurgling sound beneath my feet and I could hear, very faintly, the sound of dripping.

Drip, drip, drip.

The oddest notion came over me: that something had just climbed out of the water and was under the dock. Waiting and listening.

I backed away from the edge and bent, trying to peer through the dark spaces between the planks. A spurt of water suddenly shot up through one of the gaps, accompanied by a hissing noise.

I bolted up, grabbed my things and ran.

I was out of breath by the time I got to the top of the hill. My chest was tight and the familiar dry cough began. *Stupid asthma*. If I was going to run for any length of time, I had to use the inhaler beforehand. That's what I did for gym. Unfortunately, getting scared out of my wits didn't lend itself to taking proper preventive measures. Fumbling, I got out my inhaler and took two quick puffs. There was probably a perfectly normal explanation for the eerie noises beneath the dock. I just couldn't think of one. So I tried to forget that peculiar hissing noise and the feeling that something had been peering up at me from the dark. As the ache in my lungs eased, I looked around.

Where the steps leading up from the dock stopped, it was only a few yards to a small, gravel-covered parking lot with a few dusty trucks and golf carts. Past this was the downtown area of Trespass, if that was what I should call it. A single paved road meandered away from the parking lot, lined on either side with small houses and shops with old-fashioned-looking glass-fronted displays. There was a hardware store, a coffee shop and a place called Flo's Wave-n-Curl. At the corner closest to me, a sign read TRESPASS CHAMBER OF COM-MERCE WELCOMES YOU. A traffic sign on the other side of that warned SPEED LIMIT 20 MPH.

This wasn't what I'd expected at all. Somehow the words *private island* made me think of luxurious homes and mani-cured lawns, people drinking martinis on their speedboats. This was more like a quaint, run-down fishing village. Sun bleached and sea washed, it smelled of balsam and something sweet I couldn't pinpoint. The largest building I could see was on the corner, close to the parking area. It was a faded blue metal structure with a painted wooden sign that read GUNN'S LOBSTER COMPANY—SINCE 1898. That sign was painted with squiggly symbols and pitchforks, just like the dock. It was like some kind of weird graffiti.

I sat down on a wooden bench and propped my suitcase next to me. The lower half was soaked; it would probably smell like really bad sushi when it dried out. Thankfully, my backpack was dry. I opened it to check the contents and zipped it closed again.

I twisted on the bench and saw a small group gathered across the street. Six or seven people stood looking at me si-lently. One of them, a woman in a flowered apron, turned and whispered to a man beside her.

Okay. They were watching me like I was an animal es-caped from a zoo. Maybe not a particularly dangerous one, but unapproachable. A deranged porcupine or something.

The thought was so strange I had the sudden urge to laugh. But the humor of it wore off as they kept watching me. It was

27

as if they were waiting for something to happen, and as the seconds passed it became more and more uncomfortable.

The door of the coffee shop swung open and a girl and a guy came across the parking lot.

They looked roughly my own age. The girl had shiny waves of espresso-brown hair and tanned legs beneath frayed denim shorts. She carried her willowy form very straight and reminded me of something exotic—an Egyptian statue, maybe. The boy beside her looked more ordinary, a freckled redhead with a tall, skinny frame.

"Hi," I said.

The girl stopped a few feet away. She was tall, with striking features: high, wide cheekbones, a strongly angled jaw and a cleft in her chin. Her wide-set green eyes, heavily outlined and lashed, flicked over me. She bent and picked up a rock.

"This is private land," she said in a low, quiet voice. "You'll have to leave."

"I'm . . . visiting someone," I said uncertainly. "I'm Delia." I pushed up my glasses on my nose and dragged a lock of hair behind my ear. "McGovern," I finished in a dry whisper. The girl made no response, just fingered the rock in her hand as if trying to decide whether she should add it to some collection at home or fling it at my head. Suddenly I thought I'd rather be back in the leaky boat.

Neither of them spoke. Apparently they'd come to join the community stare and simply wanted a closer view.

"Who are *you?*" I said impatiently.

The girl frowned. "I'm Zuzu. There was no announcement about you."

"Announcement?"

"Usually we're told ahead of time if there's going to be a newcomer. So we can prepare."

"Zuzu, come off it, you're scaring her," said the gangly guy beside her, and smiled at me. Most of his face was nose, and what wasn't nose was freckles and bright coppery brown eyes. "I'm Reilly."

"Well, it's true," said the girl, frowning at him. To me she added, "We don't get a whole lot of visitors. Well . . . any. It's not allowed."

It's not allowed. That was what Ben Deare had said too. I wished he hadn't taken off like that; I suddenly felt like I needed backup here.

"What the heck is going on here?"

My head snapped around at the voice.

A woman approached with long, striding steps, kicking up gravel from the parking lot. She was tall with big shoulders and a low, heavy bosom that stressed the buttons of her sleeveless blouse. Gray hair fastened in a loose braid hung down over one shoulder. The look on her face as she caught sight of me became one of . . . I wasn't quite sure what. Horror? Disbelief?

The woman stopped short. "Who are you? What are you doing here?" she said, staring at me.

Believe it or not, I recognized her instantly. Oh, not her face; the woman had dark eyebrows that contrasted with her stark gray hair, and square, raw-boned features. It was a stranger's face. But that was my mother's *voice*. A little ragged-sounding, maybe, but the rise and fall of it was familiar and unmistakable.

I was suddenly sure that this was my grandmother.

"Are you Marianne McGovern?" I said tentatively, and smiled. "I'm Delia. Helen's daughter." But I could tell she'd recognized the resemblance already.

The woman made no movement to come closer. "Holy Mary," she whispered. She stared at me like I'd just been pulled out of a magician's hat. "How did you *get* here?"

Okay, not exactly what I'd imagined. I walked forward, closing the gap between us by a few feet, and held my arms up. When she didn't move, I let them drop.

My grandmother didn't smile. Her breath came in short puffs through her open mouth, as if she'd been running. Some of the other people headed our way, and soon I faced a rough half circle of curious faces standing behind my grandmother. The women wore mostly plain skirts and blouses under aprons or flannel work shirts. The men, dressed in T-shirts and overalls, had stern features and weather-beaten skin, as if they worked hard in the elements. This included a tall young man with sun-streaked blond hair at the back of the group. I only noticed him because he stood a full head taller than any of the others.

A chubby, red-cheeked man at the front eyed me and asked my grandmother, "Well now, who's this, Maisie?"

Maisie? My grandmother hardly looked like a Maisie to me.

A red flush tinged my grandmother's cheeks. "No one," she answered deliberately. Her hard wintry-gray eyes shot back to me.

"Ben! You stupid old fool," she hissed to Ben Deare, who'd appeared in the crowd and eased his way through. The old man's Red Sox cap was off again, this time twisted between his hands.

"What have you done, bringing that girl here?" she asked, jerking her chin in my direction.

That girl? "I asked him to bring me," I said, my voice shaky. I felt like a bug pinned beneath a magnifying lens. It didn't help that my grandmother was so imposing. She must have been almost six feet tall and had hefty upper arms. Not saggy old-lady arms either, but solid-looking and freckled.

I lowered my voice so the others couldn't hear. "I wanted to come and see you. I thought if I came maybe you would talk to me and tell me . . ." My voice died away as I waited for my grandmother to come closer, to smile. To *say* something.

But she didn't do any of those things.

The stupid smile was still stuck on my face, like something embarrassing that had dried there. "I've come a long way," I whispered.

Marianne McGovern wasn't looking at me. And wasn't

listening. She just stared at the ground and shook her head. No. No. No. As if trying to block out my voice.

Now I understood. This woman wasn't just shy or eccentric or "set in her ways," as my mother had hinted. She didn't want a granddaughter. Or at least, not me. I glanced around at the irregular semicircle of strangers. They were all looking at me.

A burning fullness began behind my eyes but I blinked hard to stop it.

No one was going to see me cry today.

"You can't come around here," Marianne McGovern said. She raised her head and looked around. "She's not staying. It was a mistake," she announced clearly, as if making a public service announcement.

She's embarrassed. The thought struck like a blow inside my chest. Marianne McGovern was worried about what her neighbors thought. What kind of godforsaken, ass-backward place *was* this?

I shifted my backpack on my shoulders. "I came here to—"

"You have to leave. Go back now," she said harshly.

Okay. It was becoming obvious what the truth was. This old woman hadn't been able to stand the fact that her daughter got knocked up at sixteen. She'd thrown her out like so much trash.

"You listen to me," I said. Louder now. I didn't really give a damn if everyone on the stupid island heard. And given the size of the place, *that* was entirely possible. "When my mother left here, she was—"

"A willful, selfish little brat," said Marianne McGovern in a loud voice that overtook mine. "Just like *you* are, I s'pose." She seemed to have gotten control of her breathing but smoothed down the fabric of her denim skirt in a nervous motion with red, chapped hands.

"That's not true!" I cried. "She was wonderful. And a good mother. Something you obviously don't know crap about."

There was a disapproving murmur from someone in the back of the crowd.

And so much for unobtrusive.

But my grandmother's voice was deathly quiet. "Was?" she whispered.

"My mother died about six months ago," I said quietly. I'd wondered if my mother had ever had any contact, contact that she'd kept secret from me. I guess she hadn't. From the devastated look on her face, I knew my grandmother had known nothing about her daughter's death.

"Helen." My grandmother's mouth twisted and it looked like she whispered something under her breath. But when she spoke again, her voice was a quiet monotone. "You have to go now, child. You don't belong here."

Even after the other stuff she'd said, the coldness of those words took me by surprise. And hurt.

"Fine," I said at last. "Mr. Deare will take me back. Don't worry. You'll never see me again."

Next to me Ben cleared his throat noisily. "Sorry, miss. We're not going out again today." He pointed out to the harbor. "Not in that."

Out over the water a heavy mist had gathered. As I stared, it rolled toward the island, spreading over the boats and the pier like a blanket of gauzy wool. The sun, piercingly bright a moment ago, was blocked out, leaving only a pale fuzzy disc behind the fog.

"She'll have to at least stay the night," Ben said.

My grandmother heaved a sigh. Her shoulders dropped as if she were defeated by fatigue, or a burden too heavy to carry anymore.

"Girl's a newcomer. We should let the mayor know," said a man near the back holding a fishing pole. There were several nods of agreement.

"No need," said my grandmother with a sharp glance around the gathered locals. "She's leaving. Ben, I'll expect you to take her back to Portland first thing in the morning."

"All right, Maisie," said Ben.

"Come on, then," my grandmother said, waving a hand.

"Hold on there." One of the island men spoke, a burly sunburned guy with his thumbs in the pockets of his jeans. He scuffed his feet. "Maybe we *should* see what the mayor has to say about this."

"That's right. Those are the rules," said the girl named Zuzu. She still wore that composed, faintly curious expression as she watched me. And she was still holding that rock.

"No. It's time to get inside." It was the tall guy at the back, the one who'd been so stern and silent up until now. "The mist is rising," he said, jerking a nod. "You know the rules.

Everybody back to your own house," he said. He gave me only a glancing look. "Let's go. Miz McGovern will take care of her own business."

My grandmother almost imperceptibly relaxed the set of her shoulders, and gave him a nod. "That's right, Sean."

Despite his youth the tall guy seemed to carry some weight of authority, because people started to disperse, still casting curious glances my way.

I looked around. Ben had disappeared too. I felt bad; the old man had only tried to help me, and I didn't want him to be in trouble over it. But it was beginning to get dark, and my grandmother crunched across the parking lot, giving me no choice but to follow.

Wordlessly she grabbed my soggy suitcase, headed over to one of the golf carts and flung it into the back as easily as if it had been a bag of knitting. I crawled into the little vehicle and sat, holding myself stiffly away from her. From the corner of my eye, I watched her hands, big on the tiny steering wheel. There was dirt under her fingernails and her hands were rough, with prominent reddened knuckles. I could hardly believe this woman had given birth to my mother. Mom had been delicate and beautiful. And kind. And thoughtful.

The apple had fallen pretty far from the tree, I thought. *Like in a different orchard. On a different planet.*

"I don't have to stay with you, you know," I said as the golf cart chugged up the street. "I'm sure I could find some-place else."

My grandmother's eyes never left the road. "Don't be foolish. Of course you'll stay with me."

It wasn't an invitation. There was no way to lend it any graciousness. Every syllable this woman uttered, every look she gave me, said I was nothing more than a burden to be tolerated.

We rode in silence up the main road past the little storefronts. The sandy terrain disappeared. Green grass and bushes with pink flowers overtook the roadside. My grandmother kept a sneakered foot hammered to the pedal, making the golf cart whine.

She kept glancing to either side of the narrow road. I followed her gaze into the densely shadowed trees. All I saw were lengthening shadows between the pines and that strange, thick mist that covered everything. We turned off onto a dirt road and then again, onto a packed track in the grass. The golf cart rolled to a stop.

A small yellow house with white shutters stood before me, hemmed in by tall bushes of lilac. I could hear the surf somewhere nearby, and the air smelled tangy with salt. A big hanging basket next to the front door held red geraniums and trailing ivy. An old-fashioned globe-style lamp glowed in the window, making a cozy, welcoming beacon against the gloom of the mist. But there was a general look of disrepair about the house; the wraparound porch sagged and there was a broken window on the second floor. The whole thing needed a paint job.

I wished I could say something cool or snide. Something that showed her I didn't care. But I couldn't.

I loved it.

I just stood looking at the house for a moment, then ran my hand along the railing as I walked up the steps with my bag. I wanted to save all of this in my mind, to remember everything later.

My grandmother only watched me silently, her expression grim, then threw open the front door and stood back to allow me to walk in. She came in behind me and heaved the door shut, leaning against it for a moment with her heavy upper body. Then she whirled around, her big hands reaching out. I flinched as my grandmother stumbled forward and grabbed me. With a hoarse sound somewhere between a laugh and a sob, she pulled me close and hugged me.

"My precious girl," she murmured. She covered the top of my head with kisses and my cheeks with kisses, over and over, and stroked my hair, all the while squeezing me so tight I became breathless. After a time she loosened her grip. She smoothed back my mussed hair and cupped my face gently in her hands. Her gray eyes looked watery and red. She gently pushed my skewed glasses back into place.

"I am so sorry," she whispered.

CHAPTER 3

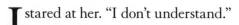

I stared at her. "I don't understand."

My grandmother gave me the ghost of a smile. "Nope. You don't. You can't. Sweetie, you never should have come. But it's a joy for me to see you." Her voice roughened. "I'm sorry I acted the way I did, but I thought it was for the best. Helen—" She broke off. "I suppose your mother didn't want you to ever come here."

"No. She didn't. But why?"

"She ever talk about this place?" Her tone was gruff and somehow hopeful.

"No. Not until she got sick. But—" I hesitated. "She wanted to come back."

Then I explained the way I'd learned about the island. How I'd found some old coins that Mom had collected in the safe-deposit box and used them to pay for my trip.

"I'm sorry," she whispered again when I was done. "I never thought she'd tell you about Trespass. I never thought I'd see her, or you."

What had happened to keep Mom away from here? I didn't know, but the heartache I saw in my grandmother's face was real. "I don't think she ever meant to," I said. "And a lot of what she said was so strange and mixed-up. But she wanted to come back here." Hesitantly I reached for my backpack and took out my mother's ashes. They were in a beautiful green porcelain vase decorated with sprigs of yellow and white flowers. "I think she would want these to be here."

My grandmother nodded and bent her head. "Thank you," she whispered, reaching out hands that suddenly looked very old and very frail.

———

We sat on the couch and talked for a long time. "There's so much I want to know about you," my grandmother said. "You've got another year of high school left. Then what? College, maybe, or work?"

I hesitated. Those kind of questions always put my stomach in knots. "I haven't decided about that stuff yet. Most of my friends seem to know, but I don't have a clue, and it kind of freaks me out that I don't but . . ."

She took my hand and squeezed it. "Course not. There's no rush."

We were both silent. Then my grandmother began again, "I'm sorry you were alone like that, after Helen died."

"I was okay. Foster care isn't that bad. But people don't really want teenagers. Apparently we're challenging. Kind of like the army."

And I'm difficult. Too outspoken. Not a good fit, I added to myself. But there was no need to spoil things.

She smiled. "I know what it is to be alone. I lost Charlie, your grandfather, about a year before Helen left."

"I wish I'd been able to meet him."

She gave me a wondering look. "I still can't believe you're here." She held the urn of ashes in big hands that were amazingly gentle. "We could scatter her ashes down at the water's edge."

"No," I said. "She wouldn't want that. She was always so afraid of the water. But I think she would want to be here, on the island. In this house."

My grandmother looked at me curiously but gave an understanding nod. "She'll stay here, then."

Hair made a frilly half curtain over my eyes as I dropped my head. "To be honest, bringing Mom's ashes wasn't the only reason I came. I hoped I'd be able to stay for the summer."

When she didn't answer, I added, "I don't need to be taken *care* of. I can take care of myself. And once I'm eighteen, Family Services won't worry about me anyway. I wouldn't be any trouble."

"Oh, I'm not worried about trouble, honey," said my

grandmother. "But this is no place for you. I'm grateful that you brought Helen's ashes home." She put a hand to my cheek. "That was a fine thing to do. But you can't stay."

Then she took my hands in her own and leaned over them, as if she wanted to tell me something important. "Just like Helen's," she said in a low voice, turning my palms up. "Little elegant things. You play the piano?"

Okay. That wasn't what I'd expected.

"Mom taught me a little," I said with a shrug. "I'm not any good—I mean, I never practiced enough."

"Do you swim?"

"Swim?" I laughed, caught off guard by the sudden change of topic and the intent look on her face. "Um, dog paddle, I guess. Not too well. Like a dog without a paddle. Up a creek." I frowned. "Are you going to tell me what's going on? What was the deal down there in town? Why does everyone react so strangely to a visitor? Or *overreact*, I should say."

My grandmother still held my hands. Now she squeezed them a little tighter. "This island is a very special place. Some folks might call it strange. But we have our own way of do-ings things. Our own rules. I acted that way down at the dock because it'll be safer for you. If they think it was just a mis-take, if they think you don't belong here, then maybe . . ." Her voice trailed away.

"Maybe what?"

"Maybe they'll let you go."

I withdrew my hands. Let me go? A sick feeling snaked

41

in my stomach and coiled tight. My grandmother might be mentally ill. What if *that* was why Mom had never come back here? *Because your grandma is clinically insane, Delia. Paranoid or delusional. Or some nifty combo of the two.*

"Who's *they*?" I asked. I kept my tone light but couldn't help glancing at the doorway, the closest exit.

"If they find out you're Helen's daughter, that she was pregnant when she left . . ." She laced her fingers together and tapped the pads of her thumbs, frowning to herself.

"What does it matter?" I repeated. "You mean because she wasn't married? C'mon, people don't really think that way anymore."

It didn't seem like she was listening to me. "This is *their* island," she said; then, with an abrupt shake of her head, as if she was clearing away some bothersome thought, she added, "It doesn't matter. You're not staying. There's nothing to worry about."

"Is there someone you're afraid of?" I asked. "Has someone threatened you or . . . hurt you?" The thought sent an unexpected feeling through me, a rush of anger and protectiveness. Strange feelings for a woman I'd only just met and, until a little while ago, hadn't even liked.

"No, no, nothing like that." My grandmother waved the idea away like a mosquito. "I'm fine. It's this place. For people who aren't used to life here, it's hard. And dangerous. Like the reef. There've been terrible wrecks on that reef you came through today. You were darned lucky." She stood and turned away, adding in a low voice, "The Hands are always hungry."

"The Hands?" I got up and followed her into the kitchen. The tall, solid woman dominated the cozy space decorated in a country style—the rooster and chicken motif was pretty strong. "You mean the reef? I don't understand. How is it hungry?"

"Not just the Hundred Hands. The sea itself is always hungry. I just mean there's always trouble, danger waiting out there." She pulled a red-checked curtain closed over the kitchen sink, blocking out the darkness beyond. "And island folks don't accept everybody right off. It can be lonely here. Especially for young people."

Would it be possible to be any lonelier than I'd been for the last six months? I didn't think so. But I didn't want to tell her that, I didn't want her pity. Maybe all these strange warnings were just my grandmother's way of saying she didn't want me around. If so, I wished she would just tell me, not make excuses. Or try to scare me away.

I had the feeling I could do that all on my own.

"None of this makes any sense to me," I told her. "You live here. You raised my mother here. If it's so dangerous and lonely, then why do *you* stay?"

My grandmother let out a little dry huff. "Me? I'm set like an old barnacle. Sometimes it's harder than you think to leave a place." She rubbed her neck as if to ease a knot in the muscle, but I saw a scar there, nearly hidden by her braid. The raised red line began under her ear and zigzagged beneath the collar of her blouse. She readjusted her thick gray braid and the scar disappeared.

"We shouldn't worry about these things tonight." She pulled a lumpy canvas sack from a low drawer and potatoes rolled out onto the countertop. "You must be half starved. We're gonna eat some lobster salad and french fries. I fry up the best you ever had. I'm going to enjoy cooking for my granddaughter. My granddaughter," she repeated. "How does that sound?"

"That sounds good," I said softly.

Maybe things would be all right after all. So what if my grandmother had gotten a little odd? Living out here in the middle of nowhere all alone would do that to a person, wouldn't it? Maybe having some company would help her.

I sat down at the little wooden table. "But I have questions. A lot of questions."

"Hmm?" My grandmother slid a cast-iron skillet roughly the size of a tire onto the stove, then picked up a paring knife and began to peel a potato with rapid, practiced motions.

I'd been waiting so long I wanted to shout it, but I didn't. In fact, suddenly, it was hard to speak. I slid a sugar bowl in the shape of a duck toward me and focused on sliding the yellow lid off and on as I spoke. "Why did my mother leave? Was it because of my father? And is he still here? Is my father on the island?" I looked at my grandmother, almost afraid to hear the answers or see something bad in her face. But I couldn't read anything in her expression, except maybe Mc-Govern stubbornness.

"You can't push a rope," she remarked, shaking her head. "You gotta give me time with the questions. Right now I'm just glad you're safe."

"Again with the safe thing. You're going to scare me."

"Well, that won't hurt you," said my grandmother calmly as she reached for another spud. "But it won't help either."

"Okay." My grandmother had some fierce skills in being cryptic. Obviously she wasn't going to tell me any more tonight.

I watched her silently for a moment. "I do have one thing I *really* have to know."

She eyed me with a look of exasperation. "What's that?"

"What do I call you?"

She looked at her potatoes and smiled. With this smile I could finally see the Maisie. She was Maisie all over.

"Call me Gran," she said. "I'd like that."

———

After supper I tried to use my cell to call Mrs. Russell, my caseworker, again. But my phone had no signal. Zero bars, no matter where I stood.

"Maybe I should go outside." Over the top of the curtains, I glimpsed the dark evening sky.

"No, you can't," Gran said quickly. "I mean, it's no use.

No reception. We don't have cell phones or computers here on Trespass. No telephones. Heck, sometimes I don't even have electric if the propane generator acts up. Guess you'd say we're kind of old-fashioned." She peered at me. "You okay?"

I must have looked a little shell-shocked. No cell phones and no computer access? How was that possible? How did these people *do* anything? This wasn't old-fashioned. This was . . . I had no words for what this was. "I'm fine," I finally managed.

After directing me to my mother's old room and putting fresh sheets and a softly faded patchwork quilt on the bed, Gran said good night in the doorway. "You'll sleep well," she assured me. "There's nothing like the sound of the waves for a lullaby."

Again the similarity to my mother's voice struck me. Despite this strange, new place, that familiar voice wrapped around me and brought me into a safe haven. A place I didn't want to leave. "About tomorrow, Gran," I began.

"Hush. We'll deal with tomorrow when it comes."

This time I reached out and hugged *her* close. It was hard to let go.

Two-thirty in the morning. And I was still awake.

A rectangle of moonlight glowed on the floor and a sweet scent billowed through the open window. Sea roses, Gran had told me, were the pink and white flowering bushes I'd seen on the roadsides and on the dunes.

I rolled over. The ocean at night wasn't like a soothing lullaby at all. It was completely annoying. I would've much preferred car horns and sirens to the faint, insistent shooshing of the waves.

It almost sounded like strange voices out there, murmuring beneath my window.

Gran was going to pack me off in the morning as quickly as she could. I still didn't understand why exactly. Except that it had to do with the people on this island. And yet I sensed Gran actually *wanted* me to stay. What was she so afraid of?

I heaved a sigh and twisted in the narrow twin bed. From my new position I saw a picture in a seashell frame sitting on the lower shelf of a little bookcase. I got out of bed, put my glasses on and clicked on the lamp.

The picture was of Mom. She laughed up into the camera, a dazzling grin on her face. The picture must have been from when she was about my age or maybe a bit younger. Sun sparkled off the rippling water around her like a jeweled tiara, making her look like some kind of fairy-tale princess. But there was something wrong.

It took a moment for it to click. My mother was in the water. The edge of a weathered dock beam was visible at the corner of the picture; she was in the *ocean*. I set the picture down carefully. So Mom hadn't always been terrified of the water.

Something had *made* her afraid.

Maybe she'd had an accident or gotten frightened by something in the water. I remembered the cold wet touch on my hand that Old Ben had insisted was seaweed, and the unseen thing under the dock, and involuntarily gave a shiver. It wasn't hard to imagine that kind of thing terrifying someone. But whatever it was must have happened to her after this picture was taken.

I went to the window and drew the white curtain aside. There was a full moon tonight, and below I could see the pale glimmer of a sand-covered path between two grassy dunes.

Suddenly the beam of a flashlight cut across the yard, and I drew back from the window. A figure appeared. It was my grandmother, carrying some kind of bundle. She hurried across the lawn with long, purposeful strides and disappeared over the rise of the dunes, heading toward the water.

Where on earth was she going? The sudden thought flashed into my head that maybe she had ignored my request and was taking Mom's ashes down to the water.

I grabbed the quilt to throw over my shoulders.

I was going to find out.

CHAPTER 4

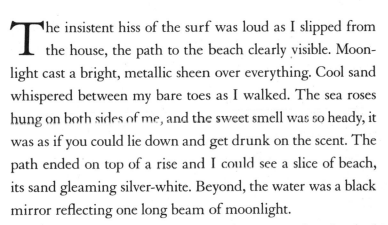

The insistent hiss of the surf was loud as I slipped from the house, the path to the beach clearly visible. Moonlight cast a bright, metallic sheen over everything. Cool sand whispered between my bare toes as I walked. The sea roses hung on both sides of me, and the sweet smell was so heady, it was as if you could lie down and get drunk on the scent. The path ended on top of a rise and I could see a slice of beach, its sand gleaming silver-white. Beyond, the water was a black mirror reflecting one long beam of moonlight.

I clutched the quilt closer. I thought my grandmother had come this way, but there was no sign of her. I'd also checked the mantel over the fireplace, where she'd placed the urn of my mother's ashes. It was still there, so whatever strange purpose Gran had for being out here at night, it wasn't that.

As I walked toward the water the packed sand felt as hard as pavement. When the first lick of cold water splashed over my toes, I gasped at the shock.

I sat down on a low outcropping of black rocks and decided to wait. Hopefully, Gran would come back this way.

Had my mother ever sat in just this spot? Probably. It was nice here. Nestled in the quilt, a pool of quiet water swirling gently at my feet, I almost felt like I could fall asleep. The only thing that prevented it were the faces, images and snippets of conversations from the day whirling in my head. Old Ben Deare's odd predictions, Gran's warnings.

It's not safe here. . . . Keep your eyes open. . . . A monster . . .

Dipping my heels by turn into the water, I found myself humming. Maybe it was because I was a little freaked out by this place that I chose to sing something silly from when I was little. I sang softly at first, as I tried to remember the tune, then a little louder, pleased with the way the cool night air lifted the sound up and away. This was almost as good as the shower. The notes vibrated in my chest and tingled on my lips.

"Down by the bay," I sang softly, "where the watermelons grow . . ."

There was a loud splash.

My eyes flew open. A few yards away something surged through the water, raising a sharp plume of spray. It was a huge fin with fanlike segments glistening iridescent in the moonlight. It came directly at me, cleaving the water like a missile.

I screamed and jumped up. And found myself in knee-deep, cold water. The tide had come in. I felt a surge of panic and splashed backward, stumbling onto the sand. The giant fin veered away at the last second, disappearing beneath the water.

What the hell was that? And how had the water come up so fast? Maybe I'd dozed off for a little while and not realized it. I stood up, clutched the quilt close to me with shaky fingers and paced back and forth on the sand, searching the water for another glimpse of that gigantic fin. What kind of a fish swims toward the beach?

I'd heard of whales or dolphins beaching themselves, but that fin hadn't looked like it could possibly be one of those. It had been strange, with long spines delineating each segment. Almost prehistoric-looking. Immediately I thought of the thing I'd seen earlier in the waters near the reef. Not just seen. Felt.

Right, I told myself. *Maybe Trespass has a sea monster. Like Nessie. Only not so shy.*

Get a grip, girl.

I was about to head back to the house, when something else broke the surface of the water. Too shocked to scream this time, I just stood behind a shelter of rocks and stared.

It was a young man. Moonlight gleamed on the wet contours of his muscled chest and arms. His skin was so pale he looked like a marble statue rising from the water. He strode forward through the waist-high water and whipped his head to clear a long hank of black hair from his face. The water coursed over him like . . . well, I didn't know what . . . but something hard and wet and very well made. He moved easily through the water, barely splashing at all. He stood still for some seconds, then began to wade parallel to the beach. It was too dark to make out his features, but by the slow, deliberate movements of his head he seemed to be searching for something.

"Um. Hello?" I called. "You should get out of the water. I just saw something out there. Something big."

He spun around and spoke into the darkness. "Reveal yourself."

His deep voice cut through the night air, clear and distinct, as if he were next to me instead of ten feet away. There was an impatient, authoritarian note to the voice, and I found myself stepping out from my hiding place without thinking.

I looked around the little inlet, but it seemed very quiet now. "You should get out of there," I told him. "Some big fish just tried to attack me."

"You were attacked," he repeated, breathing hard. "By a big fish."

I wished that I could see his face. It sounded as if he'd just swum a long distance. And also as if he thought I was crazy.

"Yes. Well, no, not exactly *attacked*," I admitted. "It scared me. Aren't you freezing? You're swimming out here all by yourself?"

"I *thought* I was," he answered in a clipped voice.

Okay, so it was obvious from his tone I was intruding. I turned and began to walk away.

"I heard something," his voice called out after me. "Were you *singing*?"

I stopped short. "What? Singing? Um. No."

As if I would admit to anyone that I was belting out Raffi tunes a capella, never mind to a complete stranger on a dark, isolated beach.

The lights and darks of his sculpted body were visible, but his face was in shadow. He was still half covered by water, and the thought suddenly came to me that maybe he didn't have swim trunks on.

Please don't come out of the water, I prayed silently. *Please.*

His voice called to me again, cutting across the water and the night air, clear and penetrating. "You're a newcomer here."

"Yes," I said. "Just visiting," I added nervously, keeping my eyes away from his whole . . . area.

"May I give you some advice?"

"Sure."

"Stay out of the water here, Lander."

There was nothing advice-like about it at all. It was an order, issued in nearly a snarl.

"Oh, really?" I snapped, lifting my head. "Well, thanks. I hope Nessie, or whatever it is, decides to have you for a midnight—"

I stopped, realizing he was gone. I mean literally gone. No splashing or kicking, nothing. The moonlit water was serene. How had he disappeared like that?

I turned and dashed up the beach and onto the path, not looking back.

CHAPTER 5

"I saw someone swimming last night," I said, picking at my breakfast the next morning. The night before, I'd lain awake until my grandmother's tread on the stairs told me she was back, and then finally slept, huddled beneath my covers while in the corner a damp quilt scented the air with salt and roses. I had such a strange dream—I was playing the piano in our old living room back in Kansas but there was no sound, no matter how hard I banged on the keys.

"Where *is* that old biscuit?" fumed Gran, peering out the kitchen window. "He promised he'd be here first thing." She turned to me. "What did you say?"

"There was someone down at the beach. Swimming out there in the dark."

"What were you doing out there?" she demanded, hands on her hips.

"Just walking. Thinking," I answered. "Why not? I noticed you went out."

She blinked and then scowled at me. "Never you mind about that. You say you *saw* somebody?"

Obviously, whatever my grandmother had been doing, she meant to keep it a secret.

"Just a guy," I said absently.

A very good-looking guy. And amazingly rude.

"And he . . ." Here Gran paused, her expression puzzled. "He *talked* to you?"

"It was more like he talked *at* me," I corrected her. "Ordered me to stay out of the water. As if I'd be nuts enough to go out there and splash around in the dark."

"And so you would be. You stay away from the water," said Gran with a huff. She clattered dishes into the sink. "Leave things alone that you don't understand."

Her sudden fierceness confused me. What was there to understand? I'd gotten freaked out by a fish and insulted by a hot skinny-dipper. It wasn't anything to make a fuss about. The only strange thing was, I couldn't get the sound of his voice out of my head.

Stay out of the water here, Lander.

Just the thought of it made me mad all over again. The jerk.

Seeing my dark look, Gran softened. "There's no harm done. It doesn't matter. Where *is* that Ben Deare?" she said, twitching aside the curtain. "Sometimes I don't think that fella has both oars in the water."

"You still want me to leave," I said, so softly I could barely hear myself.

Gran dropped the curtain. "I've got a bad feeling about this. C'mon. We'll go down to the dock and find him."

She was worried. She didn't even give me time to gather my things before climbing back into the golf cart. She remained silent, her lips pressed together tightly as we retraced our path from yesterday.

Overnight the weird mist had disappeared. Blue cloudless sky hung overhead and contrasted with the dark outlines of towering pine trees. The wind gusted, making the water in the harbor shiver with small waves and ripples. I followed Gran down the dock toward the spot where the *Belores* was tied, but stopped short as she whispered, "Oh my Lord."

Ben Deare's sailboat had been vandalized. More than that. The *Belores* was mutilated. Heavy canvas sails hung over the side of the boat, ripped into tangled shreds. Splintered pieces of wood lay in heaps on the deck. The mast was still upright but looked like it had been attacked with a sledgehammer, judging by the deep dents and gouges. Someone had destroyed the motor too: the propeller blades were twisted into a mangled mess, the thick metal plates torn like pieces of aluminum foil.

Gran sucked in a breath. "Mary and Joseph."

"Who would do this?" I whispered.

And who could *do this?* The damage would have taken incredible, explosive force. And a vicious desire to destroy an old man's property.

"Where's Ben?" I asked. The thought of him set a sick feeling churning in my stomach. Suppose he'd been nearby, or worse, on board, when this had happened?

My eyes scanned the mess. There was no sign of blood. Only a wet trail of oozy water and seaweed hung over one side of the boat.

"The other men have gone out for their hauls already. I'm going to go up and ask at the Snug if anyone's seen Ben," said Gran, hurrying away. "You'd better wait here in case he shows up."

I checked my cell phone again. She'd been right about the terrible reception—there was still no signal. How did they call 911 here? Did they even *have* 911?

I walked along the dock, looking for any sign of activity. There was no one around and only a few boats tied up. Most of the boats here on Trespass weren't as shiny and clean as the fancy ones in Portland. With their chunky, squared-off shapes and old tires tied to their sides that bumped against the dock, they said working class all the way. I walked by slowly, reading the names: *Ugly Marie, Rosebud,* and *Little Sue.*

I stopped. We'd been wrong about the dock being empty. At the very end a tall young man was loading lobster traps onto a big, powerful-looking boat. The name *Widowsong* was painted on the side, and the boat looked newer than all the rest.

With a smooth, swinging movement he lifted a large

wire trap from a stack on the dock, then turned and jumped the gap to the boat and placed it neatly on the deck.

I realized as I came closer it was the guy from yesterday in the square. Mr. Authority. I was surprised at how young he looked. Probably not much older than I was. He was also sort of nice to look at, handsomely rugged in a plain white T-shirt and faded jeans. He noticed me and stopped to stare.

Only not at me.

"Watch out!" he yelled, pointing behind me.

The dock shook under my feet. Something was coming. Something big. I whipped around as a huge black form lunged toward me. My hands shot up, too late to protect myself from the tangled mass of hair and paws and long, lolling red tongue.

I teetered backward as a shaggy black dog landed on me. Hot breath and drool slapped me in the face as I windmilled my arms, trying to get my balance. It was no good. My cell phone went flying and I landed with a slamming thud on my butt. And just in time to see my cell phone skittering toward the edge of the dock. I yelped and threw myself sideways to grab it, but I wasn't fast enough. There was a faint but unmistakable plink as my phone went into the sea.

"Buddy!" yelled the young man. "Down. Get off her!"

The mountain of dog stood over me, licking my face, his black tail wagging in a frenzy of excitement. But somewhere deep in the doggy brain the command must have registered;

with one last slobber he backed up. Wincing, I pushed myself to sitting.

"Jeez, are you okay?" The young man strode over. I put a hand up for him to help me stand, but instead he bent, grabbed my waist and without hesitating hoisted me to my feet. I think my feet actually left the ground a little. Close-up, he was even taller than I'd first imagined, cornstalk tall, with a thatch of blond hair way up high.

"Sorry about that," he said. He let go of me, removing his hands from my waist as if I were something delicate that he was afraid would fall over. "What's the matter with you?" he asked the dog sternly. The dog blinked eyes like big chocolate pools of innocence at his owner and wagged his tail.

"It's okay," I said, rubbing the animal's thick fur. "I like dogs. This one looks like he's got a little yeti in him."

"Making a good impression, I see," said Gran, coming along the dock. "Sean Gunn, this is my granddaughter, Delia, she isn't staying."

Somehow she managed to make that last phrase sound like part of my name. This was getting kind of ridiculous.

Sean nodded hello. He had a nice face with broad, strong features and sun-streaked blond hair that stood out from his tanned forehead in attractive disorder. "I saw you yesterday in the square."

"Yeah, I attracted quite a crowd. It was kind of weird."

He shook his head. "Don't worry, it's not you. It's just a pretty quiet place here."

Quiet wasn't exactly the word I would have chosen. *Weird, eerie* or *isolated,* maybe.

"It couldn't have been too quiet when Ben Deare's boat got trashed," I remarked. "Did you see who did it?"

"Nope."

"You don't seem that concerned."

He tilted his head slightly, regarding me with thoughtful brown eyes. "Why does it matter to you?"

"I'd like to know Ben is okay."

"He's taking Delia back to the mainland," Gran interjected. "He was supposed to meet us first thing at the house."

Sean nodded. "Ben can take care of himself. Better than most. And his boat will be fixed." He looked at me. "We take care of each other here. So there's no need to worry."

"But he could be—" I began, but was cut off. The dog, apparently thinking I'd sent an invitation to come back, my being upright and all, trotted over and stuck his nose in my crotch.

"Ugh. Hey!" I nudged the dog's persistent snout away.

"Buddy!" yelled Sean. "So uncool. Get in the boat."

Buddy galloped away and leapt onto the boat. Sean looked at Gran and me, seeming to be at a loss for words. "Nice to meet you," he mumbled finally. "I should get back to work. Bye."

Gran looked at me. "You okay?"

"Yes," I muttered, examining my scraped palms. "But my phone is swimming with the fishes."

"It doesn't matter about the phone," said Gran. "Let's go aboard. I want to talk to Sean again for a minute." She pointed to my raw hands. "And he'll have a first aid kit on the boat."

But apparently Sean Gunn wasn't the "welcome aboard" type. He'd already returned to stacking his lobster traps and replied with a polite, noncommittal shrug to Gran's request for a few words with him. While she went up front to talk to him, I looked around the boat.

Sean Gunn must have been doing well in the lobstering business. In contrast to Ben's floating junk drawer, Sean Gunn's boat looked brand-new, well-equipped and like a model of ruthless efficiency, right down to the spotless woodwork and gleaming hardware on the rails.

An array of heavy nets, spear guns and spike-ended poles hung on a wall of the cabin. It looked like an undersea hunting arsenal. I eyed the lethal-looking black point of a sleek metal arrow, reached up to touch it and changed my mind.

God help Nemo if this guy is looking for him.

Just then Sean Gunn strode over and handed me a plastic box of first aid supplies. Meanwhile, Gran remained up toward the front, feeding the big black hound something she took from the depths of a pocket.

"Do you need a hand?" Sean asked me, wiping his palms on the back of his jeans.

"No, thank you."

He nodded with what seemed like relief but didn't leave.

I sat down and opened the kit, which was neatly organized and well stocked, and began to apply disinfectant spray to the bloody scratches on my palms. Sean stood by, arms folded. Watching me like the Bactine police or something.

"I'm fine," I said, glancing up. "Thanks."

He shifted his feet. "I'm sorry about my dog. If he scared you."

"That is not a dog," I told him, laughing. "Did he fall into a vat of toxic waste or something as a puppy?"

Sean smiled. Just a little one that tugged the corner of his mouth. "He seems to like you."

I smiled back. "I got that impression. Still have the drool tracks on my neck." I stuffed the supplies back into the box and handed it back to Sean. As he reached for it the sleeve of his T-shirt lifted slightly and I noticed a tattoo on his upper arm. It was a dagger, entwined with swirling coils. The dense black motif against his skin looked fresh, the skin around it slightly reddened and shiny.

"Nice ink."

He frowned. "What?"

"Your tattoo. It looks like you just got it. It's nice."

"Oh." Sean ran a hand over his biceps, covering the black point of the dagger. Almost as if he wanted to hide it. His hands were big, with chafed red skin and rough fingernails bitten down to nubs.

Silence hung between us. I wondered what it would take to get Sean Gunn to smile again. Or at least relax. He had the air of someone who didn't do either one easily. Or maybe ever. "What is it, some kind of a gang thing?" I asked jokingly.

But Sean didn't smile back. His open features hardened ever so slightly. It was as if he'd tightened his face, closed it, so I couldn't see inside.

"Yeah. Something like that." Without another word he turned, went to the front of the boat and began to wind a rope into a stack of neat coils at his feet.

I was just trying to make conversation. Maybe they actually spoke a different language here. It *sounded* like English, but there were subtleties I couldn't hear.

"Thanks for the Band-Aid," I called over my shoulder, and went toward the side. No way would I ask him for a hand over to the dock. He'd made it clear he was so busy. I spotted Gran, who'd already gotten off the boat.

I was about to step across the short distance to the dock when the *Widowsong* revved to life and began to pull away.

"Hey! Stop! I have to get off!" I shouted.

Sean slammed the throttle, or the clutch, or whatever it was, forward and made me skitter backward, my sneakers squeaking on the deck. "Sit down!" he yelled.

The dog promptly sat on my feet.

Grabbing the side of the rail, I stared as the dock withdrew and the expanse of swirling black water between me and land widened. "Gran!" I shouted. But Gran only stood there, hands clasped together up on her chest. As I watched she raised one hand in a stiff, silent farewell.

Really?

She wouldn't do this. I didn't have any of my stuff. How could she do this?

I untangled myself from Buddy and crossed to Sean's side. "Turn the damned boat around! I want to get off!"

He looked down at me, his face infuriatingly calm. As if he couldn't imagine what I was making such a fuss about. "You will. Just as soon as we get to the mainland. Now go sit down."

"My grandmother put you up to this, didn't she?"

"Yeah. Maisie asked me to bring you back. So what?"

"So I *don't want to go*," I yelled, trying to overcome the loud noise of the motor and keep my whipping hair out of my mouth. "Turn it around!"

"Nope."

I glared up at him. "I'll pay you, okay? C'mon." I staggered against the roll of the deck before planting my feet. Back at the house, I still had those little gold coins. "A hundred dollars to take me back. Please?"

Sean looked down at me and for a moment there was a look of kindness in his brown eyes, like he wanted to help me. But he shook his head. "Sorry. Believe me, this is for your own good."

When I didn't move, he added, "Attention, passenger. We've turned on the No Smoking sign. The captain requests that you sit your ass down." He turned his attention back to the open stretch of water.

Jaw clenched, fists tight, I held down my temper by calling

Sean Gunn a string of dirty names in my head and made my way back to the edge of the boat. It wasn't that far, I thought, looking toward the dock. I licked my lips and eyed the rolling drop to the water. Maybe I could swim it.

Ugh. No way.

Buddy began to bark at me.

"I *really* wouldn't do that," Sean called over, obviously thinking I was a whole lot braver than I was.

"Look," he said louder, "you've got to sit down. No kidding. We're coming to the Hands. It's gonna get rough."

I just crossed my arms and remained standing; I was mad about being surprised—no, *kidnapped*—like this and felt weirdly pleased about the uneasiness in his voice. He *should* be nervous.

"I came through the Hands before with Ben Deare just fine," I shouted. "And his boat is a lot smaller. So just how bad could it possibly—"

An earsplitting scrape sounded along the length of the hull and the *Widowsong* slammed to a lurching stop. I pitched forward, scrabbling to catch hold of the curved railing even as the boat tipped sideways. Then, unbelievably, I saw the opposite deck begin to rise out of the water. Like the empty end of a seesaw.

I screamed and tumbled over the side.

The shocking cold of the water was a hammer strike on my skin. Seawater burned in my nose. Eyes shut, I swept my arms forward and kicked, reaching blindly for *up*. I opened my eyes. There was no bright surface above. Just swirling dark water and bubbles. Panic exploded in my chest and I flailed, trying to right myself. With relief I saw the large white form of the boat's bottom looming nearby. And then I saw what was under it.

While my mind couldn't really process what I was seeing, my eyes were forced to absorb it.

Two huge, scaly animals gripped the bottom of the *Widowsong,* their shapes like the dark silhouettes of a nightmare. Webbed hands. Claws. Spiked tails. One of the monsters swung and fixed me with reptilian yellow eyes. Its jaws unhinged like a bear trap, showing rows of curved, sharp teeth, and it screamed at me. The obscene roar reverberated through the water and suddenly the creature swam toward me with rapid undulating movements and a bobbing motion of its head.

I screamed, and a rush of bubbles frothed from my mouth. The creature stopped abruptly, as if startled, and swung away.

The next thing I saw was its long tail with spiky side fins whipping through the water, coming at my head. It would have been a great shot in a 3-D sci-fi movie. Unfortunately, this was real. Before I could move, the tail struck me on the side of the head and sent me spinning, drifting. The world went dark, as if someone had cupped a hand over the end of a kaleidoscope.

Stunned, I floated down. A buzzing noise filled my head, and I had the awful dreamlike sense that I couldn't move.

I had to move, to get air. But I couldn't. My arms and legs wouldn't answer the frantic commands of my brain. As a heavy burning weight filled my chest, the need to breathe became unbearable. I prayed in that moment for it to stop.

Then I saw it. From the black depths below me, something small and white and shimmering appeared. It grew larger, floating up toward me, glowing against the murk. It was an angel.

The angel was dark. Black hair floated around his face like plumes of glistening raven feathers. And he had only a single, gleaming wing. That didn't seem to matter. His deep blue eyes were all I could focus on. Brilliant and intense as a lightning strike, they fastened on me and didn't let go.

He'd come to take me.

Whether to save me from the edge of the world or take me to the other side, I didn't know or care. My chest and throat were on fire, bursting from the need to breathe.

He floated closer, his arms open. The angel's hands were warm on my skin, like the warmth of a fire when you come in from the cold.

He pulled me to him and kissed me.

With the press of his mouth, I felt a gasp of breath. Sweet, intoxicating air rushed into me. But not enough. The little taste of it brought a spasm of desperate need, an animal panic for more, and I clutched the angel's head and drank the breath from his lips in coughing gulps until he broke away. Then his long fingers cupped the back of my head. He laid a hand against my chest, calming me, slowing me down. Now his mouth returned to mine and I breathed him into me. Inhale. Exhale.

Bliss.

I wrapped my arms tighter around the angel. Something was happening to me.

Every inch of my skin pulsed with sensation at the touch of the water, his hands, his lips. The angle of his mouth on mine changed, became something else. Something dark and sweet and just as elemental as breathing.

I felt myself being pulled deeper and deeper. Into the kiss and oblivion.

Something struck the water and surged beside us in a white plume of froth. But I couldn't focus on anything but my consuming need for air. For this kiss.

A hand grabbed me and I was yanked sideways and pulled upward, upward.

I broke the surface of the water gasping. My chest ached and the side of my head throbbed. Weakly I kicked at the water as small waves lifted and dropped me. The air felt good, so cool in my throat.

But I was tired. Somehow all I wanted to do was float down once more. . . .

"Delia!" someone shouted. A strong hand grabbed the back of my T-shirt and supported me in the water.

"Are you okay?"

I sputtered and nodded, unseeing, to the voice. "Y-yes."

"C'mon."

It was Sean. He was beside me in the choppy sea. I could hardly move as he gripped my arm and dragged me toward the *Widowsong,* which rose as high as a skyscraper before us.

Back on the dock, I sat on an empty wooden lobster trap. I was swaddled inside a thick gray blanket, my hands clamped around a cup of hot liquid that I drank without tasting. I couldn't stop shivering. Or thinking about the creatures that had clung to the bottom of Sean's boat. Or the angel. I put shaky fingers to my lips as I remembered his mouth on mine.

Maybe he wasn't real. Maybe I'd just had some kind of freaky near-death experience.

I dismissed that. No one ever says, "Go toward the light—and the really excellent kisser." Whatever he was, he was real.

"Thank goodness you're all right," Gran said. "I should have known, after seeing what they did to Ben's boat, that something like this might happen. But I thought maybe—" She broke off.

What they did to Ben's boat. The words drifted over me like a vague, black cloud. *They.*

The memory of those monstrous faces swam before me again: green and black, their heads looking obscenely human. Like men, but with veiny, bald scalps and black sunken holes where their ears and noses should have been. They had elongated torsos and short curved legs that had clung to the boat.

"M-monsters," I said. My voice came out in a high-pitched waver that didn't even *sound* like me. "There were sea monsters under the b-boat."

I blinked up at the two of them, waiting for a laugh or a slap on the back to jar me out of this nightmare. I waited for them to tell me I'd imagined the whole thing.

Sean Gunn simply gave a nod. "Yeah." He looked over at Gran. "It was the Glaukos. Two of them. The First Ones don't want your girl here to go."

Gran nodded. "Guess they made it clear enough."

I could only stare at the two of them for a few slack-jawed seconds. "You mean you *know* about this?" I finally snapped. "About what's out there?" I pointed a shaky finger toward the water and then snatched it back under the blanket again. "The monsters?"

"Glaukos," replied Gran. "They serve the First Ones."

"Ow!" I winced and pulled away from Sean, who'd tilted my head and was exploring the lump on my temple with gentle fingers.

"I couldn't see much down there, but I was afraid the Glauk's tail might have gotten her," he muttered, moving my head this way and that. I felt like a melon being inspected for ripeness. "No," he said after a moment's probing. "None of the spikes broke the skin." He gave my hair an encouraging tousle. "That's good."

I cradled my head against one hand to peer up at him. "Why? Would that hurt more?"

"No," he said calmly. "But you'd probably be dead in

twelve hours. Either from the flesh-eating infection they usually carry or the convulsions."

"Oh," I said weakly. When I managed to get past the image of my gangrenous head falling off during a seizure, I asked, "Why did they attack your boat?"

Gran looked to the water with a worried frown. "The Glaukos only do what they're ordered to do."

"There was a First One down there. He obviously told them to stop the boat," said Sean. "I'll bet it surprised them when you fell out."

"Gee, I hope I didn't scare them too much," I muttered, automatically reaching to adjust my glasses. They were gone. "Just great," I muttered.

No *wonder* everything looked so fuzzy. Now what was I going to do? I didn't have another pair with me, and I was practically blind without them.

I wasn't too nearsighted to see Sean grinning at me, though. He was probably thinking *See? I told you to sit down.* It was nice of him not to say it. I'd put both of us at risk with my idiotic plunge off the side of the boat.

I pulled the blanket tighter. "That was really brave of you. You could have been hurt. Thank you."

"No problem," said Sean, wrapping the towel Gran handed him around his neck.

"Who *was* he?" I asked. "The one down there who—" I broke off, not sure of how to put it. *French-kissed me back to life?*

"He was one of them. A First One. He's called Jax." Sean's smile faded and he looked uncomfortable. Despite my chilled state, I felt hot color creep into my cheeks. I wondered how much Sean had seen of the rescue operation.

"Trespass Island belongs to the First Ones," said Gran. "I tried to tell you before, but it didn't seem like it would matter if you weren't going to be staying here. The folks who live here . . . well, we're sort of tenants, I guess."

"First Ones?" I repeated. "Are they some kind of monsters too?"

"Demigods of the sea," said Sean.

"Demigods?" I was starting to sound like a not-very-bright parrot, but I just couldn't help it.

"Of the sea," Sean added, apparently trying to be helpful. "Those're the only ones that seem to have survived to the present day. Only ones we've got *here,* anyway."

It was like some bizarre dream. But the throbbing pain in my head, the texture of the woolen blanket on my skin, those felt real enough.

Other things had felt very real too: I remembered the consuming feel of the angel's mouth, the tantalizing feel of the water, of him enclosing me in strong arms like iron bands. If Sean hadn't pulled me away, what would have happened? Would he have taken me all the way down? Drowned me?

And could I have done anything to stop him?

And would I?

I swallowed.

73

"How do you feel?" said Gran, watching me.

"I'm okay," I assured her. "Thank you," I told Sean. "You saved my life down there."

"No problem." Sean cleared his throat. "Well, I'll let you two sort things out." He hesitated, as if looking for something else to say. "Go ahead and keep the blanket," he finally told me, and left.

Gran leaned over and rubbed my arms through the scratchy wool, in a brisk no-nonsense fashion. "At least now you know," she muttered. "Part of it, anyhow."

"Know what?" I squinted, watching Sean walk away.

Gran paused. "About Helen."

My attention snapped back to Gran's face.

"Your mother didn't leave Trespass, Delia. She *escaped*."

CHAPTER 6

Right after they get hit on the head is never the best time to tell someone they're trapped on an isolated island surrounded by sea monsters. Not that there's ever a *good* time for that kind of thing.

"Seeing the Glaukos like that," said Gran. "That must have been darned unsettling."

"Unsettling?" I repeated. "It feels more like reality just got yanked out from under me and I've been tossed on my butt into the Twilight Zone." I was back at Gran's, lying in bed with an ice pack on my forehead. Maybe I wasn't poisoned by a lethal tail spike, but my headache was so bad, I almost wished I had been. "How long has it been like this?"

"The First Ones have always been here," she answered,

striding around the room. She set a tray of toast and hot tea on the side table. "This island belongs to them."

"And they're demigods," I said. "What is that exactly? Some kind of deity-lite?"

This was probably uncalled for, but at that point I felt kind of woozy and detached. How could sarcasm make things any worse? Besides, I truly wasn't sure what it meant. The little mythology I knew had never had any practical application.

Hello? Isn't that the whole point of mythology, not to have any practical application?

"They're descended from Poseidon," said Gran. "When he . . . ," Here she hesitated, pursing her lips with an oddly prim expression. ". . . *visited* a mortal woman, their offspring would be half mortal and half god. A few of their kind have survived through the ages, and live in these waters."

Maybe it was the whack on the head or being nearly drowned, but I believed it. There was no way the things I'd seen today were anything natural or normal.

"Descended from Poseidon. Okay." I thought of the strange symbols I'd seen carved in the village, and of Gran's mysterious trip down to the beach last night. "So. Do you worship these First Ones?"

Gran tossed a napkin on the tray. "Worship them? Certainly not!" Color crept up her neck. "I'm a Christian woman." She jerked a shoulder as if to shrug off the very idea. "But we live together, side by side. That's how it's always been here on Trespass."

"Side by side, huh?" I raised an eyebrow, then lowered it because that hurt the tail-whack spot. "It sounds more like they call the shots."

Gran looked uneasy. "It's true, there are rules," she admitted. "We don't leave Trespass. A few of the fishermen have permission to bring their catches into Portland, buy certain things. But we have just about everything we need right here. The island is guarded by the fog you came through, and the reef. In other ways too. Like the Glaukos. But it's just to keep the island safe from outsiders. The First Ones provide everything we need. They just ask for certain things in return."

"What kind of things?"

"Loyalty," said Gran after a second's hesitation. "It's an old-fashioned thing, and I know you won't understand, not being raised here. But they stick to their side of the bargain, and we stick to ours." She sat on the edge of the bed. "The Accord was struck hundreds of years ago by the first sailors who wrecked here. They came from a boat called the *Dover.* We follow the rules and we live in peace."

"So what are the rules?"

Gran's face relaxed into a faint smile and her gray eyes softened. For a moment I saw what a pretty woman she must have been when she was younger. I wondered at what she'd been through in her life to make her seem so rough and hardened.

Oh yeah. I forgot. She lived *here.*

"Don't make it sound so terrible. There's plenty of time for learning your way around. Now that you're staying."

"But you wanted me off the island. I thought it was too dangerous."

Gran raised her hands in a gesture of futility. "I thought you could leave before they knew about you. But now, you have no choice."

"What are you talking about?" I rubbed at my head and sat up. "That's ridiculous. They can't keep people here if they don't want to stay."

"Hush now." Gran's eyes glanced to the partly opened window beside us. "Don't talk like that. The First Ones are very powerful."

Her words brought back the image of a dark-haired angel with gleaming eyes. He didn't seem like he wanted to hurt me. In fact, he'd saved me. Or had it been Sean who saved me? It was hard to remember, everything was so fuzzy and mixed up.

"You'll grow to love it here," Gran went on quietly. "You'll see. You're home now."

Home. Wasn't that exactly what I'd wanted when I'd come here? A place where I could fit in, make friends and find my grandmother? But now . . .

This was a place of nightmares and monsters, surrounded on every side by water. And I was a prisoner.

How could I ever be at home on Trespass?

The next day I woke to sunshine streaming through the bedroom window and the sound of a bird chirping outside. The smell of something delicious and baked drifted to my nose, and I smiled. I sat up and groaned, feeling my head throb. "Oh yeah." I touched the tender lump over my right eye. Sea monsters. Island. Demigods. Check.

I'd slept late, I realized, and went downstairs to find a note from Gran on the kitchen table next to a plate of blueberry muffins. It said, *Gone to work. You should rest.*

Work? Gran had never mentioned anything about a job. I was surprised she hadn't left me any other words on what I should do. Maybe she'd thought I'd want to stay in bed, but I was far too restless to let a bump on my head confine me.

I fixed some strong tea and had a muffin for breakfast, then wandered around the small house for a little while. It was very plain and sparsely furnished, though the walls were decorated with lots of framed needlework pieces. On the mantel was a black-and-white photo of a handsome man with slicked-back dark hair. His shining eyes crinkled at the corners as he grinned at the camera. This must have been my grandfather, Charles McGovern.

It must have been very lonely for Gran here for all these years. I wondered if she'd ever considered leaving the island herself. She seemed like such a strong, determined person. If my mother had been able to escape, surely others had too.

I stood and walked over to the bookshelves, tilting my

head to read the titles. Luckily, I didn't need my glasses for reading, only driving. And it seemed like I wouldn't be doing much of *that* here. Unless you counted a golf cart.

Gran's books were a pretty varied assortment. Two Grishams. Danielle Steel. Agatha Christie. Audubon bird-watching. *Fish Species of the North Atlantic.* My finger stopped at a burgundy-colored hardcover book with faded lettering.

"History of Trespass Island," I read, pulling it out. "As recorded by Reverend Archibald Trent."

In the front there was a black-and-white photo of the author, dated 1962. He was a smiling silver-haired man with thick horn-rimmed glasses. Beneath his picture the caption read, "This book is dedicated to our brave and seafaring ancestors."

"Yeah, they would have to be," I murmured.

There was also a foldout map of Trespass. The shape of the island was sort of square, with chunks bitten out of two sides. It looked vaguely like a jigsaw-puzzle piece. In the middle the book opened to a section of photos. Most of them seemed to be pictures of the island from the author's boyhood days. A small gray schoolhouse with a line of boys and girls arranged by height.

Why did nobody ever smile in old pictures? The kids looked like they were posing for a mug shot.

The next picture was a color photo of a painting in an ornate gilt frame. It was a portrait of a couple. The man wore a white wig and was dressed in a military coat with a sash.

Next to him sat a woman on a cushioned chair. She held a small book in one hand.

Portrait of British naval officer Benjamin Deare and his wife, Isabel. Deare was captain of the ill-fated Dover, *wrecked off the coast of Trespass on March 17, 1776.*

This must have been Ben Deare's great-great-grandfather. Actually, I wasn't sure how many *great*s it would take to go back that far. I couldn't see any resemblance between the stocky, red-cheeked man in the painting and the old man I'd met.

"Knock knock," said a voice at the screen door. Before I could answer it, the dark-haired girl named Zuzu drifted in, graceful and unhurried. She wore a tie-dyed sundress that looked like it would have been more in fashion about thirty years ago. The scent of coconut suntan lotion trailed behind her.

"Morning." She looked around with her wide-set, dramatically green eyes. "Is Maisie here?"

"Um, no. She's gone out."

Zuzu nodded. "She must be down at the gardens. There are lots of preparations to do with the solstice coming. I think the strawberries are nearly ripe, and she makes this unbelievable strawberry rhubarb compote thing with—"

"Sorry." I held up my hands to interrupt. "Do you always just walk into people's houses like this?"

Zuzu swept back a length of her dark hair, making a small braid decorated with tiny blue shells and silver beads jingle with the movement. "Didn't you hear me knock?"

"You said, 'Knock knock.' It's not exactly the same."

"Huh," said Zuzu, considering this; then she shrugged. "Well, we're not formal around here."

"One big happy family, huh?"

"That's right," she said with a smile, displaying gleaming white teeth that contrasted with her tan to perfection, and I found myself smiling back at her. Zuzu tilted her head, closed her eyes and drew in a deep breath. "Did Maisie make any blueberry cake this morning? I'm crazy about that stuff."

"No," I answered. Then, realizing I wasn't being exactly hospitable, I added, "There are muffins."

Zuzu glided into the kitchen. "So I guess you'll be staying," she said as I followed. She perched herself on the counter and helped herself to a muffin.

"For now," I answered slowly. "It seems like I've got no choice."

"You chose to come here. *That* was a choice." Zuzu broke off a piece of muffin delicately and popped it into her mouth.

"Right," I said. "That was before I knew about the whole one-way-ticket thing."

"You're lucky. The First Ones want you to stay." She tilted her head to regard me. "I wonder why."

"Must be the stylish way I nearly drowned," I remarked. "So. Have you always lived here?"

"Of course. I've never been off the island."

"And you've never wanted to leave?"

Zuzu smiled dismissively and examined the muffin. "No one can leave."

"My mother did."

At this she frowned and looked uneasy. "You say that like it was a good thing, some big accomplishment," she said quietly. "But it's not. People here say your mother was a traitor."

"A traitor? To what?"

Zuzu stared at me with a pained expression. As if she couldn't believe she had to explain something so obvious. "To *us*," she declared, sweeping a hand. "To this. No one leaves Trespass. We *love* it here. We have everything."

"You say that like it's something you learned in school."

Zuzu stiffened. Then, with a faintly challenging smile, she asked, "What's the matter? Are you scared?"

"I'd be pretty stupid *not* to be scared, don't you think?"

"It's a dangerous place," Zuzu agreed. "If you don't know how to handle yourself. If you don't belong."

It was so hard to tell what was going on with Zuzu. Was she trying to test me somehow? Or just scare me? I shrugged, doing my best to look unconcerned. "Guess I'll just have to stay out of the water."

"Oh, the bad things aren't only in the water," said Zuzu, sliding off the counter.

"You're like the worst welcome wagon *ever*," I observed.

Zuzu looked surprised; then she laughed, a rich giggle.

"Don't worry," she said, pulling open the refrigerator door, "I'll teach you everything you need to know. I'm going to hang out with you." She pouted her full lower lip, surveying the contents of the fridge. "Maisie doesn't have much milk left." She swirled an old-fashioned glass quart bottle and sniffed it. "I'll introduce you around, stuff like that. We'll be friends," she added matter-of-factly, and put the milk back.

"Thanks," I said coolly, "but I don't need a babysitter."

Zuzu blinked black feather-duster lashes and her eyes went wide. "That came out wrong, didn't it? It did. I can tell. Look," she said with a sigh, "I'm not used to being around someone I haven't known my whole life. It's weird, okay? We don't do a welcome wagon. We don't do welcome *period*. They just thought I could help you get used to things around here."

"Who's *they*?"

Zuzu shrugged. "Your grandmother. The Council."

I swept up the crumbs she'd left on the counter. "Like I said, I don't need a babysitter. Especially not one ordered by any Council. And you know, it kind of freaks me out to think of strangers talking about me, *arranging* things for me," I muttered.

"It's not like that." Zuzu twined her long fingers together. "You're the first new girl my own age I've met in, well, as long as I can remember." She bit her lower lip. "I really *want* us to be friends."

She looked genuinely upset.

"Well, I guess that would be nice," I said slowly. And realized with a pang that it really *would* be nice. "Thanks."

Zuzu's smile gleamed again, this time in a grin that made her cheeks dimple and displayed a little gap between her two front teeth. "Fabulous," she said. "I can show you all around the island."

"Where do we start?"

"There's only one place," she replied with a shrug. "The Snug."

———

HAM AND BEAN SOLSTICE EVE SUPPER—
GET YOUR TICKETS EARLY!

The sign was tacked on a dark wooden door decorated with brass trim. Inside was a dimly lit room filled with tables and booths, each set with a candle flickering in a jelly jar. About half of the seats were occupied with people eating and drinking. The smell of fried food wafted through the swinging doors to a kitchen. Posters of old movies, bands and cars decorated most of the darkly paneled walls except the one lined by a set of shelves sagging under the weight of books. A man in a faded denim shirt sat on a stool in the corner playing guitar. Whatever tune he strummed was drowned out by the buzz of laughter and talk.

"Welcome to the Snug," said Zuzu. "Combination

restaurant, pub, lending library and gossip depot. It's pretty much our only hot spot."

Zuzu introduced me to two girls. Linda and Marisa were sisters, both with strawberry-blond hair and big blue eyes. Linda was the older one. I knew this because she told me so. She also seemed to do all the talking for the pair of them.

"Marisa has been dying to meet you," Linda said, "ever since we heard you came to Trespass."

"That sounds funny, doesn't it?" I said with a smile. "Coming to Trespass."

Linda tilted her head, her blue eyes looking a little alarmed. "I don't see what's so funny about it."

"No," I murmured. "Okay. Really nice to meet you."

"Hey, Reilly." Zuzu walked over and sat at a booth with the boy she'd been with when I first arrived. He had a half-finished sandwich and a rumpled magazine in front of him.

"Hi. How're you doing?" he asked me, making room in the booth. "I heard about what happened." He gave me a rueful smile. "Guess you're one of us now, like it or not."

"And why shouldn't she like it?" Zuzu demanded, taking a french fry from his plate. "What's wrong with us?"

"Nothing," said Reilly innocently. "We're a real happy little gulag. And yes, I'm going to finish this." He slid his sandwich away from Zuzu.

"You're the talk of the island," he told me with a nod. "Not too many people have faced Glauks underwater and walked away. You're lucky."

"I guess so," I said. "But I really didn't do much facing. It seems they were only trying to stop the boat. It was kind of my own fault that I fell out." Several people at neighboring tables had turned to look at me curiously. At least they weren't wearing the hostile stares I'd experienced on my first day. And nobody was holding a rock. This seemed like progress.

I leaned across the table to them. "Sorry, but this . . . this is all kind of unbelievable, you know? You live on this island with sea monsters swimming around it."

Zuzu nodded, looking bored. "So?"

"I mean, how do you live here, how do you spend your time? Do you have a school?"

"Course we do, for the little ones, but we're all done with that now," Zuzu said. "Everyone has a job. I work at Gunn's, packing lobster. Reilly works on the generators and the electric whatnots."

"Geothermal turbines," Reilly said, giving Zuzu an exasperated look. He leaned forward, gesturing as he spoke with hands too big for his long skinny arms. "We use hot water that bubbles up from springs in the center of the island to power turbines and make electricity."

"That's amazing. But wouldn't you want the chance to go somewhere else?" I asked him. "To college?"

Reilly shook his head. "Nah. My life is here." He glanced at Zuzu.

"And who needs college?" she said with a shrug. "The stuff you learn in school changes all the time. I learned a whole book, practically memorized it. *The Book of Knowledge,* a pictorial encyclopedia, BAL through CRU," she recited. "Anyway, last month we got some *Time* magazines and I found out there isn't even a Burma anymore. Exotic land of the monsoon, with chief commercial products of cinnamon, sugar and indigo?" She threw up her hands. "Gone."

"I'm pretty sure it's just called something else."

"Myanmar. I told her," said Reilly. "And Pluto's not a planet anymore," he added to Zuzu. "Get over it."

"It just seems so weird," I said softly. "You really have no telephone? No Internet? You're cut off from the rest of the world."

Reilly nodded. "The whole island is in a constant state of electromagnetic flux. We have electricity from our generators, so we can play movies that we sometimes get. We can't get any satellite feed for TV or even radio transmissions. Even compasses don't function properly here."

"Why not?"

Reilly smiled. "According to the First Ones, it's because there's a spell on this place. Personally, I think it's because this island is centered over a tectonic plate fault resulting in magma extrusions and geomagnetic anomalies."

Zuzu rolled her eyes. "I just love it when he talks like that. Makes my heart flutter."

Reilly threw a french fry at her. "Brat."

"You should know," Zuzu told me, while throwing the

fry back at him playfully, "that Reilly doesn't believe in anything."

Reilly shrugged and took another bite of his sandwich. "I just think there's scientific explanations for a lot of things people choose to see as magic."

"I'm also slightly psychic," Zuzu said, leaning toward me. "Which Reilly doesn't believe in either. My great-grandmother was a great shaman. Micmac Nation." She frowned and a crease furrowed her smooth forehead. "I sense *dark forces* at work around you." She covered her mouth.

"It might be a little more convincing without the giggling," I said.

The door opened just then, and Sean Gunn walked in. The chatter in the place died down as heads turned and Sean was greeted with a wave or a slap on the back by almost everyone in the Snug. The young lobsterman responded with a quick word or a wave as he made his way over to the table next to us.

He gave me a friendly nod. "Hello."

"Hi," I answered.

"That's interesting. Sean doesn't usually come here," observed Zuzu. She glanced at me curiously.

If she thought Sean Gunn's being here had anything to do with me, it didn't seem likely. Sean made no move to come over and talk to us. Although once or twice I did see him glancing over at me.

Sean looked out of place. The chair seemed too small for

his tall form and long legs, and he hunched over the table, drumming his fingers as if he wasn't sure what to do with himself.

"He's had to work really hard, taking over the lobstering business since his dad died," said Zuzu. She frowned. "His mom has bad arthritis and can't do very much for herself."

Soon a waitress brought over his order and Sean reached into his pocket. A number of coins spilled onto the table and I stared. It was a mix of old gold and silver coins, some that looked very similar to the ones I'd discovered in the safe-deposit box.

"Nope," the lanky bartender called over, "your money's no good here, Sean."

Sean raised his cup. "Thanks, Donnie." He scooped the coins back into his pocket.

"Everybody loves Sean," said Zuzu, with a smile. "He's such a good guy."

"Were those gold coins on the table?"

Zuzu shrugged. "I think so. Most everyone has some. The First Ones don't care much about coins. They give us the ones they find in wrecks. Sometimes Ben Deare gets permission to trade a few if we need something special from the mainland."

It explained why Sean was unimpressed with my offer of money to turn his boat around. Money obviously didn't mean the same thing here as it did in the real world.

The real world. I wondered if I would ever get back to it.

The man in the corner began to sing in a gruff, soft voice.

> "*From old Long Wharf the* Dover *sailed out of*
>   *Boston town*
> *With linen, wool and guns and gold for the*
>   *British Crown.*
> *Halifax they'll never see; the* Dover's *taken*
>   *down.*
> *The compass spins from north to south with*
>   *Trespass on the lee,*
> *But a Trespass sailor never drowns; he's only lost*
>   *at sea.*"

It took me a few moments to realize where I had heard it before. My mother had whispered snatches of this song when she was sick.

It was a beautiful tune, but sad. It seemed like most of the people in the Snug knew it well; quite a few of them joined in and sang along.

> "*The briny witch she took them all beneath*
>   *December waters—*
> *One hundred souls in coral chains, fathers, sons*
>   *and daughters.*
> *The compass spins from north to south with*
>   *Trespass on the lee.*

My heart's an anchor weighing me, never to be
   free,
For a Trespass sailor never drowns; he's only lost
   at sea."

Sean didn't sing. He swirled the drink in his glass. "Play something else, Jem," he called over. The musician nodded and changed to a song with a lively, thrumming beat.

Zuzu smiled and tapped her fingertips. "We'll dance to this at Revel," she said.

"Revel?" I asked. "What's that?"

"It's kind of a traditional celebration we have on the island every summer. It's coming soon."

"It's nothing special," said Reilly, giving Zuzu a quick look.

A woman came racing in, her face pink with exertion.

"Crates down on Wreck Beach," she shouted. "Pickin's for all."

One by one everyone rose, emptied their drinks or took a last bite of what they were eating and left the tables, making for the door.

"C'mon," Zuzu said, rising. "Let's go see."

———

On Wreck Beach the waves crashed on the sand in overlapping curls of blue and green and white.

Wooden crates and white plastic tubs were strewn across

the sand. Some containers were at the very edge of the water, tipping over and rolling in the surf.

"How did this stuff get here?" I asked, watching as people scrambled along the sand and waded through the water to claim boxes.

"The First Ones," Zuzu answered, surveying the scene with a look of excited pleasure. "They give us supplies from things they've collected."

"Collected? You mean they sink ships?"

"Of course not," said Zuzu. "That would attract too much attention. But containers are always getting lost from cargo ships. Falling off docks, slipping out of holding straps on rolling decks." Her eyes scanned the beach. "I hope they brought some DVDs; we need new movies."

It was like some kind of combination shopping spree and scavenger hunt. Boxes of tennis shoes, a case of shampoo, metal canisters of propane, and a pallet laden with crates labeled *Bananas—Product of Ecuador.* The assortment seemed completely random.

There was a woman who stood apart from the rest of the crowd. While others scurried from container to container, she remained motionless, staring out at the water. But piles of items were at her feet, and as I watched, one of the men brought a bag of oranges and added it to the rest.

"Who's that?"

Zuzu glanced over. "That's Sophia Clark. Isn't she lovely?"

She was. Sophia Clark must have been in her thirties and

had long, straight ash-blond hair. She wore a silky green print dress, and a striking gold medallion dangled from a gleaming chain at her neck. But her dark eyes held a haunted look. She seemed unaware of the activity, keeping her gaze trained on the water as if searching for something, or someone, out there.

"Finally," muttered Zuzu. She bent over a wooden crate and fished out a can with triumph. "Mandarin oranges. I'm so sick of cling peaches."

Suddenly a high-pitched wail broke out behind us. Sophia Clark pointed at the water. "It's coming." She paced through the sand, back and forth, while hugging her arms tight to her body.

I looked in the direction she was pointing. There was nothing out there except the empty, rolling water.

"Don't pay any attention," said Zuzu in a low voice. "She gets like this sometimes." She went over to the woman. "It's okay, Sophia," Zuzu said, bending to pick up some of the items at the woman's feet. "Here. Look at these. *People* magazine. Look, Brad and Jen are splitting up. Wow, that's too bad. Shall I help you get these home?"

The woman quieted and blinked. Then, as she seemed to notice me for the first time, her face contorted. "It's her," she yelled. "She's bringing it here." She covered her ears with her hands and began to cry.

"What's coming?" I asked.

"The monster," whispered the woman. "The monster."

Zuzu shook her head and said in a low tone, "Sophia gets mixed up about stuff, and you're new here. Maybe it frightens her."

"Is she going to be okay?"

Zuzu nodded. "I'll take care of her, don't worry. I think you'd better go home, Delia."

I walked away thinking exactly the same thing.

CHAPTER 7

On Trespass the water was never far away, and the sea made sure I didn't forget it. The smell of salt, the bite of wind and the rumble of the waves were everywhere, all around me. As each day passed I felt more and more trapped on this island.

I went to the dock, making sure I stayed in the middle of the walkways and well away from the edge. I didn't care to have any more encounters with anything that lurked beneath the surface—though I couldn't help but wonder about the dark-haired First One named Jax. Would I see him again?

I found Ben Deare working on his boat. The *Belores* looked more dilapidated than ever, even though repairs had begun; there were new planks in place on the deck and the smell of varnish hung in the air. Ben's back was to me, and I noticed he was moving slowly.

"Ben."

"Ben."

"Ben!" I shouted.

Ben leapt up and spun around, looking like his limbs were being jerked by puppet strings. "Hell's bells, girl! You'll kill a man with that caterwauling."

"Sorry," I said sheepishly. Then I saw that his left arm was hanging by his side in a sling. "What happened to you?"

He grimaced. "The First Ones were none too pleased about me bringing you, miss. The Council had their Glaukos guards give me a talking-to."

"A talking-to?" I repeated softly. I could see a brown stain on the edge of the gauze on his wrist. I jumped onto the boat beside him. "It looks like more than just talking. Ben, you're bleeding! They hurt you just because you brought me here?"

"St. Cuthbert save us," he muttered, adjusting the bandage and hiding it from my view. "It's not that bad, miss. They could've done a lot worse. Just wish they hadn't set the Glauks on my poor boat is all."

"I'm so sorry." The words seemed lame in view of what had happened. "I had no idea you would get hurt. Or your boat. If I'd known—"

Ben snorted. "Pshaw." His pointy chin jutted up until it nearly met his nose in a defiant expression. "I'll be fine." He patted a hand to the boat's railing. "And she'll be all right too," he added, as if that was somehow more important. He surveyed the *Belores* with affection in his flinty blue eyes. "It would take more than a few Glauks to pull *Bellie* down. And there's no need to blame yourself. I brought you here because it was the right thing to do."

The back of my throat burned with dull anger, and with the words I would've liked to use against whoever had hurt Ben. That probably wouldn't help him, though, and maybe it would make things worse.

And I'd even been thinking about asking him to take me back to Portland if his boat was fixed. But I could never ask that of him now. I couldn't ask it of *anyone,* not if this was the way the First Ones punished disobedience.

"Can I do something to help you?" I asked.

"I can't plane this smooth with only one hand," Ben admitted, tapping a plank with one foot. "I'd be obliged."

Ben showed me what to do, and so I learned how to use a planer to even out the new planks. I enjoyed the feel of the sun on my shoulders as well as the smell of the fragrant curls of wood that piled up beside me. Ben watched me work with hawklike attention, directing my efforts until a particular spot was smoothed to his satisfaction. After we'd worked for a while, I paused and sat cross-legged on the deck. The gentle rocking motion of the *Belores* beneath me was soothing.

"If I'm going to stay here, Ben, I want to know more about the island." I brushed sawdust from the plank I'd just finished. "The only map I could find that even had this place on it was in an old book about New England legends. And the only sentence in the book that mentioned Trespass Island was about buried treasures."

No wonder the ticket agent in Portland had acted so strangely when I produced those gold coins. They would have been enough to get any treasure hunter excited.

Ben didn't react, only rubbed an assessing hand over a place where two boards met. "So," I prompted, "*is* there a buried treasure?"

Ben shrugged. "Oh, there's treasure here right enough. But not the way most people think. The First Ones don't care too much about gold or jewels. They have as much as they want of that stuff, you see? Every treasure chest ever lost at the bottom of the sea is open to them. No. They protect what they see as the real treasure of this island."

"And what's that?"

"Something called the Archelon. It's buried deep inside the heart of Trespass. They say that the Archelon contains the power of Poseidon himself. He left it here, and here it will remain, until the old gods return to reclaim their world."

"And when is that going to happen?"

"No one knows that, miss," said Ben. "But they wait." He squinted out to the water. "We all wait."

There was something so resigned and sad in his voice. "Really?" I asked. "What are you waiting for, Ben?"

"Waiting for you to get back to work, that's what," he said with a waggle of his free hand at the next plank.

I sighed and kneeled over it, scraping carefully. "Yesterday a woman on the beach freaked out when she saw me. Someone named Sophia Clark."

"Yep," he answered. "I heard something got her upset. You shouldn't pay her too much mind." Ben tapped a finger to the side of his head. "What did she say, anyway?"

I hesitated. "She said a monster is coming."

"Well, no wonder everyone's in a bunch."

"And she said I'm bringing it here. And back in Portland, when I threw those bones, *you* said you saw a monster in my future. So what is this monster? Did you mean the Glaukos? Or the First Ones? Or something else?"

Ben took off his cap. "I just read the portents, miss. I don't know all the answers as to what they mean. World's full of monsters. We've got a big whirlpool called the Tor about four miles due southeast of Trespass. It's a whirlpool they say goes down to the bowels of the Earth. And all sorts of beasts live at the bottom. Imprisoned there in olden days by Poseidon himself."

I grimaced. "He left stuff all over the place, didn't he?"

"Joke all you want. Some of these stories are true."

"So why should this Sophia Clark think I have anything to do with monsters?" I asked. "She acted like she was actually afraid of me."

"I don't know," Ben grumbled. "But it don't matter. You're meant to be here. The portents said so. Look out there, now you've missed a spot."

Portents. Monsters. Buried treasure.

Trespass Island was not exactly the ideal spot for a summer vacation. I didn't belong here. But could I leave? Noooo.

It was early afternoon by the time I finished helping Ben, and the sun blazed with the kind of heat that raises tingles on your skin. I walked down the slope of dune to the beach near Gran's house and decided to explore in the opposite direction from the one I'd been before. There were hardly any waves, and quiet sheets of water rolled to meet my feet as I kicked broken shells along the sand.

If only my mother were here. She would have been able to tell me what to do, how to fit in here. But did I even *want* to fit in here?

I came to the end of the beach—or at least, as far as I could walk. An irregular wall of black rocks rose and protruded onto the sand, blocking the way. I reached out and touched the craggy surface. It was a strange-looking rock, with tiny holes in it. Like pumice. I had seen something similar— where was it? In the earth sciences lab at school.

"Volcanic," I murmured, running a hand over the sharp edges.

Since when did the New England coastline have volcanoes? It was official: everything about this island was impossible.

Something shiny lay at my feet when I turned around. It was my glasses, with beads of seawater still clinging to them.

How had these suddenly appeared? Looking around, I saw that the beach was empty and mine were the only footsteps in the sand. I turned toward the sea and saw him in the water.

It was the angel. The one who'd kissed me beneath the dark water.

A fin flashed silvery in the sunlight and he disappeared almost instantly, ducking below the surface without a splash or a sound.

"Wait!" I called. "Don't go."

His dark head emerged from the water, much closer now. How had he moved through the water so fast? He wasn't bobbing or sweeping his arms. It was as if the water simply parted around him, supporting him.

"You require those lenses for your vision," he said. "I've returned them to you."

"Thank you." I picked up my glasses, wiped the lenses with the bottom of my T-shirt and put them on, immediately feeling more comfortable.

Above the water and in daylight and now with my glasses, I really saw Jax for the first time.

He wasn't handsome. And not even faintly angelic.

His nose was aquiline but flattened and widened at the bridge, as if it'd been broken and mended badly, giving his face a leonine look. His mouth was firm, with narrow, uncompromising lips. Black hair hung in messy waves nearly to his shoulders. His eyes were the same brilliant blue that I remembered and of such a strange, deep intensity that I felt I could get lost in them.

But how did I ever imagine him as an angel? His wasn't a face you'd see in a Renaissance painting. Unless it was at the bottom, where they depicted hell. Yes, he looked like he'd be down there, mixing it up with the sinners and brawlers.

"You're the one who saved me," I said softly. "A First One."

"My name is Jax," he answered, swimming closer. "I am of the Aitros clan. Landers call us the First Ones." His voice was deep and resonant. It was the same voice that had warned me away from the water three nights ago on the moonlit beach.

"Landers?" I finally asked.

"You." There was a faintly derisive curl of his mouth as he tossed his blunt, square chin in my direction. "Air-bound mortals. Humans." His gaze swept over me. "I'm surprised to see you in the water so quickly."

"I'm *not* in the water." Then, looking down, I realized that I *was*. Water curled around my ankles, and my feet were sunk into the sand. *How did that happen?* I wriggled free and splashed back to the sand.

"You've recovered from your accident?" Jax asked. His tone was formal and courteously distant.

"Um." Unbidden, the memory of his lips against mine came back so clearly, it was almost a physical sensation.

I pressed my lips together, trying to erase the thought as heat flooded my cheeks. "I didn't have an accident," I said, fumbling to adjust the right earpiece of my glasses; it seemed to be bent out of shape and—oh, *great*—tangled in my hair. "I was dumped overboard, remember?"

"You came here without permission," replied Jax. "The

Lander Gunn did not have authority to transport you. Just as Ben Deare did not have authority to bring you."

"So you decided to sink Sean's boat?" I retorted. "Very mature. Is that how they do things on Olympus these days?"

Oh, not wise.

It was as if a storm cloud had come into his eyes, they went so dark, and his voice was the unexpected clap of thunder that makes you jump. "If I *had* decided to sink that frail husk," he snarled, "it would be another shell on the floor of the sea. That was not my intent. The Glaukos are clumsy creatures." His voice fell to an irritable grumble. "But they meant you no harm. The creature responsible will be punished."

"Punished? There's no need for that. It was just an accident. I'm fine. You . . . saved me. Thank you."

Jax frowned. Instead of saying "You're welcome" or "Don't mention it," he looked as if my owing him my life annoyed him. A lot. Maybe he resented having to give a mere mortal mouth-to-mouth. Although from what I could tell, he'd seemed to enjoy it at the time.

"There is something strange about your voice," he said, as if wanting to change the subject. "You don't speak like the Landers here."

I blinked through my glasses. They still didn't seem quite right; everything looked a little fuzzy. "Probably my accent. I'm from Kansas."

"Where is this Kansas Island?"

"It's not an island," I laughed. "It's a state."

He straightened, rising a little from the water. "Every piece of earth is an island. Some are merely bigger than others."

He didn't seem accustomed to being laughed at. Or talking to people, for that matter. "I guess that's true," I said. "I'm sorry. I really don't mean to be rude, but can you walk? I mean . . . do you have a tail?"

In reply he strode out of the water toward me, moving so fast that I backed up in surprise.

Why can't you learn to keep your mouth shut, Delia?

"You're fortunate that you risk this impertinence with me rather than one of the elders," he said. His eyes sparked with blue fire. "They're not so tolerant of Landers. No. We do *not* have tails."

Jax had a body. A very human, very male body a little over average height with a trim, muscular build. And I was grateful that part of it was covered with a dark blue garment tied around his hips. A long knife hung from his side. Handle and blade appeared to be fashioned from one gleaming, rippled mass of silver. It was fastened with a piece of leather to his powerfully carved thigh.

"We are descended from Poseidon, who had legs. Two of them," he added. "Only the children of Triton have tails. Which is very lucky for you. They like land meat. Even such a small portion."

"Good to know," I whispered, taking in other details. He had a shimmering green fin protruding from his back—the same segmented, elaborately scaled fin that I had mistaken for a wing in my loopy condition under the water. But within moments of emerging from the water, the fin flattened and disappeared, leaving only three spiny raised bumps along his upper back.

"Wow." I felt a little breathless. Where was my inhaler? I couldn't remember where I'd left it. *Please don't let me have an asthma attack now.* I took a slow, steady breath. "That's an amazing trick."

"On land we look as you do," said Jax. "In the sea our form changes. It is no trick."

I nodded. In daylight I saw what the moonlight had hidden. His chest was perfectly molded but crisscrossed with ugly scars that stood out pale against his sun-bronzed skin. I was curious about what could have made such wounds. But I thought it would have been rude to ask him.

But you had no problem asking him if he had a tail, did you?

My mind worked in weird ways sometimes.

From what I could see, only small things kept Jax from looking completely human: his hands and feet had thin webs at the base of the digits. But even these retracted as he stood before me, until they were barely visible. And on his flatly planed abdomen two vertical slits interrupted the muscles on either side of his belly button. They rippled with each breath he took.

Gills. The guy has gills. Interesting. For some reason I found it hard to tear my eyes away. He seemed full of energy and strength. It glowed in the rich golden color of his skin and the fierce intelligence of his eyes. It was almost as if I could feel the radiant heat warming me. But his face was somber.

"Do you find me dazzling, Lander?" asked Jax with a contemptuous curl of his narrow mouth.

"No," I said. "I mean . . . what?"

"You're staring."

"Sorry." Embarrassed, I looked away and felt a blush color my cheeks. "I just never saw anyone like you before. What *are* you exactly?" That sounded rude. "I mean, what are the Aitros?" I asked. "Where did you come from?"

"We are demigods. Lineage of Poseidon," he said. "We originated in the Ionian Sea, near an island the humans call Corfu."

"And how did you ever come to Maine, so far away?"

Jax's brilliant blue eyes transfixed me. "Once, the children of Poseidon could be found in all the waters of this world. But the time of man came, and as the old gods left us, the demigods dwindled away. Eventually only a few strongholds remained where the waters retained the power of our ancestors." He shrugged. "Our powers become diminished the farther we swim from this island. A source of the old power rests inside it."

"The Archelon," I murmured.

"Yes," said Jax, leveling a sharp gaze on me. "What do you know of this?"

"Ben Deare told me some of the stories about the island."

Jax nodded. "To humans they are only stories. Even to some of my people, the old gods have become distant memories. Stories."

But obviously the young man standing before me was all too real. He looked like a descendant of Poseidon, born of something ancient and powerful. But in a way he was trapped here too.

"What powers?" I asked.

Jax shrugged. "Compared to Landers we are stronger and faster. We live longer but are not immortal. We have some abilities in the water that you might see as supernatural."

He held a hand over the water and murmured something under his breath. Immediately the water beneath his hand began to churn and a thick fog rose from the surface to drift in delicate swirls around his fingers. He waved it away with a careless gesture.

"You create the mist that surrounds the island. To keep outsiders away."

He nodded. "And if they become too persistent, we sometimes must resort to other means." He cupped one hand and swept it through the water. A ripple coursed away, against the tide, traveling in the direction of the open sea. As I watched, the ripple rose higher, becoming a racing, glassy slope. Finally it crested, a dark wall of water twenty feet high. It slammed down with the sound of a thunderclap, creating a momentary craterlike depression in the sea before dispersing.

I stared as the tumult of roiling, bubbling water subsided. "You wreck ships," I whispered.

"Not nearly as many as we used to," replied Jax, his voice almost regretful. "The island has a reputation for treacherous seas and a deadly reef. People know to stay away. Most people," he added, looking at me. There was a spark of challenging amusement in the slight lift of his eyebrow and the curve of his mouth.

"You don't think very much of people, do you?"

Jax watched me. "They serve their purpose. As long as they know their place."

Our *place*? His condescending tone put my back up.

"If we're so far beneath you, why are you talking to me?"

He folded his arms across his chest. Once again my eyes were drawn to the network of scars that disfigured the smooth, broad muscles.

"I do what pleases me," he said slowly. "When it pleases me."

If I hadn't seen him underwater, I might have laughed at the proud angle of his shoulders, the arrogant lift of his chin as he spoke. But I *had* seen him. Up close and really personal. And I might have drowned if he hadn't intervened.

"Why did you tell me to stay out of the water? That was you, wasn't it?"

Jax nodded brusquely. "Landers have their own beach, your people should have told you. And why do you question the orders of a First One?"

"Orders? I thought it was just *advice*."

"It was for your safety," Jax replied. "Something has changed—there are creatures from the northern depths here.

They shouldn't be in these waters; it's as if something has called them." He looked at me curiously.

"Oh?" I said. I was thinking about something else entirely. *Why did you kiss me?*

I know I didn't imagine that kiss. I'd never been kissed like that in my life. But obviously it didn't make a big impression on Jax. And if he wasn't going to mention it, then I certainly wasn't either.

"Why can't I leave the island?" I asked instead.

Jax scowled. "I'm not accustomed to a Lander speaking to me so freely. Or haranguing me with questions. I wouldn't recommend that you speak so to the others; you won't live long if you do."

"You're the only First One that I've seen," I said truthfully. "Answer my question, please. What makes you think you can keep me here if I don't want to stay? I'm sure there must be a way for me to leave."

Jax strode back to the water, scooped one hand in and lifted it high. Water coursed through his fingers and down his gleaming, muscular arm. "This," he said. "Water surrounds you, and it's our domain, not yours. You will stay as long as the Council deems it right for you to stay."

"Maybe I could talk to this Council."

"That would not be pleasant for you, believe me," he called over his shoulder, wading deeper into the sea. "And they're occupied with more important matters right now. The clan is gathering for Revel."

"None of this is fair," I shouted. "I didn't agree to any of this!"

"There is only one thing you need learn," Jax said, turning to face me once more. "First Ones rule. Landers obey." He slid into the water on his back.

He was going to disappear again. I should have been relieved, and yet I didn't want him to go.

"One more thing, Lander," he called to me as he glided away. "Tell your people there is a dead man over there on the rocks."

I stood staring at the water and unable to move for a few seconds. Jax was gone. Had he really just said what I thought he had? Slowly, as if dragged by some invisible rope, I walked farther down the beach, back to the outcropping of black rock.

A tangle of cloth was caught in a crevice. The loose end washed back and forth in the turbulence. I went closer, my heart beating so hard and slow inside my chest that I thought I could hear it over the roar of the sea.

It was only when I stood right over the spot that I could make out a blue shirt and a pair of pants. But it wasn't just clothes. A man's body, gray and bloated, lay wedged in the rocks. He stared up blindly, his mouth open and brimming with seawater.

His eyes were gone.

I gasped and looked away—but not before the image of those two bloody, open sockets seared itself into my brain.

Leaping from .the rocks, I landed hard on the sand, my palms and knees pressing into the hard wet grit. I jumped up and ran.

"Help!" I yelled as I raced down the beach, but my voice was swallowed up by the wind and the crash of water. And soon, with my running and panic, my breath was reduced to hoarse cries.

I stopped running and tried to calm my breathing before I started a full-blown asthma attack. That wasn't going to do any good. Raising an alarm wouldn't help the poor man on the rocks anyway. He was dead.

And part of the sick panic I felt was because I recognized him.

Not from his face, which was— *No. Breathe. Don't think about that.* I'd recognized him from the patch on the tattered shirt, still with a faint brown coffee stain and stitched with a name.

Richard.

It was the ticket agent from the ferry terminal.

CHAPTER 8

Several of the island men struggled to remove the body from the rocks. One of them stood apart, yelling and gesturing instructions. The corpse was covered with a canvas tarp, but as I watched, something gray flopped out from underneath when they tried to lift it. It was an arm. I think it was an arm.

I clamped a hand to my mouth, feeling nauseated, and turned closer to Gran. I'd never seen a dead person before and really, really wished I could erase the picture from my mind. The man's skin had been sliced with deep cuts, like long talons had ripped into him. A piece of his neck had been torn away in a deep, circular wound. But the worst part was those two ragged pulpy holes.

It looked as though he'd been fed on.

I shut my eyes tight and took deep breaths of the sea air. Jax had told me where the body was. Could he have killed the ticket agent?

No. For some reason that I didn't really want to examine right now, I decided that he hadn't. He couldn't have done this.

Not that I had any delusions Jax wouldn't be capable of killing. He as much as admitted that the First Ones sank ships, and his disdain for humans was pretty obvious.

You just don't want it to be him.

When I opened my eyes, Sean Gunn was climbing down from the rocks. His cheeks were red from exertion, and sand clung to his tousled hair.

"They're getting another tarp. We'll have to take him away in—" He broke off as he caught sight of me. "We need another tarp," he mumbled, then turned to me and asked, "Are you okay?"

"I think so. Thanks. But should you move him? Won't the police be coming to investigate?"

"He'll be taken care of," said Gran. "He'll be buried up on the hill. Proper and respectful."

"But what about finding out what happened?" I asked. "His family? They'll need to be notified?"

Neither of them responded. Gran stepped closer as if to block my view of the gruesome work. "Don't you worry, everything will be handled."

"But what *happened* to him?" I asked. "How did he get here? Did those Glaukos things do this? Or the First Ones?"

114

"No," said Sean. "This was something different. An Icer killed him. They always go for the eyes."

I let out a breath and realized I was relieved. It hadn't been Jax. Though this was a stupid thing to focus on at the moment. "Icer?" I said, swallowing. "Do I even want to know what that is?"

"A sea demon," answered Sean, in that really calm, matter-of-fact way that I was beginning to realize was typical for him. And really annoying. I'd been freaking out ever since I'd arrived here. My body was probably running on adrenaline fumes by now. Meanwhile, Sean sounded like a bored tour guide.

"They come from deep waters up north. They can crawl right out of the water and slip on board, usually at night. But it's weird." Sean rubbed the back of his neck. "I've never seen one this time of year. Or an attack near the island."

"Why would it come here now?"

Sean shrugged. "Who knows? Stray current. Global warming. A tasty snack wrapped in a little boat. Icers kill pretty much anything in their path. We don't know if it's because they're hungry all the time or if it's just for fun." He peered over at the rocks. "Actually, they didn't eat much of that guy."

"Hush. Don't scare the child," scolded Gran. "Even if it was an Icer—and we're not sure it was—there's no need to get Delia worked up."

"Definitely," I said, feeling dazed. "Let's not get me worked up. I mean, maybe there's something more serious to focus on."

"Tried to tell you it was dangerous here," said Gran gruffly. She swung her gray braid behind her.

"I thought you meant like rocks and big waves, Gran. Not"—I shook my head, at a loss—"whatever this is."

Gran patted my shoulder. "There's no need to worry, child. We're safe here; Icers can't get through the Hands. The current just washed the body in on the tide. That's why we call this Wreck Beach—everything winds up here eventually." Gran twitched one of her own bulky cardigans up closer over my shoulders. "Here, keep this on. You must be in shock."

"Well, *yeah*."

Gran, impervious to sarcasm, just nodded. "You want to come inside? The men will take care of this."

"No," I said softly. "I'm not cold."

I *was* cold. But it wasn't the kind that any amount of fuzzy knitwear could change. Thick clouds blocked out the sun, and the sea whirled around the island, churned by a cool, sharp wind. We were surrounded by gray water, gray sand and gray sky all blurred together. I couldn't even see a line for the horizon.

And out there, in the swirling shadows, are monsters.

A foamy curl of surf rolled across the dry sand toward my feet. I shivered and backed away before it could touch me.

"Is this the newcomer?" The man who'd been issuing orders over the removal of the ticket agent's body strode across the sand. He was middle-aged, with a small frame and a potbelly that strained his plaid shirt.

"I hope you realize this is your fault," he said, piercing me with a glare from behind wire-rimmed glasses. His head was round and much too large for his body. A few strands of hair clinging to the top broke the shine of his balding scalp. The resemblance to an egg with a bad comb-over was striking.

"What?" I wasn't sure he'd spoken to me.

"That man's dead because of you," he said in a nasal voice, emphasizing each word by jabbing a finger at my face.

"Ed, now, take it easy," said Gran. "She had no idea. Delia, this is Ed Barney. He's the mayor of Trespass."

"My fault?" I whispered, unable to find my voice at first. "I didn't even *know* him."

"Did you give him this?" asked the mayor. He held out a white, plump hand with a gold coin in it. It was the one I'd given to the ticket agent in exchange for arranging my passage with Ben Deare.

"It was still in his pocket. And what's left of his boat is floating out near Pelican Rock, loaded up with supplies and equipment for digging. The way I figure it, the fella wanted to find some treasure. Got himself killed by an Icer instead."

"That's enough, Ed," Gran said in a voice that carried its own weight. Not in an "I'm an elected official" way but rather an "I'll kick your ass if you mess with my granddaughter" way. "Delia couldn't have known what would happen," Gran went on. "She wanted to come here to bring her mother's ashes. And now the First Ones have made it pretty clear she's supposed to stay. And *I* want her to stay."

In spite of everything frightening and bizarre that had happened, a sense of quiet happiness filled my chest at her words.

"Is that so?" Ed Barney eyed me. "Well, nobody told *me* about it. This is a breach of security. A major breach." He spoke in a fast staccato, as if tapping out his words in Morse code. "This isn't the end. No, sir. Who knows what this'll lead to? Foreigners swarming this place by sundown. Treasure hunters. Snoops. Spies."

"Why does there have to be so much secrecy?" I asked. "I think the whole world would be interested in this place. Weird sea creatures, strange climate. *National Geographic* would probably give you guys a whole issue. And maybe you could get some protection from these Icers or whatever they are."

Mayor Ed's eyes popped and he wriggled his shoulders as if I'd just dropped a poisonous snake down the back of his shirt.

"Well, girlie, that's just what we *don't* want. Prying eyes and interference. That'll be it. They'll come in here and cage us all up like animals. Or nuke the place. This is *our* world, and it runs just fine. As long as we keep outsiders away." He glared at me as if he really needed to emphasize the point.

"You call *that* running fine?" I demanded, pointing to the remains of the man up on the rocks.

Sean grabbed my hand. "C'mon, Delia, why don't we take a walk," he said, tugging me away. "You don't mind, do you, Maisie?"

Gran shot him a grateful smile. "That's fine, Sean, you two go ahead."

The mayor's querulous voice followed us down the beach. "I'll expect to see you all at the services tomorrow. Oh nine hundred. Sharp."

I was clumsy trying to keep up with Sean's long-legged strides through the sand and at the same time very aware of the warm clasp of his hand around mine. I wasn't used to good-looking guys grabbing me and whisking me away for a stroll.

"Hold on a minute!" I said, slowing down. "What's the big rush? I wanted to talk to that guy."

"Yeah. I could tell." Sean's head was down; he was full of determined momentum. "That's why we're taking a walk. Ed Barney may look like a joke, but he's not. You don't want to make an enemy of him."

I planted my feet, forcing Sean to pivot in the sand. Which wasn't easy, given the size difference between us. It was like trying to stop a quarter horse stallion. "Stop," I said breathlessly. "This place is insane. You know that, right? I got on a boat in the real world, in the twenty-first century. Now I'm here and nothing makes sense. At all." Sean opened his mouth and I held up a palm. "And I'm tired of all this 'you can't understand' and 'we're so mysterious' island crap. So don't even *go* there."

"Okay." Sean nodded. He looked out to sea. "Fair enough. Here's your quick lesson: Demigods and sea monsters are real. It makes sense fast enough when your life depends on it. Which it does. The end." He folded his arms.

"So all of this is normal for you? Bodies washing up on the beach. Getting attacked by sea monsters. Just all in a day's work, huh?"

Whatever lightness there was in Sean's expression, which wasn't much, disappeared. "No. When I was growing up, we never saw the First Ones or the Glauks or anything else. Well," he corrected himself, "only once in a while. They gave us good lobsters in our traps, left crates of supplies on the beach, stuff like that. Intruders were kept away. Non-violently," he added, to my questioning look. "To a kid they even seemed kind of cool, like superheroes or something. They protected the island."

"From things like Icers?"

"Yeah. Usually the Glaukos will patrol a three-mile perimeter around Trespass. Makes it a lot safer to go fishing, though we still have to be careful."

That would explain the arsenal of weapons on Sean's boat. Being a fisherman was probably dangerous enough. I couldn't imagine being out there with real sea monsters. "Creatures from the northern depths have come," I whispered, thinking aloud.

Sean looked at me. "Who told you that?"

"Jax."

A worried frown passed over Sean's face. "We stay separate from the First Ones, Delia. Especially him."

"Why especially Jax?"

"He's an outcast from their clan. A troublemaker."

"What did he do?"

Sean laughed. "Jeez, I don't know." He put his hands in the pockets of his jeans and hunched his shoulders against a sudden breeze. "We don't usually have any contact with the First Ones. That's one of the rules of the Accord. Well," he added, "no contact except for Revel."

I pulled my wind-fluttered hair out of my eyes. "Revel. Zuzu mentioned that. It's some kind of a party, right?"

Sean looked out to the water. "Oh yeah," he said in an odd voice. "It's a hell of a party."

"So tell me why nobody leaves Trespass," I said. "You have a boat, you go to Portland to sell your lobsters, right? Why don't you just leave here and never come back?"

Sean stopped and for a moment I thought he didn't understand the question, he looked so puzzled. "Where would I go?" he said at last. "This is my home. Besides, I would never turn my back on my family, my friends. I have to protect them."

It might have sounded melodramatic except for the delivery. Sean Gunn spoke as though he'd told me his address or phone number, just simple facts he was absolutely sure of.

What would it be like to feel like that? Like such a part of something that you would never leave it, and would protect it with your life.

"So you like living here," I said, searching his open, honest face. "Okay, I get that. But isn't there anyplace else you'd like to see? In the whole world?"

Sean stepped closer. "You know, you ask a lot of questions." His eyes weren't all brown, I noticed; when I got close I could see they had flecks of green and bronze around the irises. And the tips of his dark eyelashes looked like they'd been brushed with gold.

"Yeah, well, you know . . . tourists."

"This island might seem like a nightmare to you," Sean said. "But it can be okay. Magical, even. You'll see. Look." He bent down and plucked up something from the sand and put it in my hand. "This is sea glass. And that's a good-luck color. You can make a wish."

I looked down at a piece of glass in the center of my palm, a softly rounded triangle of hazy blue. I closed my fingers around it and smiled at the sweet gesture. "Thanks. Maybe I should save it for when I really need one."

"No way," Sean said, and folded his arms. "That's cheating."

"Well, that's me all over." I grinned up at him. "A hardened criminal in the fraudulent-wishing department. Sometimes I even make two when I blow out the candles."

He smiled at me, and suddenly he looked like a cute guy again. Not like someone carrying a world of worry on his shoulders. "Maybe you shouldn't have come here," he said quietly. "But I'm glad you did."

CHAPTER 9

The next day was the funeral service for the dead man. As if to be ironic about it, the weather turned beautiful. Blue skies twinkled overhead and the air smelled wonderful, like the whole island had been washed and tumble-dried with wildflower dryer sheets. Gran and I walked to the island's small cemetery, located on a grassy windswept hilltop and enclosed by a black iron gate.

In the center of the graveyard, one monument stood above the others, a solid pillar of silvery granite about eight feet high. The top was carved with strange symbols. Some were the same as those I'd seen on the dock and in the village.

Now I realized it wasn't a pitchfork at all, but a trident.

Poseidon's symbol.

The brass plaque on the monument read: BELOVED SONS OF TRESPASS. MAY THEIR SACRIFICE ALWAYS BE HONORED. Names carved into the stone ran in three columns next to dates, beginning in the 1700s. Many of the last names repeated again and again: Tremblay, Briggs, Vincent. And Sean's name. Gunn. The name Gunn was listed four times. The last one, Jacob Gunn, was dated two years ago. That must have been Sean's father.

"Were these all fishermen?" I asked Gran.

She nodded. "Most. The monument honors those lost at sea."

"They all drowned?" I couldn't help but think of those terrifying moments I'd experienced beneath the water. That suffocating press of darkness all around me.

Gran gave a shake of her head. "A fisherman never says that. Nope. Not drowned." She pressed a freckled hand to the granite monument where *Charles McGovern* was engraved. "They're lost at sea," she said quietly.

The ticket agent's grave was marked by freshly mounded dirt and a cross made of two pieces of driftwood nailed together. We took our places and watched as people filed in for the service. Some were the same faces I had seen down at the dock, and some were new. But everyone still gave me the same curious looks.

Zuzu arrived, dressed in a long wisp of a black dress with pieces of gauzy material trailing on the ground. Her hands were clasped demurely before her. She came and stood next to me. Ben Deare arrived wearing a faded blue suit. His baseball cap was gone, and in its place was an old-fashioned-looking blue seaman's cap tucked beneath his uninjured arm.

Sean was there, on the other side of the fresh grave, look-ing uncomfortable in a button-down shirt with the collar too tight. He kept shifting his weight from foot to foot and look-ing at me as if he wanted to tell me something, but each time I caught his eye he looked away.

Well, come over and talk to me already. But he didn't.

When everyone had gathered, Ed Barney, the mayor, cleared his throat and began to speak in his rapid-fire voice. The solemnity of the occasion didn't seem to slow him down any. "We're gathered here to mourn the loss of . . . this fella, Richard. Even though none of us knew him. And he had no business here. But we don't hold anything against him." Bar-ney took out a small, worn Bible from his pocket, licked a thumb and leafed through the pages.

"'There is a time for everything,'" he read. "'And a season for every activity under heaven: A time to be born and a time to die . . .'" As the mayor's voice ran on, I looked at the faces around me.

No one seemed upset. Granted, nobody knew the man, so I didn't expect anyone to be crying or anything, but still. The way he died was pretty extraordinary. It made me sick to think that it could have been my fault. But why wasn't anyone talking about it? Wasn't anyone the least bit freaked out? I was; I'd hardly slept last night, and even though the air was warm I'd closed and locked my window, trying to silence the endless whispering of the waves outside.

Ed Barney closed his Bible. "Right. Amen."

"Amen," responded the assembled islanders.

"Lots of unexpected things happening," Ed announced, looking around. "But no need to be afraid. We got to stick to our ways. Be vigilant." His gaze swiveled to me.

"What about Revel?" a woman from the crowd called out. "Will we still have Revel?"

"Course we will," answered Mayor Ed with a brisk smile. "It's more important than ever to keep up our traditions. We'll celebrate Revel together, just like always."

"And what about her?" a quiet voice asked.

I turned to see who'd spoken. It was Sophia Clark, the woman from the beach. Her sad, deep-set eyes were fixed on me.

"Delia's one of us now," Gran said, putting her arm around my shoulders. Her voice was loud against the eerie quiet of the graveyard. No one seemed ready to argue the point. But they didn't seem too happy about it either.

———

One of us.

It would take more than Gran and a few of the younger people welcoming me to become part of Trespass. Over the next few days, whenever I walked to the center of the village, laughter stopped, voices quieted to murmurs, and people who'd been sitting in rockers on front porches suddenly needed to step inside. I was still a stranger and got only aloof courtesy from most of the islanders. Gran insisted that I shouldn't worry about it.

"Folks on this island are just private, that's all," she said. Her big hands worked on a piece of counted cross-stitch of ducks and geese carrying a banner: *Welcome to Our Home.* It was so sweet.

"Besides that," she went on, "they're a superstitious bunch. You came and trouble followed with that mainland fella. It'll take time for them to forget." Gran squinted and poked the needle through. "Give 'em a few years. They'll warm right up to you."

I sighed, waiting for her to smile at her own joke. But she didn't. Great.

"According to Zuzu, people haven't forgotten about Mom's leaving Trespass. She said they consider her a traitor."

"That's just talk, Delia. Pay it no mind. Your mother had her reasons for leaving."

From what I'd seen she must have had a million. But I was curious to know what finally convinced my mother to leave this place.

———

Sean Gunn and his mom, Sally, were the closest neighbors to us. Sean stopped by sometimes, especially in the evenings after he'd finished work, but his mother never did. Gran said she was in poor health from rheumatoid arthritis. Gran often sent a special herbal tea over for her.

"We have to make do with what we have here," she said. "I make cough syrups, poultices, sleeping medicines from the herbs we grow." She shook her head. "But Sean insists on paying for some fancy medicine from the mainland. Doesn't do any better than willow bark tea, if you ask me."

One Saturday morning when it was raining hard, I put on a slicker and brought the tea over for Sean's mother.

When Sean opened the door, he looked surprised and almost uncomfortable to see me standing there on the porch.

"Um. Come on in," he said, leading me into a sparely furnished living room.

Sally Gunn was a thin woman who looked to be in her forties. She had Sean's blond hair and brown eyes but a small, pinched mouth. She was dressed in a thin cotton housecoat and sat on a rocking chair in their living room next to a large bay window that looked down to the sea.

"What's happened? Who are you?" she asked me nervously. She made no move to stand and I noticed that she wore large black shoes with thick soles and had a metal brace on one ankle.

Sean picked up the plaid blanket and arranged it over her lap. "This is Delia, Ma. She's Maisie's granddaughter. She brought your tea."

"Oh." She looked from me back up at Sean. "Thanks, honey," she murmured.

"Have you taken your pills today?"

"Pills?" she repeated, furrowing her brow. "Oh, Sean. I don't think I need those pills every day." She took her hands from beneath the blanket and laid them on her lap before her.

Sally Gunn's hands hardly looked human. The joints of her fingers were red, swollen knobs, and her wrists were twisted sideways so badly they looked like broken claws. "Grammy never took a pill in her life except aspirin," she said. "And she did all right."

She gave Sean a worried look. "And I don't want you to get into any trouble, getting things like that. From away."

"Hey. Stop worrying. Didn't I tell you that you're going to have everything you need?" said Sean. "Everything is going great." He motioned for me to follow him.

"She hasn't been the same since my dad died," said Sean in a low voice as he put a kettle of water on the stove. "Just sits by that window, watching like she thinks he's going to come back or something."

"I'm sorry," I said. " How did your father . . . ?"

"His boat wrecked in a storm November before last. I've been trying to keep things going." Sean blew out a frustrated breath and took a mug from the shelf. "Man. Looking back now, I don't know how he did what he did." He spooned some of the loose tea into a small strainer and set it on top of the mug.

"You have an awful lot to handle," I said.

Sean looked at me and smiled. His deep-set brown eyes were warm and friendly. "Don't worry. Things are gonna get better."

It was a good attitude. I only wished I could be half as confident about my future here on the island.

In some ways life was very quiet. Just as Zuzu and Reilly said, everyone on Trespass Island was expected to work to support the community. A lot of people worked on the fishing boats or at Gunn's, shelling and packing lobster meat. Repairing nets and lobster traps was a full-time occupation for many of the islanders, as was raising animals for milk and meat. Many of the women went out at low tide to dig for clams, and a few worked at the island's little school or in one of the small stores in the village. Gran's job was gardening. One day she took me with her to the fields, located on the southern side of the island.

"I take care of the herbs, mostly, and a few vegetables," she told me. "You can help me with that for now." Gran strode ahead through a neatly organized garden plot. Tall fronds of savory-smelling plants brushed my legs as I followed along behind. A flash of bright color caught my eye, and I spotted a hummingbird hovering over the trumpet petals of a purple flower.

"You probably noticed it's warmer here," said Gran. "Our winters are mild, and we have a real nice long growing season."

"Yeah, why is it so warm?" I asked, brushing away a mosquito. Even for summer, the air seemed unusually heavy, almost tropical. There were plants here that I'd never seen before, and the sweet, spicy scent of flowers was everywhere.

"Why?" Gran stopped short and looked surprised. "Heavens, I don't know, child. Must be something to do with the currents or the airstream or some such. That's just the way it is."

As I was learning, that phrase pretty much summed up my grandmother's outlook on life as a whole. *That's just the way it is. Deal with it. Keep going.*

But I'd bet Reilly had a scientific explanation for the strange climate. I'd have to remember to ask him.

"That's dill," Gran said, moving on. "And here's sage, parsley, some basil." She knelt down. "And here's rosemary. That's for remembrance." She chuckled. "Only wished it worked better; my memory's not what it used to be."

Gran moved on and began to cut leaves from a bushy plant. It was strange-looking, with glossy green leaves and tiny flowers of a lighter shade of bright, nearly fluorescent green. Soon our basket brimmed with the cuttings. A sweet, slightly resinous smell wafted up.

"What's this?" I asked.

"Trapweed. No. Don't touch it, dear. It'll give you a rash." Gran snipped another clump with her gloved hands and dropped it in the basket. "There. That should do it. Gosh, look at the time. It's nearly high tide; they'll be waiting."

"Who?" I asked, but Gran didn't answer me as she tossed her gear and baskets into the back of the golf cart, and soon we were rattling over the dusty road to a part of the island I'd never been to before. We stopped and I followed as she crossed a grassy meadow that ended in a bluff overhanging the sea. I came close to the edge, cautious of the soft, loose ground. Far below, waves crashed against the rocks with cracks and booms and jets of water. The water churned with black eddies. At first I thought some heavy current or a rising wind was whipping it. But it wasn't that.

The water swarmed with Glaukos monsters. There must have been hundreds of them. Scaly arms, dark misshapen heads and tails thrashed together in a tangled, boiling mass.

Gran reached into her basket and threw out a handful of the leaves. They fluttered down to the water's surface and disappeared. Below, the thrashing increased, accompanied by a chorus of high-pitched, chirping cries as the Glaukos gnashed at the floating leaves.

"You *feed* them?"

"Oh yes." Gran had a contented expression as she tossed out the clumps of greenery. She looked like one of those people at the park, feeding pigeons. Really big, nasty, poisonous pigeons. Obviously the creatures had immunity to the spikes on each other's tails, because it was pretty wild down there.

"I'm kind of surprised that they're . . . vegetarian," I said, watching the scene below.

"Oh, they're not," said Gran. "A Glauk will eat meat. But they love this trapweed. It's part of what ties them to this island. They can't come out of the water for too long, so they need us to provide it for them." She upended the basket and shook out the last few leaves. "We help each other."

"This is where you came, that first night I was here."

Gran nodded. "We aren't too far from the house here if you follow that path." She pointed to a break between some arching bushes. "They were overdue for a feeding that night, so I took a bundle of the dried trapweed I keep on hand at the house. Glauks can't go too long without trapweed. They start to get real agitated. This keeps them calm."

I stared as one of the Glaukos swam closer to the rocks at the cliff's base to reach a clump of trapweed caught there. It raised its leathery head and stared up at me with yellow, unblinking eyes. Suddenly it bared curved rows of teeth at me and let out a series of high-pitched trills. I shuddered at the noise. It was like a weird, angry birdcall that drilled right into my ears.

"Step away now, Delia," Gran said. She turned to go. "They don't like to be watched."

She didn't have to tell me twice. I was only too happy to leave the bizarre creatures to their meal.

CHAPTER 10

I'd been on Trespass Island for a little over two weeks and had begun to venture out on my own whenever I had spare time. There was a shed behind Gran's house stuffed with yard tools, clay pots, fishing poles and other odds and ends, as well as an old bicycle. Calling it a bicycle might have been generous: it was basically two wheels and a wire basket, held together by chipped black paint. But it got me everywhere I wanted to go.

Invitations to explore were everywhere. And what I liked best about exploring the island on the bike was there was no one to say "That's not allowed." I never got tired of discovering new places, from winding paths that twisted along the grassy bluffs to hillsides covered with wild blueberries.

There were even sea caves on the opposite side of the island from Gran's house; from a jagged curve of the coastline, I could see their dark openings at the base of the rocky cliffs below. Seeing them made me think once again of the legends of treasure on the island. The caves would make a likely hiding spot. But they appeared to be inaccessible, except from the water. Even at low tide water churned at the mouths of the caves. Exploring the caves would have meant swimming out to them. So. Definitely not an option.

But I decided that I did need to try new stuff. So one day I took a pole and a box of equipment from the shed and decided to go fishing from the beach.

Yeah. Fishing wasn't as easy as it looked. Not that I'd never *watched* anyone fish, but the principle of it seemed simple. You threw the line with the hook into the water, right? Voilà. Fishing.

Unfortunately, when I tried to do this, the fishing line didn't fly out over the water and plop in like it was supposed to. Instead, the line and the hook snapped back with a *zing!* sound in an angry little ricochet. I reached up instinctively, trying to catch it.

"Ow! Crap!"

The hook, I realized when I got brave enough to look at my hand, was buried in the meaty part of my palm, at the base of my thumb. The pain was actually not as bad as my irritation at myself.

I heard barking. Perfect. Sean Gunn was striding toward me. His dog raced around him in crazy circles, chasing gulls. I held on to the pole but stuck my left hand behind my back. I smiled, nodded at Sean and mentally begged him to pass by.

Pain throbbed in my palm, but all I could focus on was how much Sean had seen of my performance. And how handsome he looked in a simple white T-shirt and cargo shorts.

The giant black dog waggled his way over.

"Two words for you, Buddy," I told him, glaring. "Personal space."

"Hey," Sean called with a wave. "What're you doing?"

"Oh." I tried to look relaxed. And not impaled. I couldn't show him my hand, now that I'd stuck it behind me. This was so stupid. "A little fishing."

Sean nodded, surveying the opened tackle box and its disgorged, tangled contents. "For what?"

"Tuna," I answered, training my eyes on the water. "Preferably solid white albacore. I don't like the other kind, it smells like cat food."

Sean threw a piece of driftwood for Buddy. He seemed to be enjoying this way too much. He must've seen.

"Oh yeah?" he asked pleasantly. "What're you using for bait?"

"Can opener." I swiveled to face him. "You know, I think I just want to concentrate on my fishing. Alone. You know, relax, get Zen with it?" I looked around pointedly. "It's a big beach."

Sean shrugged. "Small island."

"Really? Gee, I hadn't noticed."

He didn't seem fazed by my sarcasm and took hold of the line. "What's the matter, is there a knot in it? That happens all the time. Let me help you."

Sensing that he might pull on the line, the other end of which was *stuck in me,* I let out a shrill "No!" and showed him my hand. "Don't laugh."

But Sean didn't laugh. "Jeez. Why didn't you show me right away? You can get a nasty infection from something like this," he said, gently probing the skin around the hook. His hands were big. Reddened calluses and small cuts marked his knuckles. "I'll get it out. Buddy, sit," Sean ordered the dog, who'd circled back, dragging his driftwood. Sean took a Swiss Army knife from his pocket.

"Whoa. Wait a minute!" I said, and swallowed. "What're you going to do with that?"

Sean looped the fishing line next to the hook and cut it with a quick tug. "You've got half an inch of stainless steel buried in your hand, Delia. You can't pull it back. The barb's got to be pushed through."

"Is it going to hurt?"

Sean eyed my hand critically. "Oh yeah. Definitely."

"What's the matter with you? You're not supposed to say that!"

"What," he said, putting on a wounded look, "you want me to lie?"

"Yes," I practically hissed. "You're supposed to lie. And distract me."

Sean thought this over for a second. "You want a stick to bite?"

I laughed. "Hmm. Somehow I don't think grinding my molars into a piece of dirty wood is going to make me feel better. You should tell me a joke or something."

He took a pair of pliers from the fishing box. "I'm not very good at jokes."

We sat down on the sand next to each other. He must not have worked on the boat today: his skin was freshly shaved and bronzed from the sun. I breathed in.

"You smell nice," I said. "I mean, not that you smelled bad before. Or that I was . . . smelling you."

Okay. Could *not* believe I just said that.

"Pay no attention," I told him. "It's the excruciating pain talking. Just do it."

Sean gave a nod for me to look the other way. "Okay, I've got one. There was this tourist couple visiting Maine, Fred and Betty. From Schenectady."

"Schenectady?" I winced as I felt the pliers grasp the hook, and looked at Sean. He frowned in concentration, teeth catching his lower lip. There was a snap as he clipped the end off the hook.

"Yeah. Don't interrupt. Joke in progress here. Fred and Betty from Schenectady went out to eat and Betty is looking at the menu and she says to Fred, 'Let's get the twin lobster special.' And Fred says, 'Are you crazy? It's thirty-nine bucks.'"

I felt Sean's hand grip mine tighter. "Hold on," he murmured.

A sharp pain.

"And Betty says, 'Well, of *course* it's expensive, Fred. They're *twins*. What are the chances?'"

I let out a breath, smiling despite myself at the corny humor. "Is it over?"

"Yeah, the hook is out."

I smiled at him. "I mean the joke. Is it over?"

Sean smiled when he looked up, and the sun glinted on his blond hair.

"Thanks," I said.

"No problem. You're going to need to disinfect that when you get home and bandage it up good."

Sean Gunn was like some super-sized Boy Scout, only with the Hotness badge added.

We sat silently for a minute, Sean looking out to the water and running his fingers through the sand. Buddy gamboled around the beach, barking at gulls. "God, I love this place," Sean whispered suddenly. The sudden emotion in his voice surprised me, and for a moment I felt awkward, as if I'd heard his private thoughts out loud.

"I can understand that," I said softly. The feeling of being trapped and helpless that I'd had when I first came here was lessening. I was beginning to appreciate the beauty of

Trespass. "I saw some caves on the northern part of the island," I told Sean, glancing at him. "But it looks like you can only get there from the water. Could you take me to see them sometime?"

Sean gave an exasperated-sounding laugh. "You must have a nose for trouble or something. The sea caves are totally off-limits. Those belong to the First Ones."

"Oh, that figures."

"You know, if you like, I could teach you how to fish. There's some fine striped bass running lately."

"That would be great."

"No problem," said Sean. "I'll bring the Band-Aids."

———

Zuzu and Reilly invited me to come to the beach with them on Saturday. I agreed, on the condition that actually getting into the water wasn't required. I couldn't imagine swimming here, not after what I'd seen.

"It's perfectly safe, as long as we're inside the reef, of course. This is Lander's Beach," said Zuzu as she pulled her hair into a ponytail.

"That's okay, I'm good," I told her. "Really. I don't swim much."

As in ever. I brushed sand off the blanket and, wrapping my arms around my knees, surveyed the beach. A number of the islanders were out enjoying the hot, sunny weather; blankets, colorful umbrellas and coolers dotted the sand, and a handful of people *were* swimming. It looked so normal.

"We go swimming all the time, don't we, Reilly?" said Zuzu, prodding him with her toe.

"All the time," Reilly muttered, lying next to me on the blanket. He was covered from neck to toes by an oversized towel, wore sunglasses and a UV-protective hat with earflaps, and had smeared zinc oxide over most of his face.

"Well, I'm going in," Zuzu announced. "It's too hot to sit here and melt. Look, there's Derek. I'm going to go say hi." She stripped off her T-shirt to reveal a daring pink-and-white-striped bikini and strode off toward the water.

"Have fun," Reilly mumbled.

As soon as Zuzu was gone Reilly sat up. "God, I hate swimming," he sighed. Then he got up and followed her.

I smiled. Reilly might have hated swimming, but that wouldn't stop him from sticking to Zuzu. For a while I watched them swim and saw them join another group: a guy and two girls who were tossing a small football across the water to each other. I was hoping I might see Sean, but there was no sign of him.

I scanned the sparkling water out to the horizon. The smooth expanse was peaceful, unbroken. Idly I let warm sand run through my fingers. This place seemed like another world. I might as well have fallen into the Bermuda Triangle. Who knew? Maybe I had.

Closing my eyes, I lay back and listened to the sounds of laughter and waves and enjoyed the feel of warm sun on my skin. For the first time since coming here, I began to relax. I thought about Sean Gunn. It wasn't hard to let myself picture his warm eyes and gorgeous smile.

But almost instantly another face drifted into my mind. Searing topaz-blue eyes. Dark, roughly carved features. I felt Jax's mouth on mine again. And tasted the pulsing air and water and life in our kiss. I was never going to get over that kiss.

I squirmed beneath the hot sun and flipped over, but that was no better. It felt like I was being slow-roasted over a fire. The back of my neck itched with sweat, and sand was stuck to the sunscreen on my legs. I sat up and drained the last sip of my bottled water.

Reilly and Zuzu were far off down the beach.

The water *did* look inviting: cool blue-green in color and frosted with sparkles of sunlight.

"Cowboy up, Delia," I muttered, laying my glasses on the blanket. I was grateful that Jax had returned them to me, but something must have happened to them—they seemed not quite right, and I found myself taking them off more and more.

I made my way down toward the water, feeling awkward. In contrast to Zuzu's, my bathing suit, the only one I owned, was of the practical, no-nonsense variety: a navy blue one-piece Y-back designed for the swim lesson set. When you're struggling to dog-paddle and keep your face out of the water, the last thing you want to worry about is your suit giving you a wedgie, or losing your top.

Though on Trespass, those would probably be the least of my problems.

As I stood facing the water, Zuzu waved from a distance, then, breaking away from the group, she dove under the water and came up, swimming smoothly over to me. "Yay! You're coming in!" she shouted.

"Yay," I echoed halfheartedly.

I put my feet into the water and stifled a scream. "This is freezing!"

Zuzu ducked down until only her head was visible. "It's best if you just dive in."

"Right," I said. "Like *that's* going to happen. This is as far as I'm going." My feet were already aching from the cold, and they sank into the sand as it shifted. I took a step in farther, just to where it felt more solid. "Okay, *this* is as far as I'm going."

"At that rate you should be in by Tuesday," observed Zuzu as she passed by, doing a backstroke. She stood up and smiled mischievously. "I could splash you. I'm willing to do that to help you."

I wrapped my arms around myself. "Splash me and die, Zuzu. I mean it."

The water was up to my knees now, and I had to admit it felt good, but it was still a shock when the small waves broke against my thighs. I went in a little deeper, where the water was smoother. I couldn't see the bottom. What if I stepped on something? What if there was something . . . lurking under there? With teeth? All of a sudden the familiar, menacing notes of a movie theme began to play in my head.

Dunh-dunh, dunh-dunh . . .

"What jaws?" asked Zuzu sharply.

"What?" I jerked my head up and spun around.

"You said something about jaws."

"Oh. Did I? It's just a movie. About a shark." I looked around. "Let's not talk about it, okay?"

"You started it," she said in an arch tone. "We don't joke about that stuff."

"Got it."

To my surprise I was in up to my chest now. The cool water was such a relief on my skin. With each rise of an oncoming wave, the water lifted me off my feet and set me down gently again. What a strange sensation. Weightless. I realized I'd been holding my arms up stiffly, out of the water. I let them drop.

When the water covered me, I didn't feel cold anymore, and I let myself sink down and, without thinking, pushed off from the bottom and began to swim.

I was actually swimming. In the ocean. Admittedly, it was my signature style—an awkward, lurching paddle with my chin stretched up high—but it was swimming. It wasn't so bad.

My arms cut through the water in tentative strokes, and then stronger ones as my confidence grew. Suddenly, I came eye to eye with the dark, rippling surface of the sea. It was such a strange, exciting view. And unlike a pool, it went on and on.

On impulse I dove under and kicked, exulting in the forward surge that my legs provided. This felt amazing. My whole body tingled and I laughed out loud when I broke the surface. I felt so *alive*.

"Delia!"

It was Zuzu's voice. Sounding worried. And distant.

Disoriented, I lurched upright and gasped when I realized my feet couldn't touch the bottom. Zuzu was a small figure near the beach. I saw her wave to me.

I'd swum the distance of a football field in a matter of seconds.

My legs flailed, the smooth, strong movements disappearing in panic. I paddled more awkwardly, but still covered the distance back to the beach pretty fast. It must have been a burst of adrenaline fuelling my muscles. My breaths came in nervous gulps. Thankfully, I didn't feel the tightness of an asthma attack coming. I hadn't even thought to bring my inhaler.

When I got close enough, I could hear Zuzu yelling. "What the hell was that? You scared me to death." She grabbed my arm to steady me as I lurched out of the water.

"I have no idea," I gasped. My arms and legs were trembling as if my muscles had just been pushed to their limits.

"I thought you said you weren't a good swimmer," Zuzu said accusingly. "I looked up and you were halfway to Nova Scotia."

"I—I'm not," I stammered. "I mean, I didn't do that. I couldn't have. A current must have carried me out there or something."

"I didn't feel a current," said Zuzu, frowning.

Reilly ran over. "We were all calling you, Delia. Didn't you hear?" He looked ashen, the freckles on his face standing out in dark patches on his pale skin. "You've gotta be careful," he said. "Sometimes there're rip tides that can pull you right out to sea."

"I'm sorry. I must have gotten distracted," I said. I took the towel Zuzu offered and wrapped it around myself. "I've never swum like that before."

I looked out to the sparkling water and felt a chill shake me. Something was happening to me, but it wasn't anything I could explain to Zuzu and Reilly. I didn't even understand it myself. Something was pulling me out there, calling to me.

But what was it?

CHAPTER 11

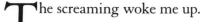

The screaming woke me up.

At first I thought it was a human scream, but it was too high-pitched. It was more like the cry of an angry bird. Maybe a seagull.

"Gran!" I called, running downstairs. "Do you hear that? What's going on?"

Gran sat at the kitchen table, her hands gripped tightly together in front of her, her eyes closed. It looked like she was praying.

"It's got nothing to do with us," she said. She got up and strode around the kitchen, taking out pots and pans and banging them on the stovetop as if to block out the noise. "I'll make you some breakfast."

But the cry grew louder.

"God help us," Gran said. "There's nothing to do for the poor thing. Nothing to do."

"I'm going to see what it is," I said. "Gran? Okay?"

But she seemed to hardly hear me. Her face was blank and she was fixed on her preparations, as if the only thing in the world that mattered was breaking eggs into a ceramic bowl.

I ran outside and down the path to the beach, following that eerie, wailing cry.

The sun was rising in a blaze against the gray sky, and the tide was way out.

I could see something big and dark moving against the rocks. I stopped short as that unearthly scream came again and I saw what it was. A Glaukos.

The thing was *chained* to the rocks with a thick manacle fastened around one leg. I walked closer, repelled yet fascinated. The Glaukos was even more frightening now than it had been under the water; I could see its massive size and the grotesque details of its face. The long torso and short arms and legs looked reptilian, like a crocodile, while the leathery head with its vivid yellow eyes looked almost human.

The creature's yellow eyes, rimmed with swollen red lids, fixed on me as I came closer. The Glaukos snapped and let out a scream of rage that made the hair stand up on the back of my neck. The spiked tail thrashed sluggishly against the rocks with a wet, smacking sound. Heart pounding, I took a few steps closer, being careful to leave a wide circle for the reach of the tail, which must've been eight feet long. The spikes were vicious-looking things, like the pointy parts of a medieval weapon. I recalled Sean's warning about how poisonous they were.

How long had it been here? A while, judging by the spatters of blood and slime marking the rocks. The Glaukos had battered its own flesh trying to escape. I searched the beach for any sign of life, but it was empty. The creature had been chained and left here.

As I watched, the Glaukos slumped back on the rocks. Bloody froth oozed from the gill slits on its face and neck, and the yellow eyes closed. A sickening smell of blood and decay wafted over me. It smelled like something already dead and rotting.

Gran told me they couldn't survive for long outside the water. The sun was up now, and its heat warmed my face. The tide wouldn't return to this level for hours.

It was going to die.

"Hey," I yelled.

The Glaukos didn't respond.

I climbed up the rocks. Close enough to see the creature more clearly but away from the deadly tail. "Hey, you!"

The thing lifted its head and let out a weak rasping sound. I couldn't help but cringe at the folds of leathery skin, now cracked and bleeding. The yellow eyes opened and blinked; they were covered with a hazy film. I could hear wheezing coming from the gills as its chest moved very faintly. The webbed digits of its claws twitched, looking pathetically like fingers trying to grasp at something.

Scrambling back down to the water, I scooped some with my hands and tossed it upward, splashing it onto the Glaukos. It didn't seem to have any effect.

I ran to the house and dashed inside. Gran wasn't in the kitchen anymore. I pulled out the first container I could find: a plastic dishpan from under the sink.

When I got back, I couldn't see any sign of life in the creature. It hadn't moved at all. I filled the pan with sea-water and struggled up onto the rock until I was close to the Glaukos's head.

"C'mon," I whispered, and poured a stream of water onto its face and gills.

The water rinsed away some of the blood and algae from the gills, but they didn't move. Blood trickled from the gills and mouth, tingeing the water.

"What are you doing?"

I turned around to see Jax a few feet away, leaning back on the rocks, his arms folded.

"What does it look like?" I turned away and splashed the rest of the water onto the Glaukos. "It's going to die."

"That's the general idea. This is the creature that harmed you; I told you it would be punished."

I looked down at the collapsed Glaukos. It was no longer the monster that had terrified me under the water. It was a pathetic, dying thing.

"You're not punishing it." I glared at Jax. "You're *killing* it. What is this supposed to prove, anyway? It's an animal. It probably doesn't even understand what it did. And I told you that it wasn't necessary."

"Let me clarify. This is not being done for *you,*" said Jax. "The Accord guarantees the safety of Landers from First Ones or their slaves." His face was as cold, as implacable as stone. "The injury must be recompensed."

"Recompensed? Yeah, well, I think it's recompensed enough," I muttered, and stumbled past Jax with the dishpan. I lugged another panful up the rocks as water leaked through the crack in the side. "Besides," I panted, "the Glaukos were under your orders. Shouldn't *you* be the one chained to a rock?"

"No one would dare touch me," Jax said almost absently as he watched me. He frowned. "The spikes are poison to Landers. Only the Aitros are immune."

"I know. I'm being careful. Besides, it's so weak it can hardly open its eyes. I don't think it would hurt me."

"Then you're a fool," Jax said sharply. "Glaukos are mindless beasts. If it revives, it will react like any injured animal. Blindly, and without thought of your safety."

"Then why don't you help me?" I retorted as water sloshed down my front. "You must be able to unlock those chains."

Jax shook his head. "You're interfering with a punishment ordered by the Council."

"Well, they don't have to know about it," I said. "Right? We could keep it on the down low."

Jax didn't move, only glowered at me with his face like a

battered prizefighter's and his eyes like dark diamonds. "You don't know your place."

I pushed past him and tipped some of the water on the Glaukos. "Yeah. That's very true."

"You're not going to stop?"

"No." I was breathing hard, but surprisingly, I didn't feel any tightness from my asthma. The sea air must have been good for my lungs. But still, how long could I keep this up? And would it make any difference? Even if the tide came in, the Glaukos would still be trapped here. I wondered if there was something in the shed I could use to cut the chain.

"Come on," I urged, nudging the Glaukos's leathery black head with my foot. "Wake up, little Susie." I tipped the pan of water so the contents sluiced once more over the gills.

This time there was something. The gills closed with an audible snap. The Glaukos's head arched up and it emitted a squawk.

Encouraged, I scrambled back down the rocks and scooped more water, being more careful now to keep an eye on the tail. As I climbed back up I stumbled next to Jax, and the dishpan went bouncing down into the water. Jax straightened, moving so quickly it was a blur, and grasped my arms to steady me. For a moment we stood as if locked together, my hands splayed against the bare contours of his chest.

I was soaking wet. He might as well have been pressed to my naked skin. I couldn't meet his eyes; instead, I found myself staring at the raised scars beneath my fingertips.

Immediately, I was brought back to the first moment I'd seen him. The sensations were different this time, and yet the same.

I wasn't drowning. *So why can't I breathe?*

"You are a very annoying little human," Jax said in a low voice, and released me. He strode past and stood over the Glaukos. With one swift motion he pulled his knife from its sheath, raised it high and hacked off the creature's foot.

A jet of black blood arced and the air shattered with the animal's scream of pain. I could only watch in horror as the severed webbed foot of the creature rolled toward me.

The Glaukos recoiled from Jax and pulled the gory stump of its leg from the shackle. With a screeching cry it leapt from the rocks and splashed into the water, disappearing beneath the rolling surface without ever looking back. I felt sick.

"You *animal!*" I cried, turning on Jax. "You didn't need to do that!"

The Glaukos's foot on the ground twitched. Jax picked it up and tossed it into the water.

"I know. You're welcome."

Suddenly a sound like the hiss of rain on hot pavement filled the air. We both turned to see a ten-foot spiral of water rising up from the surface of the sea. Inside the whirl of water stood a figure. The walls of water quieted to rolling waves that spread from a central point beneath the figure's feet. It was a man. Another demigod, I realized, but one very different from Jax.

Long silver-blond hair fell down his shoulders like the smooth mane of a prized stallion. His face was unearthly, gorgeous with elegantly sculpted features beneath quicksilver eyes. He seemed to stride over the water, carried on a rolling white-capped wave.

I was too surprised to take my eyes from the newcomer, but I heard Jax mutter beneath his breath, "Mikos. This is not good."

The newcomer regarded Jax and smiled. It was a smile of pure beauty and it seemed to glow, lighting his handsome features like a candle. I found myself smiling in return before he even looked at me. When he did, I felt at first warmed, and then uncomfortable under that incandescent gaze. I averted my eyes.

"You released the slave," said the pale demigod to Jax. "Why?"

Jax shrugged. "The creature's squawking annoyed me. I meant to kill it. I missed."

I was trying to figure out why Jax would lie about freeing the Glaukos when the stranger turned back to regard me. "You've frightened the little oyster," he said to Jax, rebuke in his tone.

Jax made a derisive sound and resheathed his knife with a smooth, practiced motion.

"Come here, Lander," the newcomer said, extending his hand. His voice had the same rich, deep quality as Jax's. And yet underneath the warmth was something steely and detached. Something inhuman.

Still, I stepped into the water and walked toward him. There was something irresistible about the voices of these First Ones. Maybe it was like some kind of hypnosis. And this demigod certainly looked the part. I'd never seen such a beautiful man in my life. But the calculating gleam of his eyes set off alarm bells in my head. It was as if he enjoyed some secret joke at my expense.

The demigod drifted closer, water curling in gentle ripples around his legs. Like Jax, he wore a garment tied low on his lean hips, though his was pieced together from silvery plates that rippled and reflected as he moved. His skin was burnished gold, perfect and gleaming.

"My name is Mikos," he said, brushing a cool finger down my cheek. His touch somehow elicited a reaction from nerve endings that I never knew I had. A frisson of sensation that mingled fear and fascination. He leaned closer. "Would you like to come with me?" His breath caressed my cheek and made me shiver.

Suddenly Jax was in the water beside me. "I was the one who released the Glaukos. Not her."

Mikos glanced at Jax and his smile narrowed into something harder. "Always causing trouble, Jax. I would have thought the Council's lesson would still be fresh in your mind."

A muscle in Jax's jaw tightened, making his chin look even more square and bullish. "I remember it, Brother."

Brother? This surprised me. The two demigods seemed nothing alike in either appearance or manner. I decided I

155

preferred Jax's brusque, unpolished ways to Mikos's glittering charm. They couldn't be very close; Jax didn't seem very happy to see his sibling.

"The Council wishes to see the new human," said Mikos. Jax looked at me, seeming torn by some inner argument with himself; then he shrugged. "Take her. It's no concern of mine."

Mikos gave Jax a look of faintly puzzled surprise. "Did I ever suggest that it was?" He laced an arm around my waist; it felt like a band of cool steel. "Come, little one," he said. "Let's go swimming."

CHAPTER 12

I pushed against Mikos, trying to free myself, but it was like pushing against a concrete wall. He felt cool and hard and he seemed calmly unaware of my frantic struggle, it was that pathetically weak against him. So I took a gulp of air and held my breath, preparing for him to pull me under the waves. Instead he extended one hand and secured me with the other. Without any visible effort on his part, we began to move through the water. The water parted and swept to either side of us in blue, arcing waves, as if Mikos's hand were the nose of a high-speed boat. The last thing I saw before the waves of water rose high and obscured everything was Jax staring at me, his eyes shadowed and unreadable. Some desperate inner urge made me reach out my hand to him, but Mikos pulled me closer as walls of water enclosed us.

I felt our violent speed over the water. Spray blew into my face like sharp pellets, blinding me, and my feet bumped against the rolling surface. The roaring sound of water surrounded me, as if I were standing behind a waterfall. Where was he taking me? Was he going to drown me or drop me into the middle of the ocean somewhere? Before I had a chance to even worry about the possibilities, we stopped. The walls of water splashed down around us. Mikos released me and I plunked down hard, knee-deep in water, gasping for my breath and my balance. It was warmer water. And warmer air, without the freshening breeze of the beach. And the sound of the surf was gone; there was an eerie quiet around me. I wiped my face and blinked into what at first seemed like inky darkness. The blue sky overhead was gone; we were inside a cave. After a few seconds my eyes adjusted. The water surrounding me and even the walls were lit with a glowing, phosphorescent green light. A faint echoing plink of water dripping came from somewhere in the shadows.

"This way," said Mikos. Again it seemed as if the water simply parted around the handsome demigod; he strode through it like air.

Wading behind Mikos, I struggled to keep my footing on the slippery cave floor as he guided me along a twisting tunnel. I had no idea how much distance we might have traveled to get here.

"Are we still on Trespass, or *underneath* it, I mean?" My voice sounded plaintive and small. Mikos didn't answer.

I followed him through a narrow opening between two massive stones. The area opened up and we entered a colossal domed space divided by towering pillars of tapered stone.

The walls seemed to stretch up into nothingness as their upper limits were lost in the darkness. I blinked, trying to take in the details of the cave in the dim light as well as keep my footing behind Mikos. All the stone surfaces radiated that faint, eerie green light.

"Glow stone," said Mikos impatiently. He picked up a rock from the ground and scraped the wall. Instantly a line of neon light flared along the line he'd drawn in brilliant orange and red. After a moment it faded. Mikos dropped the stone with a plunk and proceeded.

I turned and through the gloom spotted shadowy mouths of tunnels branching off from the walls like the spokes of a wheel. We were inside a huge warren of interconnected caves with an underground river of seawater running through it.

These must be the sea caves that I'd seen the openings to. The domain of the First Ones.

When I turned back, Mikos was watching me. He smiled. It was the same smile as before, only now the gleam of his teeth, lit with the cave's emerald glow, made him look like something feral. "Don't think about running, Lander," he said, his voice echoing around us. "Not even the First Ones know all the passages of these caves. You'd be lost in a dark maze, until something sharp and hungry found you." He took my elbow in a hard grip. "And we wouldn't want that."

We approached a platform of rough steps and walked up. Well, Mikos walked. I scrambled after him, half dragged by his hold on my arm. At the top the surface was a smooth plateau of rock inlaid with an intricate mosaic of multicolored shells. Whatever the picture was, I couldn't make it out. It was on too big a scale for me to see, and I was way too preoccupied by the three figures sitting on stone benches before us. Three of the First Ones regarded me silently.

They were two men and a woman. They *looked* like two men and a woman, anyway, but they weren't. The First Ones all shared a striking characteristic, I realized: the gleaming, otherworldly intensity of their eyes. The three were dressed in more elaborate coverings than either Jax or Mikos, their shimmering tunics fastened by heavy golden clasps at the shoulders.

A row of Glaukos monsters stood behind them. The creatures' hulking forms glistened in the dim light, and their yellow eyes glowed like bare bulbs in the dark.

The demigod in the center was massively built, his chest rounded like a barrel and furred with silvery hair. "Lukus," said Mikos, addressing him with a bow. "I've brought the new Lander, as you requested."

Lukus eyed me with fiery green eyes that mirrored the phosphorescent walls around us, and gave a very slight nod. By the deferential way that Mikos had addressed him, I got the feeling that he was the leader of this Council, or maybe of the whole clan, as Jax had called it.

Mikos turned to bow to the woman. "Dona," he said, his

rich voice practically a purr. "As always, you look as beautiful as Aphrodite herself, rising from the foam. Lukus has truly been blessed with you as a mate."

The woman Dona *was* beautiful, with skin as pale and luminescent as the inside of a shell. Her black hair tumbled over breasts only barely concealed by her sheer blue tunic. She leaned forward and smiled at Mikos, showing teeth like a perfect strings of pearls.

Pearls weren't sharp, though, and Dona's gleamed like tiny blades.

. Lastly Mikos bowed to the man on the end. This man was very ordinary-looking at first glance: short, with sparse salt-and-pepper hair and a visible paunch beneath his gray tunic. "Father," said Mikos, bending his golden head briefly. This surprised me too. If Jax and Mikos were unlikely as brothers, it seemed absolutely impossible that this man had fathered them. He looked like an accountant. Or a dentist. Though his eyes did gleam with the same silvery color as Mikos's.

The man inclined his head to acknowledge Mikos but said nothing.

"She looks weak," announced the woman, Dona. She considered me with a pout of her arched red lips and dabbled her toes in a rivulet of water that ran at her feet. "And small," she observed. "Even for a Lander."

With this comment she seemed to dismiss me and turned her attention to running a jeweled comb through her cascading hair.

Lukus stood up. He was impressively tall. Thick cuffs of silver encrusted with jewels circled his muscled arms. "This is an unusual step for this Council, to address a Lander face to face. But these are unusual circumstances, and I wished to see you. The Council suffered you to come to Trespass without permission and live." He spoke in a ringing voice made even more powerful by the echoes in the huge cavern. "Yet now you have interfered with a judgment of the First Ones."

I shivered from fear as well as the cling of damp clothes to my skin. "It was dying. I only tried to help."

"Silence," Lukus said, his tone icy. "I did not ask you to speak, Lander."

If the Glaukos standing behind the First Ones had any understanding of what was being discussed, or if they cared, they gave no sign of it. They stood so still they looked like statues, or some kind of macabre Halloween decorations.

"My lord," said Mikos. "Jax was there, aiding the human. He set the slave free."

"Really," said Lukus, his mouth set in grim lines. "No wonder he doesn't dare show his face. Jax grows more distant from this clan every day. Xarras." He addressed the older man beside him. "I will leave you to manage your son."

"Adopted son," murmured Mikos beside me. Softly but distinctly.

I looked at Mikos's bent golden head and for some reason felt like punching him.

Xarras cleared his throat almost apologetically and spoke

to me. His gaze was shrewd but not unkind. "Did Jax harm you, girl?"

"No," I answered. My voice was steady, which surprised me. I didn't feel steady. My wet clothes clung to my skin uncomfortably. I wrapped my arms around myself.

"Well," Xarras said, letting out a sigh. "That is something, anyway." He looked at Lukus. "I apologize, my lord, for the shame Jax brings to the house of Aitros. He is passionately headstrong. It has always been his great failing."

"It is not your shame to bear, old friend," said Lukus.

"My thanks," said Xarras, bowing his head.

"But now we must decide about this girl." Lukus regarded me. "There's been discontent among the Landers over her. And now she interferes with a punishment ordered by the Council."

"Tie *her* to the rocks," said Dona. She splayed her toes like fingers, displaying the delicate white webbing between the digits. "And let the crabs and the sea stars feast on her flesh."

Lukus gave her an affectionate smile and chuckled. "You have always loved the old ways, my dear."

This is not happening. My knees felt as if they might crumple any second. I looked around. Screaming wouldn't help. No one on the island could possibly hear me. There could be hundreds of feet of rock over my head. And even if they did hear me, what could they do? I thought of running. Mikos might have only been trying to frighten me into submission with his talk of mazes. I looked down the long flight of steps, toward the dark openings to the tunnels. I couldn't even be sure which of those he'd led me through. And I had no desire to test the land speed of the Glaukos. I had a feeling they might surprise me.

Meanwhile, Xarras watched me. "They tell me she was born of a Lander from Trespass," he remarked. "A woman who fled years ago. After the Revel."

For some reason this comment seemed to surprise the others.

Dona sat up straighter, her eyes flashing. "Show me."

Mikos turned to me and, before I could react, lifted my shirt.

"Hey!" I clutched the material and wrenched away from him, but not before he had run cool, hard, probing fingers over my belly, as if searching for something.

"Lander," said Mikos, releasing me roughly. His voice held an unmistakable tinge of contempt.

"Of course she is," said Dona, sitting back.

"You are the eldest of my counselors, Xarras," said Lukus. "What punishment would you suggest?"

Xarras sighed and tented his fingertips together before him. "Let us not act in haste, my lord," he replied at last. "Our community is a fragile one." He leaned forward and spoke to me directly. "Listen to me, girl. Your people and ours need each other, do you understand?"

"No. Not really," I answered, still angry and flustered by Mikos's sudden strip search. Or whatever that was.

Xarras smiled. "I enjoy honesty. But as you get older you

will learn that sometimes silence is better." He regarded me for a moment and added softly, "I am curious, though, as to the interest that my son Jax has shown in you. That is something unusual." He turned to Lukus. "The Revel is coming. In my humble opinion, we should not create discord with the Landers at such an important time. I think the girl can serve our needs alive more than dead."

Lukus nodded, eyeing me. "Yes," he said. "I believe you're right, Xarras. She will pay tribute at Revel, along with the rest." He waved a hand toward Mikos. "Take her back."

Mikos took my wrist in a grip of cold steel and brought me back in the same maelstrom fashion as before, storming across the sea within a corridor of water before setting me down on the beach. I sank to my knees, feeling nauseated. The speed and tumult of traveling that way wasn't good on my nerves, or my stomach.

"There. That wasn't so bad, was it?" he said, a smile lighting his eyes mischievously. With sun sparkling on his gleaming skin and away from the gloom of the sea caves, he looked as spectacular as before. Like Mr. July from the Greek gods calendar.

I pushed his hands away. "Thanks. Next time I want to be abducted, I know who to call."

His smile broadened. "My pleasure. Goodbye for now, little oyster. I will see you at Revel."

That smile frightened me, but I didn't want Mikos to know it. "Goodbye," I said, hoping that my voice sounded calmer than I felt.

CHAPTER 13

"This isn't good," said Gran. She paced in long strides across her porch, the boards creaking beneath her while I sat on a wicker chair.

I'd just finished telling her about my encounter with Jax and Mikos and then with the other First Ones in the sea caves.

"Having the First Ones take an interest in you is dangerous enough." Gran rubbed the scar on her neck in a nervous, repetitive motion. "Offending them is worse. I should've told you not to interfere with that Glaukos on the beach. There was nothing you could do to help the poor creature. And you might have been killed. Whatever possessed you?"

"I just couldn't stand seeing it suffer like that." I pulled my knees up and curled myself deeper into the sagging embrace of the chair. "Or hearing those cries. It was horrible."

Gran looked at me with warmth and sympathy in her eyes. "I know," she said. "You've got a good heart, bless you, child. But you're impulsive, just like your mother. Be careful taking things into your own hands like that. The tide can turn on you awful fast."

"If something is wrong," I argued, "Mom raised me to do something about it. Not sit by and be quiet."

Gran sighed and leaned against the corner post of the porch. "Sometimes it's not so clear what's right and wrong. You mustn't be too quick to judge."

There were some things that my grandmother and I might never agree on. Maybe the fact that I wasn't raised here would prevent me from ever really understanding the way of life on Trespass. I changed the subject.

"Tell me what the First Ones meant about Revel, Gran. What is this *tribute* I'm supposed to pay?"

Gran stopped her movements and became very quiet. "I'd hoped that you wouldn't be involved with that. At least, not this year." She passed a weary hand over her eyes. "Let me think on it a bit, Delia. I'm awfully tired. We'll talk about it later."

———

A few days after my encounter with the First Ones, Sean invited me out to lunch. We were supposed to meet Zuzu and Reilly at the Snug, but they hadn't shown up yet. We'd been sitting together over bowls of savory clam chowder and slices of corn bread. Sean seemed quiet and distant. His brown eyes were as warm and attractive as always, but there were shadows beneath them, as if he hadn't slept well.

"I really like you," he said, looking at me suddenly.

I smiled and felt warmth color my cheeks. "Thanks, Sean. I like you too."

"I wish you'd never come here."

"Okay." I coughed to clear my throat. "Let me explain the whole concept of a segue. You say something leading into a topic. Usually the next thing is sort of related to that *same topic.*"

"Yeah. I'm sorry." Sean dropped his head back and blew out a frustrated breath. "That came out wrong. It's just that I can see how hard things are for you here and I feel bad. You must be homesick, right?"

"Well, yes," I said. "I guess so." I picked up my spoon and swirled it in the milky broth of the chowder. "I miss some stuff. Going to the movies with my friends, shopping at the mall, *not* getting swept into underground sea lairs. That kind of thing."

Sean nodded, the corner of his mouth pulling into a crooked smile. I'd told him about facing the First Ones in the sea caves.

"But I'm fine," I told him. "I've done a lot of exploring around the island, and I've been helping Gran with the gardens. And building a pretty impressive shell and sea glass collection. I made this." I lifted a necklace from my throat and leaned forward.

The necklace was made from the piece of blue sea glass he'd given me, entwined in silvery wire. But if Sean realized it, he didn't show it or comment.

He only nodded. "That's pretty."

"So what about those fishing lessons?" I asked, letting the necklace fall back into place.

Sean grimaced apologetically. "Sorry. Things have been kind of crazy these last few days." He stared at his chowder. "Work and stuff."

"Why don't you tell me about it?" I asked. "Look. I know you're doing more than just fishing out there, Sean. I mean, your boat is fitted out with all those weapons, and you're out there at times when the other fishermen are all back with their catches. Are you hunting the Icers?"

"That's part of it," he said. He looked reluctant to say anything more, and I didn't want to push. These people were raised on traditions of secrecy.

"Just be careful, okay? Please? I think you're the only guy around who's brave enough to be near me when I'm holding a fishing pole. But there's no rush on the lessons." I smiled. "I'm not going anywhere, right?"

"Right." Sean picked up his spoon but dropped it and it clattered under the table. "Damn it. No, it's okay, I was done anyway."

"But you've hardly eaten anything."

He straightened up and leaned over the table. "I need to tell you something," he said in a low voice. He spoke fast, as if he wanted to get it off his chest. "Things are different here, ever since you came. Before, everything was on an even keel, right? I knew where I stood. Now . . ." He rubbed his hands over his fatigued-looking eyes. "I'm not so sure."

This conversation was *so* not going the way I had expected.

"I don't understand," I said. "Have I done something to upset you?"

"It's just . . ." Sean hesitated, seeming to search for the words. "You seem to think you can live your life any way you want."

"Well, yeah," I said. "Hence the name *my life*."

Sean didn't smile. "You can't *do* that here. We have to think about how our actions will affect everyone."

"But I haven't done anything to hurt anyone," I said in a low voice, hating how it suddenly trembled. "I wouldn't do that."

"I know you wouldn't, not on purpose," said Sean. His voice was gentle. "But what about that guy from the mainland? The ticket agent. He died because he helped you get here and then came snooping around. He broke the rules and got killed by an Icer. We still haven't figured out how the Icer got into our waters without the Glaukos intercepting it. And Ben is lucky that the First Ones didn't do more than rough him up a little and ruin his boat." He leaned over the table. "And what about interfering with the punishment of that Glauk? The First Ones could have killed you, Delia. And I don't even want to think about what would have happened if that Glauk had gotten loose and cut you with its tail."

"But they didn't," I said. "And *it* didn't. And I'm fine."

I took a gulp of my ice water to ease the tightness in my throat. Apparently Sean had only invited me here to give me a lecture.

"Yeah, well," he murmured. "I wouldn't want anything to happen to you." He reached to take my hand and his thumb brushed over my knuckles. "I *won't* let anything happen to you. I promise." He turned my hand over in his. "Wow, you heal up pretty quick, don't you?" he remarked, staring at my palm. "I can't even see the mark where we dug out that fishhook." He smiled. "You're so *tiny*. Like a little china doll."

"Yeah," I said softly, "so I've been told." I withdrew my hand from his, still hurt by his remarks.

Maybe my coming here had set off a chain of events. Bad events. But it wasn't like I'd deliberately done anything to harm anyone. Sean had no right to make me feel like . . . like a *monster*.

"What do you want me to do?" I asked quietly.

Sean lifted his head, a look of relief on his face. "For starters, just stay away from the water for a while, okay?" He smiled. "Every time you get wet, it spells trouble."

I returned the smile uncertainly. When I'd first come to Trespass, his advice would have been unnecessary. Of *course* I would stay out of the water. Duh. But now . . . Sean's request made me feel uncomfortable. The water held an appeal for me that I couldn't deny. And I knew Sean's protectiveness was well meant, but he was treating me like some wayward child.

"I'll try," I said at last. It was the most I could promise.

Zuzu breezed into the Snug, followed by Reilly. "Sorry we're late," said Reilly. He nodded toward Zuzu. "Some kind of hair-care emergency." He sat down, folded his long arms together and rested his elbows on the table.

"I don't care what you say, that is not an oxymoron," Zuzu told him. She eyed my chowder. When I put a protective hand over it, she smiled. Then her eyes widened.

"I love your necklace," Zuzu said. "Blue's a really lucky color, you know. You can make a wish."

"Thanks," I said, glancing at Sean. He'd told me the same thing when he'd given it to me. But Sean seemed distant and only stared past me, as if he wished he were somewhere else.

Something was going on with Sean. If only he would trust me enough to tell me about it. I cared about him. He did so much to take care of everyone else around here, but in some ways he was like an island himself. Strong, self-sufficient and remote. At least from me.

CHAPTER 14

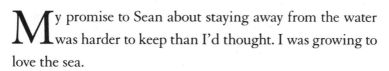

My promise to Sean about staying away from the water was harder to keep than I'd thought. I was growing to love the sea.

Every morning the tide made a new beach, washing away whatever had been there before and leaving new treasures. And the water was never the same color twice. Some days the waves were rich indigo blue, sparkling with winks of sunlight; on others, a bleak gray as cold and heartless as stone.

It was a hot summer, and the island's strange climate made the air even more sticky and humid. I'd asked Reilly about it and he confirmed my suspicion about the volcanic rock I'd seen on the beach. The island was located over a volcano with enough remnant activity to have superheated underground springs. Trespass had its own distinct ecosystem within the otherwise cold North Atlantic. He'd gone into way more detail than I could remember or understand, but the fact was that here on Trespass and in the waters nearby, we had a variety of plants and animals that were tropical, all year round. Zuzu had countered his scientific explanations, telling me that it was the powers of the First Ones that kept the waters warm and melted the snow and ice in winter.

I wasn't sure which one to believe, and finally decided that it might be a combination of the two. Perhaps the ancient sea gods had chosen this island for safekeeping of their powers just because of its special qualities. The idea satisfied me somehow. A combination of magic and logic.

The weather was certainly great for flowers—hyacinths and rhododendrons and sea roses grew everywhere—but I always felt wilted.

And my hair. Gah.

Most days it looked like I'd been the victim of some home-perm guerrilla warfare. The best option seemed to be pulling the curls through a baseball cap, the visor of which gave the added benefit of sun protection.

I would sit on the sand and look out at the water. At first just seeing it and feeling the cool breeze was enough to refresh me, to take away the gritty heat of the sun. But every day I ventured a little closer.

One afternoon I just couldn't take it anymore. It was so hot. I'd collected a handful of sea glass to make a necklace for Zuzu. The pieces were sandy and needed to be rinsed.

Besides, I hadn't exactly *promised* to stay out of the water, as I recalled. I'd only said I would try. Sean Gunn couldn't just tell me what to do—that was ridiculous. I would put my feet in to the ankles; there was no harm in that.

The sand scrubbed against the soles of my feet as I stepped in, and cool water wrapped over my skin in ribbons. I let out a long breath and closed my eyes. Bliss.

Scooping water over my arms, I sighed with the sheer pleasure of the coolness. It felt like my skin drank it in, slaking its own thirst. I yanked off my hat and tossed it to the sand, then pressed a handful of water to the back of my neck and let it trickle down my spine.

"I've been waiting."

I turned to see Jax standing in the water and felt my heart begin to beat faster. Or maybe it wasn't that fast, I was simply conscious of it all of a sudden. Really conscious. Like my beating heart took up all of me.

"Waiting? For what?" I managed to ask, sliding into deeper water. The cooling effect seemed to have disappeared.

Jax strode closer, his powerfully built body sparkling with drops of water in the sunlight. The ugly scars across his torso stood out in painful-looking detail. "You. Why haven't you come swimming again?"

"The water's not safe. You told me that." I looked around. "And this isn't Lander's Beach. It's all about the rules here, right? I'm learning."

"Rules," Jax murmured. His eyes shone like crystallized

seawater from some azure depths. "Yes, the rules. But you don't follow the rules, do you?"

"Apparently you don't either."

"What do you mean?" he asked, his square-cut jaw hardening.

"Well, you're talking to me," I said. "Isn't that against the rules? The Accord?"

"I suppose it is," he said gruffly.

"Why *are* you talking to me?" I wasn't trying to flirt or be coy. If Jax was here because of some order of the First Ones to keep tabs on me, I wanted to know. And I didn't think he would try to hide it. He was more brazen than that. More proud.

"I'm not sure," Jax said, after a moment. "I like the sound of your voice. Even from the first night, when I heard you singing that ridiculous song."

"Oh, that," I said, embarrassed.

Jax frowned, inspecting my face. "You look different. Where are your eye lenses?"

Startled, I reached up to touch the bridge my nose. "I must have forgotten them," I said. "That's weird." It wasn't the first time I'd left the house without noticing their absence. And yet I could see Jax perfectly clearly. What was happening to me?

"Show me what is in your hand."

I'd almost forgotten what brought me to the water. I lifted my hand and showed him the pieces of sea glass. With the sand washed away, they sparkled in the sunlight. Amber, green and frosty white.

"Why do you pick up those bits of glass?" he asked. "It's only trash."

"I think they're pretty," I said, letting them tumble softly in my hand. "Like little jewels."

"Jewels from broken bottles," he said dismissively.

I shrugged. "It doesn't matter how something starts. It's what it becomes. After all, diamonds come from lumps of coal."

"Would you want some?"

"Lumps of coal?"

"Diamonds." He looked at me steadily, as if trying to puzzle something out in his mind.

"Uh, no. I'm good. Thanks." I turned away, heading back to the sand.

"Mikos said I frightened you. Is that true?" Jax's voice was subtly altered. He sounded awkward. Unsure.

I looked at him and remembered the cool savagery he'd displayed with the knife at his hip. Plus he was a demigod and probably capable of things I couldn't even imagine. Did that frighten me?

"Yes," I confessed. "You frightened me."

"Because I'm ugly," Jax said. He spoke without heat or resentment. As if he just wanted me to confirm what he already knew.

"No," I answered swiftly, narrowing my eyes. "Because of what you *did*."

Jax seemed baffled. "You wanted me to help you free the creature. I thought you would be pleased."

"You cut off its freaking foot!"

Jax shrugged. "They grow back."

"What?"

"The Glaukos can regenerate lost limbs if they are severed. I thought you knew this."

"Oh," I said, taken aback. "No, I didn't." I hesitated. "I'm not sure it makes a difference."

"I suspect it does to the Glaukos," Jax said gravely.

The spark of amusement in his eyes made me smile despite myself, and I waded into the water until I stood near him. After all, it wasn't every day that I got to see a demigod up close. My T-shirt and shorts felt heavy and ungainly as they clung to my body.

"You remind me of a fish," he said.

"Gee, thanks. You really know how to charm a girl, don't you?" I walked past him, tugging my hips against the small waves.

"No," he said gruffly as I passed, "I don't."

Jax followed me into deeper water until we faced each other. "There is a blue fish that lives in the coral," he said. "The female is very small but fiercely protective of its children and home. And its mate. We call it *diabolika*." His blue eyes roved over my face. "'Small she-devil.'"

It sounded suspiciously like the Tasmanian Devil's wife from Looney Tunes. And not very complimentary. "Does she spin around and gnash her teeth a lot?" I asked.

"No. She's actually . . . very beautiful," Jax said in a low voice.

"Oh," I managed to say. I had that breathless feeling again, and there was a peculiar sensation in my knees, as if they'd been shot full of novocaine and Jell-O.

The water held me and I let it, sinking into the buoyant embrace until it covered my breasts. I had to close my eyes just for a second to simply feel it as I breathed in the clean scent of the ocean. It felt like heaven.

I opened my eyes to see Jax watching me.

Ugly? Maybe compared to Mikos's plastic-looking perfection. But Jax was anything but ugly to me; in fact, his face kind of fascinated me. It was . . . arresting. He seemed young to have a face like that. His broad forehead had two creases that became rolled-up furrows when he frowned. Beneath his proud, battered nose was a mouth of narrow precision, making him look reserved and somehow vulnerable. A dark stubble of beard roughened the raw-boned angle of his jaw.

I swam closer, wondering why I did, yet at the same time understanding it completely. When Jax was around, everything I did was based on impulse, on instinct.

And every instinct was the same.

Closer.

I couldn't help but let my eyes drift to his chest and the network of horrendous scars. "How did you get those?"

He glanced down. "There was a time when I cared about something, very much. This was the price I paid for caring."

"What was it that you cared about?"

"My clan," he answered. "I once sought to be leader. In part to please my father, Xarras. He's a brilliant man, but quiet and reserved, always in the shadows of those louder and more aggressive than himself. But he thought I would be a good leader. He approved of my ideas to change things, to bring progress to our people." Jax gave me a grim half smile that accentuated the hard contours of his face. "We've lived so long by the old customs that we don't know anything else. And the old ways don't really fit this world anymore."

I remembered Xarras from when Mikos brought me before the Council. He did seem quiet, more statesmanlike than Lukus, the clan leader. But Lukus seemed to respect his opinions and listened to his advice. Good thing for me. Otherwise, Lukus might have followed Dona's idea of feeding me to the crabs. Apparently one of those good old ways Jax was talking about.

"What are you thinking about?"

I looked at him. "I was thinking that your father was right. You *would* be a good leader."

I would follow you. Anywhere.

The thought came into my head without warning. I cleared my throat and tried to get my mind back on the subject. "What happened?"

"Someone betrayed me," said Jax. "Someone, I don't know who, told the clan leader that I was raising a revolt against him. I was punished for treason." He looked down at himself. "I was entombed in the Eluvian Trench for three days. So deep and dark that the only life inside it are the ravenous giant squid. Their tentacles cut like razors."

"But you're a demigod. Don't you have miraculous healing powers or something?"

Jax's smile was rueful. "We are not invincible. Any god-like qualities we inherited from Poseidon have been diluted through the generations. We are much closer to mortal than to immortal."

The admission obviously irked him.

"Besides, the Eluvian Trench is a hundred leagues from this island. I was weakened by my distance from home."

"From the Archelon."

"Yes."

As Jax spoke, I had the almost irresistible urge to reach out, to touch one of the scars. As if I could soothe it or make it go away. Silly.

"Who betrayed you?" I asked instead, although in my mind a shadowy image of his brother Mikos was forming. I could imagine him doing something sneaky like that. Maybe he had plans to be leader himself, even if it meant having to eliminate his brother.

"I have my suspicions," said Jax, as if he echoed my own thoughts. "But it doesn't matter anymore. I have no designs on leading this clan. They spend their time on frivolous amusements. Hunting and fighting and all the while wait-ing for the day when the glory of our ancestors will return. I simply don't care anymore."

"You must care about something."

Jax looked down at me. "No." He frowned. "I don't know

why I tell you these things. It has been a long time since I've had someone to talk to."

"Sometimes it's easier to tell things to a stranger."

"Here, it's very calm. Lie back in the water," he said. "If you want to."

I shook my head. "No. I can't float. I'll get water up my nose and it will be a whole thing. With flailing."

Jax smiled. It made his eyes crinkle at the corners and transformed his face into something almost beguiling. Somewhere a lightning-rod switch got flipped. An electric current sizzled between his eyes and mine and some hot, melty place in the center of my chest.

"You'll be safe. I promise you." Jax came closer and, almost tentatively, put one hand on the small of my back.

Somehow I believed him.

I leaned my head back and felt the water creep over my scalp and tug gently at my hair. My arms drifted.

"Now let go," he said.

My feet left the bottom as I arched my back deeply, feeling Jax's hand, warm and firm, inside the curve of my spine. The water closed over my ears, blocking out everything but a soothing hiss. I closed my eyes and floated, moving with the gentle rise and fall of the water.

Let go.

I did. The water no longer felt like something separate from me. I was weightless. Untethered from the world. The only thing that held me, my only anchor as the whole earth turned beneath me, was Jax's hand against my skin.

I'm not sure how long we stayed like that; it probably wasn't the lifetime that I imagined. But when I opened my eyes, the sun had dropped lower and lit the air; everything seemed highlighted with gold. Jax stood looking down at me, his silhouette etched against the twilight.

I'd never felt so exposed.

I'd never felt so powerful.

I wanted him to kiss me.

"What?" he said.

"What? I didn't say anything."

God, did I?

I stood up unsteadily, clumsy and dripping again. I was aware of him just behind me, his hand still on my back. I turned my head, searching for something to say, but Jax put a hand to my neck, urging my head back as he bent forward and kissed me.

Our lips touched. The rest of my body completed a slow half circle as he turned me in his arms to face him. His kisses were gentle, tasting caresses on my mouth.

"You've done something to me," he said. His breath was ragged as his lips traced a line to my ear.

"I think it's the other way around," I whispered, pulling him back to my mouth.

I twisted my fingers through the dark coils of his hair. Just like before, I was floating. Only two words in my mind.

Closer, Jax.

He broke away gently, putting arm's-length distance between us. He was looking at me oddly.

"What's wrong?" I whispered.

"This is," he said. He stepped back. "You're a Lander. I apologize for any offense." He turned away, going deeper into the water. As he did he transformed, the fin on his back growing and spreading like a magnificent wing.

"What? Wait. When will I see you again?" I asked. My mind fumbled for something to say. "At Revel?"

He stopped in the water and turned. He looked a little shocked, I thought.

"Revel?" he repeated in a voice that had grown much colder. The smile was gone. The Jax who stood before me now was the fallen angel with hard, brooding eyes. "Yes," he said at last, "if you wish. Goodbye, Lander."

With that he twisted and dove away, disappearing beneath the water.

CHAPTER 15

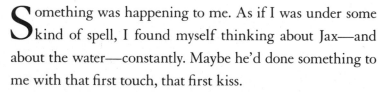

Something was happening to me. As if I was under some kind of spell, I found myself thinking about Jax—and about the water—constantly. Maybe he'd done something to me with that first touch, that first kiss.

It was becoming a big problem. Easy enough for Sean to tell me to stay out of the water. He didn't know how it *drew* me. Beyond the sheer physical pleasure I had in being immersed, there were other things. I tried to stay away, but after a little while my throat began to feel scratchy. My voice was hoarse no matter how much water I drank. My skin felt dry, and my clothing felt like sandpaper against it.

Maybe it was all in my head. I was fascinated with Jax and he was in the water, so naturally that was where *I* wanted to be. But after his abrupt farewell the other day—no, more like his *dismissal* of me—I seriously doubted this was any more than a game to him.

If I was a Lander, as he called me, maybe I should start acting like one. I should hang out with my own kind of people, not some moody demigod.

———

Down at the dock, Buddy started barking as soon as he saw me, and came bounding to greet me like a canine King Kong. I bent down to hug him.

"Yeah, you're growing on me," I whispered as he licked my hand, and whatever else he could reach before I blocked him.

I found Sean working with the lobster traps on the *Widowsong*. The sight of him, so tall and strong and competent, so *normal,* made me feel at ease. I didn't have the crazy, breathless feelings I had when I was near Jax, but maybe that was for the best.

"Do you need any help?" I asked.

"You want to bait lobster traps?" Sean asked dubiously. "You must really be bored."

I wasn't bored, simply trying to stay out of the water, and out of trouble, as Sean had put it. I shrugged and said, "I want to learn about what you do, that's all."

"Okay, sure. Here. Stuff this bag with fish guts."

He pointed to a bucket at my feet, filled with cut-up fish.

Little bulgy eyes stared up at me and little mouths gaped. "Um." I swallowed. "Maybe I'll just watch."

Sean laughed. "Sure."

"How does it work?" I asked, eyeing the lobster trap.

He tied a mesh bag filled with bait and hung it inside the front part of the cage-like trap. "This is called the kitchen," he said. "Where we put the food. And this is the parlor." He pointed to the end of a funnel-shaped tunnel that opened into another chamber of the trap. "Mr. Lobster comes inside the parlor, then he can't get back out."

I sighed. "You had to call him Mr. Lobster, didn't you? Now I feel bad."

"Yeah, well," said Sean, quirking a smile. "I throw all the cute ones back, okay?"

"Great. Now I feel bad for the homely ones." Buddy nudged up against me and I rubbed behind his ears, then scratched the thick ruff of fur at his neck. "How long does it take to catch them?"

"We set the pots in the morning and collect them the next day," said Sean. "The Glauks usually help out, herding the lobsters toward the pots. That's how we get the biggest and the best. Gunn's Lobster is the finest on the coast," he said, with obvious pride. "The wholesalers in Portland can't figure out what our secret is."

"Bet they'd be pretty surprised if they did." I pressed the toe of my sneaker against the railing of the boat. "Could I come lobstering with you sometime, when you go out?"

"No," said Sean. "Sorry. It's . . ."

"Let me guess, not allowed," I finished with a huff of impatience.

"I was going to say *dangerous,*" Sean replied. "But, yeah, it's against the rules too."

I nodded. "Why dangerous? What's going on? Have there been more Icers?"

"No," he said uneasily. "It's been quiet. Don't worry about that stuff, Delia. Okay? That's my job."

I sighed and fluttered my lashes. "My hero."

His face grew somber as he looked at me. "Well, yeah," he said softly. "I'd like to be."

Something in his expression deflated all my sarcasm.

He peeled the heavy yellow gloves from his hands and seemed to choose his words carefully.

"After you lost your mom," he asked, "how did you keep going?"

I hesitated, wondering why he was asking me this. Maybe Sean was still grieving for his dad, I thought with a pang. Or maybe his mom's condition was more serious than I'd realized. Maybe sharing would help him somehow.

"For a long time it seemed like I *didn't,*" I told him. "Keep going, I mean. Everything just went on around me, past me. And I didn't really care. After a while I started moving again, you know, inside. But slowly. Sort of on autopilot."

Sean nodded and looked at his fingernails. "And how long did it hurt?" he asked quietly.

"It still hurts," I said. "But I'm okay."

Sean always seemed so strong, so independent. I wished he would let me in a little. "You know, if you ever want to talk about your dad or anything, I'm a pretty good listener."

Sean nodded. "Thanks. I'm good." He frowned. "What made you want to come here to Trespass?"

"I wanted to bring Mom back to where she was born," I said softly. "And I wanted to find out if it could be a home for me too."

"So what do you think?" asked Sean. "You like it here a little bit, don't you?"

I smiled at him and nodded. "Yeah, I do like it here."

———

"Revel is in less than a week," Zuzu said dreamily, resting her chin in one hand. "I can hardly wait."

We were at her house, one of the small bungalows that sat on the cliffs overlooking Trespass harbor and the dock. Zuzu's mother was a plump, friendly woman with curly black hair who fussed over Zuzu constantly. "I'm so glad that Zuzu has a nice girl like you to spend time with," she told me in her soft, fluttery voice as she poured us iced tea. "And I don't pay any attention to those things people are saying in the village. We're very open-minded in this household."

"What things?" I asked.

"Oh, Mom," said Zuzu.

"Well . . ." Zuzu's mother patted her throat nervously. "The way your mother left, of course. And all the strange things that have happened since you came, dear." She turned to Zuzu. "Do you know that Ned Laquinn went out to pull traps yesterday and there was not a single lobster in them? Not one."

I frowned. Sean hadn't told me anything about trouble with the lobster catches. Then again, maybe he wouldn't. "I don't have anything to do with that," I told her. "How could I? And you don't always catch something when you go fishing. Surely that happens sometimes."

"Not here," Zuzu's mother murmured as she adjusted a crystal barrette in Zuzu's hair.

"You two are going to be the prettiest girls at Revel," she said, smiling and giving her daughter's shoulders a squeeze. "And the First Ones will smile on us and give their blessing on the fishing boats. It's going to be a good year, I can just feel it. Why don't you girls take your drinks upstairs? You could show Delia your dress."

When Zuzu and I were alone in her room, I asked, "So what's the big deal about Revel anyway?" I'd seen the preparations taking place in the village center. Strings of little white lights were being wrapped around anything standing, and green and blue starfish decorations hung in the windows of all the shops. "Gran goes all inscrutable about it every time I bring the subject up."

Zuzu took a cardboard box down from the top shelf of her closet and set it on her bed. "Revel is the ceremony we have every year on the night of the summer solstice. This is the first year I'm eligible; you have to be sixteen."

I hadn't realized that Zuzu was actually younger than me. Maybe because she always seemed so confident, so sure of herself and her place here on the island.

"Reilly seemed kind of upset when you brought it up," I said.

Zuzu rolled her eyes. "Reilly likes to pretend he's my older, wiser brother or something. You wouldn't know it by looking at him, but the guy's kind of intense." She opened the tissue-lined box and lifted out a tunic-style dress. It unfolded in a graceful cascade of silky white fabric. "They're passed down from mother to daughter," she said with pride.

"It's beautiful."

Zuzu raised a corner of the material to her cheek and smiled. Then she tossed a fall of mahogany hair over her shoulder and leaned toward me with a conspiratorial look, her green eyes gleaming. "So. The Revel. Every year, any unmarried girl over the age of sixteen from Trespass gets presented."

I took a sip of my iced tea and sat on the edge of her bed. "You get presented? It sounds like a debutante ball or something."

"For sex."

I choked.

Zuzu slapped me on the back. "Watch the dress, Delia. Are you okay?"

"No. Not really," I sputtered. "You're . . . not kidding. You mean with them, the First Ones? That's just wrong. It's barbaric."

"It's an honor," Zuzu declared, raising her chin.

"Oh, really. For who?"

She didn't answer me, only folded her dress and, with a last reverent touch of the smooth fabric, put it back in the box. How could Zuzu treat this so casually? How could this whole community look the other way as this happened? Not even that, I realized. They seemed to encourage it.

It was obscene.

"Don't worry. I don't think they would choose you."

"Good," I exclaimed, and then sat back and reflected on this. "Why?" I demanded. "What's wrong with me?"

"There's nothing wrong with you," said Zuzu in a reassuring tone that made me want to heave something at her. "I just mean being a stranger and everything." She sighed. "I shouldn't have said anything. I knew you wouldn't understand. And now you're upset."

I was sick of people on this island telling me I wouldn't understand. "I'm not upset," I said, in what I thought was a pretty calm voice under the circumstances. "Why don't you explain it to me."

Zuzu folded her arms. "The First Ones need us to strengthen their bloodlines. It's some kind of inbreeding thing. If there aren't some human genes mixed in there somewhere, they end up having monsters for children. Every summer at Revel the young men of the clan can choose to visit with the girls of Trespass. It's only for procreation. First Ones only choose one of their own kind as mates."

"But why would you *want* to do this?"

"Because it's important," said Zuzu, her eyes shining. "For the good of all of us. And," she added, after a moment's hesitation, "if you get pregnant and deliver a healthy baby to the clan, well, you're pretty much set for life. Anything you want. You live like a queen."

"But I thought you and Reilly were together," I said.

Zuzu smiled. "Really? Well, maybe someday, I think," she said, her cheeks turning pink. "He's incredibly smart, you know?" She shook her head. "But that doesn't have anything to do with this. It's separate. This is for the island; we have to remember that."

I closed my eyes, trying to wrap my head around Zuzu's twisted notions of community service. What had made me think I could ever fit in here?

And Jax.

Oh my God. I put my face in my hands as I remembered my words to him. *See you at Revel?* How would he interpret that little gem? Only one way.

Slutty much, Delia?

"I feel sick," I whispered.

"What's the matter?"

"Nothing. I'm okay."

Zuzu sat down beside me and ran her fingers over the nubby surface of her bedspread. "Just between you and me," she said in a low voice, "I can't wait to get out of here."

"But I thought you never wanted to leave Trespass."

Zuzu shook her head. "I don't mean leave the island. I mean change. Get out of my mother's house, this *smallness*." She spread her fingers and tilted her head to regard the glittering blue polish on her nails. "To be someone important. If I'm chosen and I have a baby, I'll be given a fine house and be taken care of for the rest of my life. Like Sophia Clark."

"Sophia Clark," I repeated. "You mean the crazy woman down at the beach."

"She's not crazy," said Zuzu, looking irritated. "She's just delicate. She was chosen at Revel six years ago. Afterward she . . . had a hard time."

"With what?" I said, but my heart pounded fast and I felt light-headed.

Because I thought I already knew the answer.

"Giving the First Ones her baby," said Zuzu, looking away.

CHAPTER 16

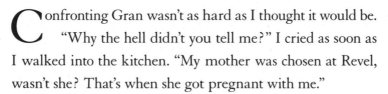

Confronting Gran wasn't as hard as I thought it would be. "Why the hell didn't you tell me?" I cried as soon as I walked into the kitchen. "My mother was chosen at Revel, wasn't she? That's when she got pregnant with me."

Gran nodded, staring at me. She sat down, putting her hands on the table and lowering herself, as if she was suddenly weak. "I Iclen couldn't stand the thought of giving you up," she said in a dry half whisper. "That's why she left when she discovered she was pregnant."

Now I understood at last why my mother never wanted me to know about this place. Why, in her delirious state, she relived memories of Trespass. Though they were probably more like nightmares. *Don't let them take the baby.*

"So my father was one of those *things*," I choked out.

"A First One," Gran said. "You're the child of a demigod. It's nothing to be ashamed of, Delia. If anything, it's a gift."

"And this awesome gift wasn't something that, I don't know, might be important to *tell* me about?"

"I *couldn't* tell you," Gran said. "Because I didn't know for sure. It's true your father was a First One. But Helen ran away while she was still pregnant with you. I figured if nothing"— she hesitated—"*unusual* had shown up in all this time, maybe it never would. You might never become like them."

Like them. The words made me tremble. I remembered Dona and her sharp little teeth. I didn't want to be anything like her.

"Who was it?" I asked, touching my incisors cautiously.

Gran shook her head. "He's gone, Delia. He was the leader of the clan when he and Helen . . . But he's dead now."

I wasn't sure how I felt about that right now. But something else made sense as the unpleasant encounter with the First Ones in the sea caves came back to me. When Mikos had lifted my shirt, he'd been looking for signs that I was one of them. He'd been looking for gills.

"And what's going to happen to me?" I asked. "There's something that happens when I get into the water. I can sense it already. Am I going to turn into something disgusting? A monster? A freak?"

"Of course not," said Gran sharply. She straightened up in her chair and her face took on that familiar stern, tough expression. "Stop that talk this instant. You can't become something you aren't already inside. And you're no monster."

"But something is definitely happening to me, Gran," I said, pacing the small kitchen. "I don't even know where I put my glasses. But I can see just fine without them. What's that about? And I haven't used my inhaler in more than a week."

"I guess you don't need 'em anymore," said Gran matter-of-factly.

"Yes, I *do*," I insisted, waving my arms at her. "I *need* those things. I'm a normal, nearsighted human being with exercise-induced asthma, okay?"

"Fine," said Gran, throwing her own hands up as if trying to humor me.

Suddenly the feelings I'd experienced with Jax made me feel so angry. All that crazy, weak-kneed stuff. Maybe the First Ones exerted some kind of seductive mind control over human girls, luring them into the water.

He was probably laughing about it right now. In some sleazy underwater grotto bar, maybe. If they had such a thing.

That was it. I was going to stay away from the water and away from Jax.

"And this Revel thing," I said, half to myself, "is so not happening."

"But I think you'll *have* to go, Delia," Gran said, breaking into my inner rant. "You said yourself the First Ones told you to be there. Chances are nothing will happen. Only a few girls are chosen for the ceremony."

"The sex, you mean."

Gran pursed her lips and knitted her dark eyebrows. "Now, there's no need to be crude about it."

"It's hard to put a classy spin on the whole virgin-sacrifice thing," I retorted.

"No one is forced," said Gran.

"No," I said, thinking about Zuzu. She acted like Revel was some kind of magical prom, for God's sake. "They're just brainwashed into thinking that it's for the greater good. And if they have a baby, wow, that's like winning the lottery, isn't it?" I was breathing hard now. I felt tired, spent and bitterly angry. "I'm not doing it."

"You have to be there, Delia," said Gran. "We all have to be there. If you're not . . ."

"What?" I demanded. "They'll punish me? I don't *care*!"

"No," said Gran calmly. "They'll punish *all* of us."

CHAPTER 17

It turned out there were a lot of ways that the First Ones kept the islanders compliant with the tradition of Revel. Gran told me all of them in quiet, insistent detail.

They could ensure the success or complete failure of any net, trap or hook sent into the water to catch fish. They could blanket the island with chilling fog or wash away houses with titanic waves. They could have the Glaukos monsters sink every boat in the little harbor, taking away the livelihood of the fishermen and their only contact with the outside world. They could withhold all supplies of food and flood the gardens with salt water, essentially starving everyone.

Or they could be nice.

No wonder everyone went to their damn party.

It seemed I had no choice but to go to Revel. Didn't mean

I had to be happy about it. I lay awake that night listening to the waves as I had on my first night on the island. If I'd known back on the dock in Portland about all this, would I have still come to Trespass?

I fidgeted. Turned. Sighed.

Yes.

Because of him.

I groaned and pulled my pillow close to me, imagining his blue eyes, deep as midnight, his heated touch on my skin.

Hot tears spilled over my cheeks. I despised the fact that despite everything, I still yearned for that sensation of floating in the water, quiet and protected in Jax's arms.

———

I might have cried myself to sleep over Jax. But that night, I dreamt of Sean.

"Hold on," he said, his breath warming my ear. He stood close behind me, his arms wrapped around my waist. The solid bulk of his frame felt safe—as tall and strong and sure as a fortress.

We flew up, soaring into a bright sky. I laughed at the sheer joy of it as cool wind whipped past me, skimming my skin and stealing my breath. But I was warm and secure in Sean's arms. We flew over the spiky green treetops of the island and over the edge of the black cliffs. Then water rushed below as we dove down and flew over the sea, close enough to see the dip and shadows between the waves. Close enough to smell the water.

We rose higher, so high I could see the clouds. They were pure white, like wisps of cotton.

But something about the clouds frightened me. "Not that way," I said, pulling at Sean. "We can't go into the clouds."

But he didn't hear me and he let go of my waist. We still flew side by side, but now I held on to only his hand. Then only his fingers.

"Don't let go of me!" Sean yelled. His fingers were slipping from mine. I tried to speak but couldn't. The wind was in my ears, my throat. It stole my breath as I tried to cry out, to tell him to hold on, to come back.

Then he disappeared, swallowed up by a white cloud.

And I was alone, and falling. The water was rushing up at me so fast. When I struck it, I knew I would die.

I woke up, covered in a sheen of clammy sweat, my heart pounding. I released my clutch on the sheets.

Why did dreams sometimes feel so much more real than life? And dreaming like that about Sean . . . I had no idea what it meant.

CHAPTER 18

Zuzu and I walked together toward the center of the village.

"Afternoon, Zuzu."

"Nice day for a walk, Zuzu. Lookin' good."

"Hello, girls."

I knew the greetings we got were only because I was with Zuzu, but it made me feel good all the same. I was still treated as an oddity by most of the islanders. Gran fussed over me in her own way, I think trying to make up for this. And I know she was trying to get me to accept my "specialness," to come to terms with having some demigod blood in me. She baked something practically every day and put vases of daisies on my dresser.

Despite her stern demeanor, I was learning how much

Gran cared. She loved me. And yet I still couldn't understand how she could live with the things that happened here on Trespass. Maybe I never would, and would just have to accept that fact.

"Are you going to the band concert tonight?" I asked Zuzu, picking my way carefully over the old cobblestoned portion of the road in my flip-flops.

"Absolutely."

Routines were a big part of what held everyone together on Trespass, and the band concert was one that I really liked. I'd been twice so far. The musicians set up in a small gazebo near the center square every Saturday of the summer from eight till ten. People would bring blankets and snacks, then relax and listen to the music while gazing up at the stars and chatting with their neighbors. It was nice.

I wondered if Sean might show up tonight; I hadn't seen him at any of the concerts yet. I didn't think he was actually avoiding me; he was just constantly working, or busy doing patrols around the island. I hadn't seen him since our talk on his boat. And not since I'd found out the truth about Revel.

What did Sean think about it? I wondered. Would he care that I was going to take part in it?

———

All over the island preparations for Revel were evident. Even the Snug was decorated with crepe-paper streamers of yellow and blue and strings of tiny white lights strung along the ceiling. When I walked in I saw Reilly reading an electronics textbook, muttering and making notes to himself in the margins, while Zuzu swayed in her chair to the rhythm of "(Sittin' on) The Dock of the Bay." She beamed at me and then gave a puzzled frown. "Hey. Where are your glasses? You lose them?"

"What? No. I mean yes. Yes, I did," I said. "But it's okay, I can see without them. It wasn't a very strong prescription." It was one thing that Gran knew about my watery birthright and the odd changes I was going through. It was something else entirely to tell my friends.

Reilly looked up from his book. "I thought something was different." He smiled. "Gee. I never noticed how bright your eyes are."

Dropping my gaze to the table, I suddenly wished that the lighting was a little dimmer in here. Were my eyes changing in appearance too? I was *so* not ready for any of this. I'd just started to feel accepted here, to make friends.

Maybe it was too soon to call Sean and Zuzu and Reilly my friends, but that was the way I felt. And I wasn't going to take the chance of alienating them all over again by being, well, *alien*. I just wasn't ready to tell them yet.

"So are you ready?" asked Zuzu.

"For what?" I asked, looking up in alarm.

She rolled her eyes. "For Revel."

"Oh. I guess so," I said quietly. I kind of wished Zuzu would talk about something else.

"You don't look so good," said Zuzu, searching my face. "Do you feel okay?"

"Just tired, I guess." I hadn't been near the water in days. Part of my new program to stay out of trouble, avoid Jax and prevent myself from getting any special creature features.

But I felt awful. It was like my body was going through withdrawal. And maybe not just for the water. For Jax.

I wanted to hear his voice again. Be near him again.

"You want to dance?" said Zuzu.

"No. Thanks. You and Reilly go ahead."

"Come on," said Zuzu, holding out her hand to Reilly. "It's you and me."

"Are you going to let me lead this time?" he grumbled, but got up immediately to follow her onto the floor. I smiled at the sight of them dancing together.

They made a really cute couple. Though I wasn't sure if they were a couple. I suspected that Reilly wanted to be. But it was obvious they were friends. That was probably the best way for love to start. As something warm and strong that grew over time.

Not some mindless, crazy impulse.

On that note I put my head down on folded arms and tried not to think about Jax.

CHAPTER 19

It was the twenty-first of June. The summer solstice and the day of Revel.

"I know that this has been real hard for you," said Gran. She sat on the couch, clutching a piece of white fabric in her hands. "All I know is this island, this life," she said gruffly. "I can't change."

"I know that, Gran."

The dress she held out to me was a strange contrast to her weathered hands. It was a featherlight tunic of diaphanous white silk. I held it up and it shimmered in the streaks of sunlight coming through the window.

"Helen wore this eighteen years ago," Gran said. "Promise me that no matter what happens tonight—" She stopped, her eyes on the floor. She cleared her throat. "You'll stay. Promise me you won't run away."

Like she did.

The unspoken words hung in the air between us.

"I promise," I whispered, even though the words felt like a chain around my throat. And how could I make a promise like that when I had no idea what lay ahead? But I wanted to comfort Gran, to let her know that I loved her.

"We should go," she said, nodding. "Let me get my things together."

Gran had prepared a lot of food for Revel. I didn't know if she always made this much or if the tension between us had amplified her baking/coping mechanism, but her kitchen table was laden with food.

Special things to celebrate the riches of the island were prepared for this celebration. Like cakes studded with dried cranberries and blueberries, apple pies, and pots of herbed goat cheese. There was also a huge, glistening loaf of bread, carefully sculpted into the form of a fish, its scales and texture made from slivered nuts and poppy seeds.

We filled the back of the golf cart with the food, and lastly Gran put in a satchel that contained her bags of dried herbs.

On the day of Revel, all the island women spent the day in preparation and separate from the men. The girls who were eligible were initiated into the "rites of tribute," and the older women helped them. The location for these solemn preparations was the Grange Hall, which struck me as kind of funny. It sounded more like a place to hold bingo games or 4-H displays than preparations for an ancient ritual.

"Rites of tribute" also sounded kind of ominous; my palms

were clammy when we arrived at the Grange Hall. The scene inside was a relief: it looked more like a noisy sorority party than some solemn initiation. A breakfast of scrambled eggs, sliced breads and fruit was laid on a table alongside insulated carafes of drinks.

"Delia!"

Zuzu ran over, her cheeks flushed and her large eyes sparkling.

She hugged me close. "I'm so glad you're here," she whispered.

There was a lot of giggling and nervous laughter among the girls, while the older women sat and chatted over cups of strong coffee. I learned that there were twelve young women, including myself, who were eligible to take part in the tribute this year. Two of them were the sisters I'd met in the Snug, Marisa and Linda; the rest I hadn't met yet.

After breakfast we went outside. A wagon waited there, hitched to a tractor that looked about a million years old. I was surprised to see Ben Deare standing beside it. The sling was gone from his arm, and he looked spry as he clambered up to the driver's seat.

"Miss Delia," he said, touching his cap to me as I followed the rest of the women to climb into the wagon.

The wagon carried us out of the village and up a winding, bumpy road until we stopped on a high plateau with a grassy field. It must have been a high point of the island; turning in all directions, I could look down and see Trespass sloping to the blue sea below. We walked to the center of the field, where a stand of tall oak trees stood, some of them with trunks as wide as a barrel. Inside this ring of trees was a pool of clear greenish water. Steam rolled off the bubbling surface.

One by one the girls got undressed and stepped in. I did too, but held a towel wrapped around myself until the last moment, tossing it aside and stepping down into the pool so quickly the heat of the water nearly made me swoon. I edged around cautiously, feeling my way for a spot on the natural shelf of smooth stone that circled the pool. I sat down and leaned back, my neck resting on a pillowy growth of moss that grew at the edge of the pool. The water bubbled at my feet, tickling its way between my toes.

Gran and two of the other older women were there with packets of soothing herbs that they sprinkled into the water. Lavender and roses, chamomile and valerian. I'd helped harvest and dry many of them with Gran, and the familiar scents calmed me.

"This hot spring comes from the heart of the island," said Marisa, her face rosy beside me. "It's supposed to have healing properties."

Her sister Linda splashed some onto her face and neck. "Not just healing. It's supposed to make you irresistible."

Marisa held her nose and dunked beneath the bubbling surface, getting a round of laughter from everyone.

Zuzu, though, was more quiet and solemn than I'd expected. I guessed this was an important day for her and she wanted to treat it with the pomp and circumstance she thought it deserved.

I didn't know about healing or beauty benefits, but the water was relaxing. The warmth seeped into my body, into my bones. I closed my eyes and drifted happily, letting the talk around me subside into a comforting hum of companionship.

The distraction was welcome. It kept my mind off the night and what it would bring. But I was curious too. In my imagination Jax's strong face appeared. He'd said he didn't believe in all of the traditions of his clan. Was Revel one of them? Maybe that was why he'd looked so shocked when I told him I'd see him there.

When our soak was done and we emerged from the water, the cooler air was a shock. My muscles felt pleasantly loose and my skin tingled. One of the older women handed me a towel and I covered myself quickly.

"We're all females here," she chided with a twinkle in her eye. "No need to be shy."

Zuzu had already left the pool and was holding a crystal wineglass with metal scrolling around the rim. She held the cup with both hands and took a small sip, closing her eyes as she swallowed. She wrinkled her nose delicately.

"Revel mead," she said, and passed the cup to me. "It's very strong. Take just a little."

I stared at the gold-colored drink for a second, inhaled the sweet heady scent, then put it to my lips and took a taste. "Ugh. Tastes like cough medicine."

"Come on, it's time to get back," said Gran, putting a robe over my shoulders.

We returned to the Grange Hall and the rest of the preparations went by in a haze. The older women gathered around each of us, tending to our appearance with clucks of admiration and advice. Hands and feet were massaged with oils. Lips and eyelids were painted with an iridescent paste that contained ground mother-of-pearl. My hair wasn't long enough to have some of the elaborate braids that the other girls wore, so it was brushed and smoothed and twisted into a gleaming coil at the nape of my neck, then pinned with tiny combs that dangled crystal stars.

Finally we were painted.

An old woman with blood-red hair curled in a bun sat behind a card table in the corner of the hall, smoking a thin brown cigarette. On the table before her sat three shallow clay pots. "That's Flora," Zuzu told me. "She does the symbols for each girl."

"What symbols?" I asked.

"She picks something special for each us. To give strength, confidence, good luck, whatever it is that we need."

"How does she know what I need?" I wondered aloud.

One by one each girl approached the little card table. Flora scooped a portion of paint into her palm, stirring it with one finger as she tilted her head this way and that, deciding what symbol to use. The paints from each of the pots looked the same to me, like some kind of thick, waxy mud.

Each girl was marked in three places: on the forehead, between the breasts, and on the back. I watched as the girl ahead of me was painted. It was Marisa, I realized, and after scowling at her for a minute or two, Flora waved her closer. She made a circle on Marisa's forehead and then a star shape on her chest, all the while murmuring something to her in a low voice. Finally Marisa turned and Flora made twin spiraling lines down her back. "Your sister is your strength," she said.

When Marisa's symbols were done, Flora wiped her hands and turned to me.

"You're the newcomer," she said in a scratchy voice. She squinted at me as though peering through a haze of smoke, probably just from habit, because she'd already stubbed out her cigarette.

"Yes."

Flora considered me, her penciled eyebrows pulled together in concentration. Then she waved me forward, dipped a thumb into one of the pots and smeared my forehead. I lifted a small hand mirror from the table and saw she'd drawn a triangle shape, then a line cutting through it. The paint felt cool and sticky on my skin, and it smelled like seaweed.

"For transformation," she said. "So changes can be for the good."

I stared at her. "What changes?"

"Big changes," said Flora with a shrug of her bony shoulders. "Little changes. Everything changes. Everything stays the same." She hacked a cough and motioned me to open the top of my robe.

The shape she drew on my chest was a green ellipse with a circle inside. "The inward eye," Flora said. "So you'll know your heart."

The last symbol, on my lower back, seemed to take Flora a lot longer. Some kind of a circle but I couldn't see it very well. "What is it?" I asked, twisting to try to see.

"Hecate's circle. So the moon goddess will give you bravery," said Flora. "I made it bigger than the others, and darker." She gave me a thoughtful look and leaned closer. "Because you'll need that one the most."

"Thank you," I told her. Even though her ominous words might have undone all the good of Hecate's circle in the confidence-building department.

After the paints were thoroughly dry, we put on our dresses. The fabric slid over my skin like water. One knot fastened it at the shoulder.

When I looked in the mirror, the girl wasn't me.

My cheeks were flushed and my skin glowed with a sunburnished tan. The dress fit perfectly, molding to me in draping lines that would have suited an ancient Greek statue. Dark outlines drawn around my eyes accentuated their tilt and made their pale blue color gleam. And the painted symbols added a savage element.

I saw Gran's face in the mirror behind me. There were tears in her eyes that she brushed away with a careless hand before helping one of the other girls with her dress. Were they for me or was she reminiscing at seeing my resemblance to my mother?

Examining my appearance, I decided that I looked like a priestess from some lost civilization. Going to war.

Did priestesses go to war? Probably not.

Unless they were really pissed off about something.

Yeah. The girl who was not me in the mirror nodded back in agreement.

I felt so weird. Like none of this was real. I didn't know what was in that Revel mead, but I had a suspicion it had been spiked with something from Gran's herbal medicine cabinet.

"You look beautiful," said Zuzu. Her eyes were as bright as matching emeralds as she spun in front of me, her gleaming hair accented with gold and pearls. She looked so happy.

"So do you, Zuzu." I grabbed her and hugged her close.

"One last thing," said Gran, returning with a basket of greens. She took a small circle of pine sprigs and fastened it on top of my hair. Then she did the same for Zuzu.

"A tribute to Poseidon," she said, and smoothed a strand of my hair with a gentle touch.

"It's time to go," someone said.

Suddenly girls who had been giggling and talkative the entire day were quiet. Anxiety hung in the air like the smell of something burning.

But I was in a reckless mood. It was as if I could feel the

blood coursing through my veins. I was past being afraid, being quiet or submissive. If that's what they expected from me tonight, well then, they were going to be surprised.

"Woohoo!" I shouted, lifting the folds of my sacrificial robes and jumping up and down. "Party time, ladies. Am I right?"

I might have actually done a fist pump, I'm not sure.

"Delia!" said Zuzu in a shocked tone. "Hush. It's time for Revel."

CHAPTER 20

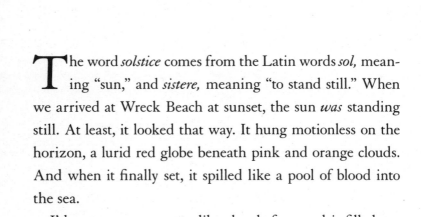

The word *solstice* comes from the Latin words *sol,* meaning "sun," and *sistere,* meaning "to stand still." When we arrived at Wreck Beach at sunset, the sun *was* standing still. At least, it looked that way. It hung motionless on the horizon, a lurid red globe beneath pink and orange clouds. And when it finally set, it spilled like a pool of blood into the sea.

I'd never seen a sunset like that before, and it filled me with a sense of dread for what was to come.

As darkness fell, the scene around me became a spectacle of light and bodies and movement. The men had spent the day preparing and had transformed the small beach for Revel. Towering piles of driftwood and pine logs were arranged for bonfires, and tiki-style torches illuminated the sand every few yards. Up on the dunes more torches marked the shoreline in a necklace of light.

It must have been a spectacular sight from the water.

The thought made me shudder as I imagined the eyes out there in the dark, watching us. Waiting.

Electrical generators hummed and music pulsed from speakers set in the sand. The town band was performing on a platform especially constructed for the night, while couples danced on a makeshift floor of plywood laid in the sand and lit with poles of sparkling white lights. The scene was surreal. Especially when the band starting cranking out the Beach Boys tunes.

Really?

But maybe that was just me, because everyone seemed to be having a good time, and someone even asked for an encore of "Surfin' USA."

According to the advice we got at the Grange Hall, we were free to mingle and enjoy ourselves until they signaled the arrival of the guests, meaning the First Ones. Even so, most of us clung together. Zuzu didn't seem nervous, though; she drifted through the crowd, looking perfectly at ease. I just stood there, probably looking like an awkwardly posed store mannequin.

We were close to the water's edge, but for the first time since I'd been on Trespass, I couldn't hear the waves. The laughter and talk of the hundreds of gathered people, the blaring music and the crackle of fire drowned out the surf.

The smell of smoke and cooking food drifted over the beach. Five huge pits as deep as a man is tall, lined with rocks, seaweed and hot coals, were being used to cook the vast quantities of lobsters, clams and corn it would take to feed the crowd. Long picnic tables set end to end ran along the sand, forming a giant banquet table. Bowls of fruit and bread, pots of melted butter and pitchers of iced drinks were piled on the tables. The dining wasn't formal; it was more like grab food and sit when you liked, drink, dance and then eat some more. But I couldn't eat. I was just too jumpy.

Cool, salty air licked my skin and I shivered. There was nothing to be afraid of, I told myself. My friends were here. So was Gran. Somewhere. People mingled, walking barefoot through the soft sand. The islanders laughed and talked quietly about their kids and their gardens, the day's catch, tomorrow's weather. The little kids ran in shrieking gangs, kicking up sand and skirting the adults as if they were traffic cones. A few yards away the ocean's surf glowed blue-white in the dark.

I looked down at myself and clasped my hands together, feeling a little silly in the white tunic. Finally I sat down on the end of a bench, watching and listening to the festivities but not really being there. I still felt a dull sense of detachment, probably thanks to that Revel special sauce Zuzu had given me.

A shaggy black body came frisking through the crowd. "Buddy!" I called out with a smile. "Come here, boy." I held out a hand.

Buddy lowered his head at me and growled deep in his throat.

"What's the matter with you?" I asked, puzzled. Then, as if he'd suddenly realized who I was and felt ashamed, Buddy whimpered and ducked his head beneath my hand. "Did the toga freak you out?" I asked him, ruffling his fur and searching the crowd for Sean. He couldn't be far behind. Through the crowd of faces, dim in the flickering lights, I glimpsed him. I thought he saw me too, but when I made my way over to the spot, I couldn't find him.

Ben Deare was standing off by himself near the water's edge, facing the sea. As I watched he raised his glass silently before him.

"Who are you toasting?" I asked him.

"Old friends," Ben replied.

We stood silently for a moment. The stars over Trespass were brighter than I'd ever seen before, fierce and white against the night sky. Ed Barney walked up to us. He was beaming officiously, a plastic cup in his hand, and his round head gleamed in the reflected light of the bonfire.

"Miz McGovern," he said pleasantly. "Shouldn't you be over there? With the other young ladies?"

I really didn't like Mayor Ed. Suddenly I felt like this was a good time to let him know. That reckless, detached feeling still pulsed in my blood. I didn't know if it was still the effects of the Revel mead or the nearness of the water or the tension that made me feel so giddy. I poked him with a finger. "You have an *egg* like a *head*."

219

Ben Deare snorted and I frowned. That didn't come out right.

"I beg your pardon?" Mayor Ed demanded, blinking at me from behind his glasses.

At that moment a low horn sounded and all the noise on the beach stopped abruptly. I hurried to join Zuzu and the other young women where they stood in an uneven group. This was away from the central part of the beach and more dimly lit, with only one tall blazing torch.

We all watched as the First Ones came from the water, a handful of the young men of the clan. Looking at them, I couldn't help but be a little awestruck. They were beautiful. As a race they could be cruel, domineering, even barbaric. But there was no denying that they were beautiful too. As they emerged, firelight glimmered on their pale, strong bodies and on the shimmering fins that protruded behind them like multicolored plumage.

They were dressed in the same fashion as we were for tribute, wearing garments of pure white tied around their waists.

My tongue felt thick and dry and my breath came in fast little gulps through my open mouth. My earlier joking in front of the others came back to me like bile in the back of my throat. I wasn't brave. I was terrified.

Instinctively I reached for Zuzu's hand, but she was standing as we'd been instructed to do, her hands crossed over her, palms on her chest. I tried to do the same but found my hands would not release from their own position: clenched into fists.

At that moment someone extinguished the single torch overhead and there was a gasp. In the darkness our skin glowed.

The ceremonial paints must have had some luminescent dye. The mysterious whorls and lines lit up in eerie colors and moved with us. I looked around me and it was as if the girls weren't even there. Our bodies were cloaked in night and the symbols seemed to move on their own, suspended in the air.

From the shadows, Mikos came. He looked like the pinnacle of gorgeous young manhood, or demigodhood, his long blond hair streaming behind him in the night air. I could see his hot silvery eyes as they cut across the crowd and fastened on me.

I looked away as Mikos approached, but felt him take my hand and brush his lips lightly over my fingers. The kiss sent a current of jittery sparks racing along my skin. But not in a good way. His large hand was cool and hard and he smelled of the water and some heavy, spicy scent. Diverting my eyes from his stare, I searched the line of First Ones, looking for Jax. He wasn't there. Why wasn't he there?

"By the right of the Accord, I choose you." Mikos still held my hand as he bowed before me. He looked up and smiled. "For this night you're mine."

I pulled my hand away. "Where's Jax?"

Mikos frowned. He took my wrist and he pulled me closer. "I said I *choose* you."

"But I don't choose you." I lowered my voice until it was

only a whisper between the two of us. "Please. Not like this. I need to see Jax. Where is he?"

"Jax does not attend Revel," he snarled. "He objects to the old customs and has never lain with a human. You will be with me."

"What? No."

An almost foolish look of disbelief contorted Mikos's classically sculpted features. "You can't refuse me. You cannot break the Accord."

"I'm sorry. I do. Refuse, I mean."

He pulled me closer still, his arm circling my waist, pressing hard.

I shook my head. "No one is forced," I whispered.

Mikos smiled his terrible, beautiful smile down at me and nodded once. "True enough," he said. "No one is forced. Because *no one refuses.*" With a growl he scooped his other hand behind my knees, picked me up and began to make his way to the water.

"No!" I yelled. But there was no longer silence; people were talking and somewhere music had begun again. I couldn't fix on anyone's face that I recognized in the flickering dimness. "No!" I screamed louder, and tried to wriggle out of Mikos's arms.

Suddenly I heard Sean's voice. "Let her go."

I could have cried with relief.

Mikos turned. "Don't interfere, Lander. You know the rules."

In the light of the bonfires, I saw Sean's face. Calm, strong and kind. "She's not one of us," he said. "She doesn't understand. Please. Choose someone else."

I saw movement from the corner of my eye. The other Aitros men had chosen their partners as well. I saw Zuzu holding her chin high as a tall, lean First One approached her and bowed.

"She is a Lander on Trespass," said Mikos, tightening his grip on me so I could hardly breathe. "And subject to the Accord. By the mark on your skin, I should think you would understand this."

Sean frowned and lifted a hand to the tattoo on his arm.

"Unless you want war, do not speak again," snarled Mikos. "Don't worry. She'll be returned to you." With this he stepped into the water.

I kicked and punched at him but Mikos was changing. The muscles of his back writhed beneath my fingers as his form changed. A low black-spiked wing emerged from the center of his spine, stretching and bristling out.

His skin felt harder. It deflected my blows like raindrops bouncing off pavement.

"Help!"

"Delia!" As if he were bursting free from some unseen restraint, Sean charged toward us. He swung at Mikos and I heard the wet, dull crack as his fist struck the demigod's jaw.

Mikos never tried to evade the blow and didn't even flinch when it struck. Sean staggered back, clutching his hand, but then lurched toward us again. Mikos, with a muttered oath of annoyance, reached one hand out, almost gently, and placed it on Sean's chest.

And pushed.

Sean flew backward. His head snapped forward as if a cannonball had struck his chest. His limp body arced up through the air and slammed down, driving into the sand ten feet away. And then he didn't move.

"No!" I screamed. But Mikos was moving relentlessly into the water. And I was going with him.

My limbs thrashed and I scratched, trying to get some purchase, some leverage to pry myself loose. "No one is forced," I gasped. Mikos's skin felt as hard and slick as glass. "No one is forced," I repeated wildly, stupidly, as if the words themselves could protect me.

I caught a glimpse of people gathered around Sean. A sickening fear froze me as I imagined him dying there. I went limp. A mindless, helpless thing.

Then the water touched me.

It slipped over my feet first, as they dangled down from Mikos's hold. A wave splashed up over my hips as he carried me deeper. The lights of the beach were receding and I saw only the black night and the cold stars overhead. But I felt the water all around me. A sense of calm came over me. And strength.

"Mikos. Put me down," I said in a low voice.

Mikos cocked his head and glanced back, as if he'd heard

something odd behind him. Then he shrugged and waded deeper into the water.

He was making fun of me.

Fury filled my lungs. "Put me down!" I shouted.

Mikos staggered, a look of astonishment contorting his face. Somehow I'd startled him with my voice. Even after the way I'd acted, did he expect meek compliance? He stared down at me, his silvery eyes looking wide and almost goofy. His grip around my waist and legs drooped and for a moment I thought he was going to release me. He shook his head, as if trying to clear it, then resumed his grip on me and started walking again.

I took the deepest breath I could and screamed.

It was something obscene. And something Mikos had apparently never been called before, hard as that was to believe.

Mikos let out a high-pitched shriek and dropped me in the water. He still had a grip on a piece of my tunic, and I felt the delicate fabric tear as I tumbled away from him, going under the surface for a second. When I stood up, Mikos was doubled over with his hands to his ears.

I didn't wait to see what he'd do next. I just ran, splashing through the water toward the cluster of people around Sean.

Reilly was there, helping him to sit up. I heard Sean's breath come in harsh, labored wheezes. But he was alive. Thank God.

I turned just as Mikos emerged from the water behind me, his body hunched over. He clutched his head in both hands and staggered onto the sand as if disoriented, making no motion to come toward us.

"Delia!" Zuzu ran toward me across the sand. "Are you okay? What happened to Sean?"

Reilly stood up beside Sean's hunched form. "Shark Boy over there pushed him," he said, nodding at Mikos. "I'd say he's got three or four broken ribs."

The tall First One who stood by Zuzu edged her aside roughly and snarled at Reilly. "Watch your tongue, Lander, or I'll cut it out."

Behind the First One, I saw Zuzu's eyes go really wide. She blinked once, twice, and then yelled, "You leave him the hell alone! You big jerk."

A shocked silence followed her words. I think Zuzu was as shocked as anyone else, and she scuttled closer to Reilly, who put his arm around her.

Mikos twisted toward us and he lowered his hands, staring at them with a look of disbelief.

"Lander witch!" he said hoarsely. "What have you done to me?"

I stared at him. What *had* I done?

Crimson blood flowed from both of Mikos's ears, spilling down the smooth, gleaming contours of his skin and onto the sand.

CHAPTER 21

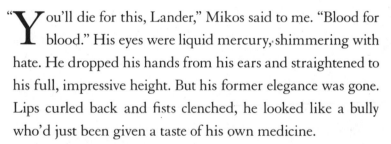

"You'll die for this, Lander," Mikos said to me. "Blood for blood." His eyes were liquid mercury, shimmering with hate. He dropped his hands from his ears and straightened to his full, impressive height. But his former elegance was gone. Lips curled back and fists clenched, he looked like a bully who'd just been given a taste of his own medicine.

The First One that Zuzu had insulted was sputtering his outrage.

Mikos snapped at him, "Quiet, Darius. You will have your satisfaction as well."

We found ourselves gathered in two knots facing each other by the flickering lights of the bonfires and torches. Mikos and the other First Ones against me, Zuzu, Reilly and Sean. The rest of the islanders formed a deep circle of on-lookers around us.

I held my torn dress, trying to cover myself.

"The Accord is broken!" Mikos shouted, addressing the crowd. "This Lander girl has defied the custom of Revel and injured a First One."

A stunned silence answered him. But it didn't last long, as Mayor Ed pushed his way through to the front.

"I knew she'd be trouble," he shouted in a nervous, tinny voice. "She's a traitor. Sent here to ruin everything."

"Silence!"

Everyone turned to see the source of the deep voice that boomed the command. Jax emerged from the water. Fists clenched, he ran as if he meant to plow us all down. His fin splayed from his back and his eyes glowed searingly blue against the darkness. He looked like some kind of alien armored assault vehicle.

"What's happened?" he demanded, slowing down as he strode to me. His eyes flashed briefly over the condition of my clothes, and his mouth pressed in a tight line.

"The little human did something to me," Mikos shouted in a voice that was too loud. Like he'd been standing too close to the speakers at a heavy metal concert. He cupped his hands over his bloody ears. "She screamed at me and—"

"I wasn't asking you," said Jax, with a dismissive glance at Mikos over his shoulder. He turned back to me. "Are you all right?" He kept looking at my dress and frowning.

"I—I'm okay. I don't know what happened."

Jax narrowed his eyes dangerously. "Try to know."

"I told him to put me down," I said, glaring at Mikos, "and he wouldn't. Then we were in the water. I got mad and screamed. Then it looked like he had a seizure or something."

"A seizure," repeated Jax. He seemed furious, but I couldn't tell if it was at me or Mikos or both of us. "You came here tonight of your own free will. Surely you knew what would happen."

"No one is forced," I whispered. "That's what Gran told me."

Mikos snorted.

At the sound, Jax turned and looked fully at his brother for a long moment. I don't know what Mikos saw in Jax's face, but his gray eyes widened and he took a step back as if he'd been pushed.

"She's right," said Jax. His eyes returned to fix on me. In them I saw the reflected lights from the fires making kaleidoscope flames in his eyes.

His voice lower, he said, "In the days of our ancestors, no human woman would ever be forced. Revel was a celebration. First Ones and humans consorted if they *chose* to, not because they were forced to. The old ways have become perverted." He turned a disdainful glance on Mikos and the rest of the First Ones. "Twisted."

Mikos's arrogant sneer returned. "This is no concern of yours, Jax. You've made your contempt for our traditions clear enough. No one even considers you part of this clan anymore. This girl has broken the first article of the Accord. No

Lander shall willfully harm a First One," he said, then added with obvious satisfaction, *"on pain of death."*

"I'm surprised that you'd care to admit harm from such a tiny foe, Mikos," Jax said. He tilted his head to regard me. "From such a—" He broke off, frowning. *"What* was it you called her again?"

"Little oyster," I said, shooting a dark look at Mikos.

"Ah yes," said Jax. "Little oyster." It was hard to tell, but there might have been a softening in the hard line of his mouth. I couldn't tell for sure if Jax was amused, but several people behind us were. There was a muffled titter of laughter.

"She used some hidden device, some *trick* to deafen me," shouted Mikos in his still-too-loud voice.

"Beg pardon, uh, sirs," said Ed Barney, breaking his silence and ducking his head in a fawning way toward the tall forms standing before him. "This girl ain't one of us. We shouldn't be blamed for what she did. We never wanted her here."

"That's not true," said Sean. He looked at me. "She's one of us." His voice was hoarse and he held a hand to his battered chest. "She belongs here."

Ed Barney shook a finger at him. "Don't get yourself mixed up in this, Sean. Or go soft on this girl. You know we're all depending on you."

"Shut up, Ed," said Gran, who'd now joined the circle. She stood behind me and put her big hands on my shoulders.

"This is *not* the way Revel is supposed to go," said Zuzu

miserably. Her makeup was smeared and her pine wreath was dangling from the side of her head. She put her head on Reilly's shoulder.

"There will be war between us," Mikos said. As if to echo his intent, the waves behind him began to surge higher, crashing on the sand with such pounding force that the sand trembled and shifted under my feet.

This galvanized the crowd, and people began backing away, surging up the dunes. They ran, sinking into steep shelves of sand and fumbling through the thickets of sea grass and briars. Whatever punishment the First Ones were planning, nobody wanted to be here to see it.

Mayor Ed wasn't going to be left behind, and I saw him pushing people out of his way. Soon everyone had gone, leaving only my friends and Gran and me to face the First Ones.

"Put your hands *down,* Mikos!" Jax shouted to his brother. "You know as well as I that this is for the Council to decide."

"Maybe," said Mikos with a snarl. "That doesn't mean I can't have a little fun in the meantime."

"Stop it!" I shouted. "Mayor Barney was right. I'm not one of you. I tried to go along, to fit in. I wanted you to accept me."

Sean spoke up. "Don't say that, Delia. We do accept you. You belong here with us."

Be quiet. Go along. Fit in.

How I wanted to, but I just couldn't.

"No, Sean, listen to me. This is my fault," I went on,

"all of it. Maybe I never should have come here. But it's too late now."

I took a deep breath.

"My father was a First One," I said in a loud, clear voice. "And so am I."

CHAPTER 22

Jax's breath seemed to come in labored gasps as his eyes traveled slowly down my body. His eyes flared in the firelight and he muttered something under his breath that might have been a prayer or a curse.

"No," said Sean. He stared at me, then turned his face away. As if I'd struck him.

"Yes," I said, feeling weary.

Zuzu lowered the hand she'd clapped to her mouth. "Why didn't you tell me?"

"Things have been happening to me," I said, to no one in particular. I guess they all had a right to know my change of status.

Yeah, to amphibian.

"Ever since I first touched the water here, I've been

changing. My eyesight, my breathing, are better. My swimming. I'm turning into something else."

"You're Aitros," said Jax. There was something triumphant in his expression. "You were born of Revel, Delia. It's only because you've been kept from these waters that your true nature hasn't emerged."

My true nature? The thought scared me. I remembered Ben Deare's words, the portent he'd read in the bones about a monster. Hadn't Zuzu said that sometimes the children of First Ones came out . . . wrong?

Monster. Maybe that was what I was.

As if he could read my thoughts, Jax interrupted them. "You're one of us," he said, stepping closer. "Father Poseidon. I should have known. And there is something else—"

"One of us?" interrupted Mikos. His eyes roamed over me with contempt. "Hardly."

"No," I said, shaking my head. "I'm not one of you either. Any of you." I glanced toward Sean. He said nothing, only stared at the sand. "I don't know what I am." With shaking fingers I tried to put my dress back in order. Behind me, Gran came to my rescue and helped, knotting the torn portion together.

"As far as I'm concerned, this changes nothing," said Mikos. "Perhaps she is the dried-up spawn of some distant Revel. It's for the Council to decide her fate. But I *will* have retribution." He strode to the water and dove in like a spear, followed by the other First Ones.

It felt like every bit of strength had drained out of me now. I was so tired. "What do you think they'll do?" I asked Jax.

He shook his head. "I don't know. Mikos values his pride more than almost anything. But the Council will judge fairly. No one can call you a Lander anymore. So how can you be subject to the same rules as a Lander?"

"So," said Zuzu, looking around at the shambles of the celebration. The beach was nearly deserted and scattered with overturned tables, discarded plates and cups. "That's it? It's over?" She looked lost.

"Yeah," said Reilly. "It's over. C'mon, princess, why don't we help Sean get back home. Here's your tiara." He held out the circlet of pine that had fallen from her hair.

Zuzu took the small wreath, looked at it for a moment, then shrugged and tossed it into the sand. "I'm kind of glad." Then she tucked herself under Sean's shoulder, supporting him. "Revel kind of sucked, didn't it?"

"Totally sucked," agreed Reilly. "But your dress is great."

"Wait for me," I said, moving to take Sean's other side.

"No," said Sean, finally lifting his head to look me in the eyes. "Don't you think you've done enough for tonight?" He nodded to Jax. "Looks like you're on their side now."

His face stopped me more than his words. There was a coldness, a wariness there that I'd never seen before. Like I was his enemy and he'd just discovered it.

"C'mon, Sean," said Reilly. He braced Sean's arm on the opposite side of Zuzu.

"Well," Zuzu said. "I'll say one thing for you, Delia. You know how to clear out a party."

The three of them made their way across the sand without another word. Perfect. It wasn't enough that I was changing into some kind of a freak. The only friends I had were turning their backs on me.

Gran still stood behind me and now reached a hand out to pat my shoulder. "C'mon. We'll go home now."

Jax turned sharply to the water. "What was that?"

I listened and thought I could hear a faint hissing. I followed the line of his gaze. A tiny yellow light bobbed in the water. I stared as it came closer.

"What is it?" I asked. It looked like some leftover part of the Revel celebration. A floating candle, maybe.

I heard Jax's shout at the same instant I saw a dark form lurch out of the water.

"Icer!"

CHAPTER 23

The creature stood on hind legs, dragging a short, thick tail on the sand behind it.

The Icer was enormous, maybe eight feet high, with a head like some grotesque deep-sea fish. A protuberant lower jaw jutted forward with curved fangs that interlaced the set from above. Warty growths on pendulous stalks protruded from its head, and on one of these a tentacle-like blob of tissue glowed bright yellow.

That was the light I'd seen in the water. A lure.

I let out a faint cry of disgust. At the sound the Icer's head twisted in my direction. Flat, milky eyes stared at me. It charged.

Long arms reached out with claws swiping the air like scythes. I staggered backward and crashed into Gran. With one strong movement she grabbed my shoulders and flung me aside just as the Icer reached us.

I fell to the sand hearing Gran cry out from deep in her throat. I looked up and saw the thing on top of my grandmother. It was worrying at her head with a horrible digging, pecking movement. It was feeding on her.

Jax pulled the Icer off Gran and smashed a fist into the creature's head. The impact made a wet, explosive thud and the Icer spun away with a sibilant hiss. It turned back, jaws gaping, and sank its teeth into Jax's shoulder.

Jax grimaced and fell to one knee before the Icer wrenched upward, pulling him off the ground.

I ran to my grandmother's still form.

"Oh my God!"

Her right eye was a pulpy mess and her face was covered in blood. But she was still breathing. Her limbs trembled. "Get away," she croaked, the words bubbling through the blood seeping into her mouth.

A few feet away the Icer still held Jax in its jaws. It shook him, then dropped him and lurched toward us again.

Kneeling next to Gran, I watched it shamble closer. I was frozen in place, fascinated by the horror of it. The thing was a walking nightmare. Its gray skin had an almost gelatinous, transparent quality. Blood vessels were visible, coursing and pulsing beneath its surface. It wasn't moving as fast as before.

"Delia!" shouted Jax. "It can't see much. Get up. Quietly. Don't make a sound. Go close to the fire! The light and the heat will repel it."

At the sound of Jax's voice, the thing wheeled around and lurched toward him again.

"C'mon, Gran," I said. "We have to get up. C'mon," I said. But she lay limp, barely breathing. She couldn't move. And it was coming back.

"It smells the blood!" Jax shouted.

The Icer was closer now, moving more purposefully toward us. My chest contracted with fear as I tried to think. I wasn't going to let that thing near Gran again. I wiped my hand against her cheek and it came away wet and red. I stood up and took a step to the side.

"Hey!"

The warty head with its expressionless eyes turned toward me.

"Yeah. Over here!"

I plunged farther away from Gran, into the water, shouting as loudly as I could. Jax yelled something at me but I couldn't hear him.

"Hey, you! Over here. Come and get me!" I screamed, and splashed and waved my blood-scented hand until I saw the thing veer away from Gran and come at me.

The water washed over me and I took comfort in the dark embrace. I ducked down deep, my frenzy overtaking logic. As if I could hide from it here. *This is a sea creature, Delia.* I kicked back hard, swimming away as it surged toward me. Filmy eyes with a central dark circle of black loomed closer. The mouth gaped, forming a ring of glistening teeth. The yellow glow of the luminescent tentacle lit the inside of its mouth. The red, rugated gullet contracted obscenely, as if it was already anticipating the food to come.

As I saw the horror that was going to end me, a single coherent thought shot through my mind. It was clear and as brilliantly intense as a laser.

Hate.

My hate for this creature was pure. There was no fear. It had attacked Gran. I wished it dead.

I inhaled deep, through my mouth.

"Die!" I screamed at the top of my lungs.

The Icer's head exploded in a burst of yellow gore.

CHAPTER 24

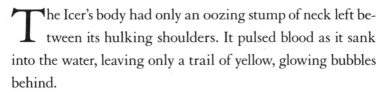

The Icer's body had only an oozing stump of neck left between its hulking shoulders. It pulsed blood as it sank into the water, leaving only a trail of yellow, glowing bubbles behind.

What just happened?

The water was quiet. My frantic breaths grated the air. I spun, looking for whatever had killed the Icer. It looked like a gunshot had taken its head off. Had Jax done it somehow? Had Sean come back to the beach?

Jax waded into the water. Blood streamed from the gash in his shoulder. He stared at the gruesome remains of the Icer that floated past him on the waves.

"Did you do that?" I panted. "How? Never mind. I need to get Gran out of here. Get help. Her face, Jax. I think it's her eye. It nearly killed her!" I practically bounded through the water toward the shore.

Jax put a hand on my shoulder, stopping me. "You're safe."

"I know. I'm okay. But Gran . . ." I shifted away, impatient, trying to move past him.

"Wait." Jax bracketed me with two strong arms. He pulled me to him, wrapping me in a sheltering embrace; then he laid his palm on my chest. It was a gesture I remembered from the first time he touched me. It had calmed me then, just as it did now. "Shh," he whispered close to my ear. "Your grandmother is alive. She will recover. But you have to calm yourself before you go to her." He paused. "Do you have *any* idea what you just did?"

"Wh-what? No."

What I did?

Maybe I did know, but my brain couldn't accept it. My teeth began to chatter and my legs felt like they weren't there anymore.

"You killed the Icer with your voice," said Jax. "I should have known, from the very beginning, that first night." He drew back and touched my hair, my cheeks, my arms, as if taking a gentle inventory to make sure I was okay. "There was something about your voice that drew me. You're a siren, Delia. Listen to me. This is very important . . . ."

Jax's voice was coming from far away. So far away that I couldn't hear the words. But he'd said that Gran would be okay. And I believed him. That was enough.

My vision contracted into a small dark tunnel.

And then I was gone.

CHAPTER 25

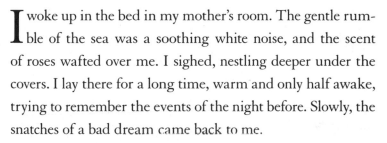

I woke up in the bed in my mother's room. The gentle rumble of the sea was a soothing white noise, and the scent of roses wafted over me. I sighed, nestling deeper under the covers. I lay there for a long time, warm and only half awake, trying to remember the events of the night before. Slowly, the snatches of a bad dream came back to me.

Blind, milky eyes. Gaping mouth. Teeth. Blood.

You killed it, Delia. With your voice.

Restlessly, I turned. My muscles ached. I was sore all over.

I opened my eyes, cold sweat dampening my forehead. I was still wearing the Revel dress. It was dry but dirty and clung to me in gritty, wrinkled bunches.

"Gran?" I shouted, sitting up in the bed.

"Down here. No need to yell."

I could have cried with the relief of hearing her gruff voice.

I stumbled downstairs to Gran's room. She was in bed. A bulky white bandage covered her right eye, and her head was wrapped with gauze, obscuring the entire side of her face.

"Oh my God, Gran," I said, rushing over to put my arms around her. "Your eye!"

She shook her head. When I started to cry, she patted me on the arm. "There, there. No time for blubbering. My other one's sharp enough for two. I'll be fine."

"It must hurt. Do you have something for the pain? We should take you to a hospital."

"I'm fine, Delia," she said. "Ben Deare brought a boatload of fancy medical supplies over and has had Flora fussing over me for the last two days. That's how long you've been asleep. My whole dresser over there's cluttered up with antibiotics, morphine pills, sterile bandages. Makes me look like some kind of dope fiend."

I tried to smile but couldn't.

"But I'm gonna be fine," she said firmly. "Jax, that's the First One's name, isn't it? The one that pulled the Icer off me?"

I nodded.

"He told me what happened. What you did." She folded her hands together. "He said you're a siren and that there hasn't been anyone like you in these waters for hundreds of years." She huffed. "I could've told him that."

I sat on the edge of Gran's bed and smoothed the coverlet over her. "I don't want to think about that right now. I can't."

"You're gonna have to. You saved yourself from that thing,"

said Gran, tilting her head in a cautious way to look at me. Her left eye was just as strong and commanding as ever. "And you saved *me*. Whatever it is you've got, it's nothing to run away from. You need to use it."

Standing up, I looked down at myself. "What I need is a shower," I muttered.

Gran nodded approvingly. "That's my girl."

I collected some clean clothes and went into the bathroom. It felt so good to peel off the sandy dress. Looking at the soiled and torn garment on the tile floor, I had a feeling its Revel days were over. It certainly wasn't going to get passed down to anybody. Stepping into the shower, I lifted my face to the warm spray of water, grateful for the cleansing, soothing pressure. My arms ached and the muscles in my abdomen throbbed as if I'd done a hundred crunches. With a washcloth I scrubbed the remnants of the Revel symbols from my skin. Rubbing the soap over my belly, my fingers suddenly stopped. Something was different. I looked down and swept away the suds.

I took a breath in on a hiss.

About an inch to either side of my belly button, my skin was sliced open.

Maybe my brain just refused to accept what I saw, but my first thought was that I'd cut myself somehow. I had that sickening feeling that comes after you stub your toe, right before the pain comes. But it didn't come; there was no pain. The two cuts just felt raw and sensitive. Open.

Trembling, my fingers slipped on the controls as I shut off the shower and stared down at my abdomen. Where my skin was split, tiny, clear bubbles formed and popped. I took in a surprised breath and saw the slits pucker and lift. Felt the air ache inside me. Felt the thirst of those tiny mouths. For water.

They were the same slits I'd seen on Jax's abdomen.

Okay.

I had gills.

———

I stood in front of the mirror and surveyed the slits that enclosed my belly button like long, pink parentheses. "This is just gross," I said softly, tilting my head. I had holes in me. New apertures that opened and closed when they wanted to. My body had betrayed me, changed without my consent.

What was next? The fin, I supposed.

Maybe even scales. Or a tail.

I felt myself breathing hard with distress, imagining the freakish possibilities, and as I did, the gills fluttered, breathing too.

Don't hyperventilate.

Then I let out a semi-hysterical laugh at the irony of *that*.

I had gills. Hyperventilating was probably what I did best.

The first thing I did was run down and show Gran. She was unfazed, of course, and told me that everything would be fine, everything happens for a reason, and I would be healthy and strong, no matter what changes I went through. All the nonsense that I desperately needed to hear.

I dropped my head to her lap, feeling comfort in the warm bulk of her.

"How did you get to be so brave, Gran?" I whispered.

I felt her long exhale as she ran a hand over my hair. "I'm not brave. I just keep going."

"But what if *I* keep going?" I asked, closing my eyes tight. "What if I get, I don't know, scales or a tail? Or another *head*?"

Gran sounded tired but still had the same wry spark to her tone when she gave a gentle yank on my curls and answered, "Then I'm sure it'll suit you just fine."

"Do you think Mom knew what I was going to be?"

A monster.

"I don't think so," said Gran. "How could she? She just didn't want the life here. For either of you. But I'm proud of you, Delia. Proud of the way you spoke up on the beach. You be what you are."

"What should I do?" I asked.

Gran reflected. "Times like this, I usually make coffee."

CHAPTER 26

I was glad to take care of Gran while she recovered. Her right eye was lost, the mangled skin of the lid healing in a thickened red scar. Helping her gave me something to concentrate on other than turning into a merwoman-siren-demigod, or whatever the heck I was. I took on most of the housework, and when it was time to go down to the gardens, I drove the golf cart for her. This made Gran furious, but with sight in only one eye, she had terrible depth perception and would have run us right off the path.

She still collected the trapweed and insisted on feeding the Glaukos creatures herself from the high bluff. It was as if she didn't trust anyone else to do the job. We also brought a basket full of the resinous leaves home to be dried on a wooden rack and stored in airtight containers in the cellar.

The only thing I didn't like doing for Gran was taking the

occasional trip into town for supplies. If I thought I'd been treated coolly when I first arrived on Trespass, then this was the Arctic tundra. No one said hello or waved. They didn't even look at me if they could help it. And they crossed the road to avoid me. I knew the islanders weren't accustomed to mixing with the First Ones. But they *knew* me. Sort of.

Were they afraid?

It couldn't have been what happened with the Icer, because nobody except Jax and Gran had seen me kill it. The Icer's body had been discovered, washed up on shore the next morning. Everyone just assumed it had been killed by a Glaukos. As for how the Icer had gotten through the Hundred Hands, Mayor Ed was apparently launching an investigation and had placed, as he put it, a moratorium on swimming for all islanders.

Though I decided that his swimming ban didn't apply to me, because I was a First One now. Plus I was pretty sure Mayor Ed wouldn't mind at all if an Icer got me.

So the islanders weren't shunning me because I had this siren voice thing. They didn't know about that. It was just the fact that I was Aitros, a First One. Sean had certainly made it clear that *he* saw me differently. How had he put it? Oh yeah. I was on "their side."

Terrific. Now we had sides.

I tried a few times to find Sean at his house, but his mother always told me he wasn't there. It made me angry that Sean could turn his back on me like this. I was still the same person inside. Despite my extra . . . attributes. Zuzu and Reilly didn't come over either. Not even to see Gran, and that hurt. Everyone on the island knew by now that she'd been injured. They'd seen me assisting her, seen the patch that she would wear over her eye for the rest of her life. Just because they wanted to avoid me, my grandmother shouldn't have been punished too.

I thought of going over to Zuzu's house, or to the dock to look for Sean, but I was afraid of making things worse. On top of everything, we were still waiting to hear what the fallout would be from Revel.

So far, according to Ben, the Council had remained silent. Just as Jax had said, I wasn't a Lander, so the rules about offering myself as tribute didn't really apply. Apparently they hadn't yet decided what was to be done with me.

Gee, didn't *that* have a familiar ring to it.

Zuzu's insult to the First One called Darius, on the other hand, was a punishable offense. Not physical punishment, thank goodness, but her family wouldn't be allowed to take their share of supplies from the deliveries the First Ones made to Wreck Beach for a year. Gran said that they would be able to manage; the other islanders would look out for them and make sure they had what they needed.

It seemed ridiculous to me that Zuzu's whole family could be punished just because she called someone a jerk. It wasn't fair. I would've liked to tell Zuzu that, or done something to help, but maybe she wouldn't want my help. Maybe she thought I was responsible for the whole mess.

I wouldn't really blame her.

It was one week after Revel when the nor'easter struck. Gran had an old-fashioned-looking barometer on the wall near her back door, and that morning the needle swung down to *Stormy* and trembled there all day. In the afternoon the sky turned dark. Not just storm-cloud gray, but with an acid green tinge that was unbelievably eerie.

"That can't be good," I said, closing a window.

Gran told me to fill buckets with water in case the electric pump for the well died. She also had me check the batteries in the flashlights and fill the kerosene lamps.

It was evening when the storm struck. Gran was in bed; she got tired in the evenings, which was no wonder, given how hard she pushed herself all day. I heard the wind first, battering branches of the lilac and forsythia bushes against the windows. When the rain began, it came in pelting icy drops. Then the wind picked up and moaned. Really moaned, like the air was distressed, as if it were having a heart attack or something. The lights flickered and went out.

"There it goes. Like clockwork." I was sitting in the kitchen. Gran's bedroom door was open; I could hear her muttering. "I've got the candles ready in the kitchen," she called out in the darkness.

"I'm right here, Gran," I answered. "Don't get out of that bed."

With the candlelight it was a little less spooky, but I still jumped when a knock came at the back door. I carried my candle, set in a mason jar, to answer it.

Sean stood outside in the darkness holding a lantern in one hand and a plastic bag in the other. His tall frame filled the doorway and was backlit suddenly when a flash of lightning streaked across the sky. "I thought I'd check on you, see if you need anything," he said, his voice raised against the wind and the battering rain. "That's what I usually do when we get a bad storm like this," he added, as if he had to explain himself.

"Come in." I clutched my robe closer and waved him through, then nearly shut the door on Buddy, who yelped and wriggled past me.

"Buddy, sit," Sean ordered. He twisted the plastic bag in his hands. "I've got some D batteries here, extra kerosene in the truck if you need it."

"Thanks," I said with a smile. "That was really nice of you. But I think we've got it covered. Gran told me what to do."

"Is that Sean?" yelled Gran.

I stepped over to her bedroom door. "He's checking to see if we need anything."

"We're just fine," she answered. "Take the Tupperware on the counter, Sean. The tea for your mother's in there."

"Thanks, Miz McGovern," Sean called to her, and tucked the container into the plastic bag and set it by the door. He pointed to the living room and I nodded, following him in.

"How's she doing?" he asked in a quiet voice when we stood by the window.

"Okay. She's healing." I shook my head. "She's amazingly

tough." I looked up at him. "I'm glad to see you, Sean. I was hoping we could talk." I peered at him. "Are you okay?" In the wan light afforded by my candle, Sean's face looked different, the bones of his face more prominent, his eyes more deep-set. But it could have been a trick of the shadows.

"I'm fine," he said.

"I never got a chance to thank you. For what you did at Revel."

"I didn't do anything but get my ass kicked," said Sean with a rueful smile.

"I'm sorry you got hurt. Are your ribs okay?"

He shook his head. "I'm fine, Delia. Really." He paused. "You look good."

I let out a surprised laugh. "Um, thanks. Where've you been all week?"

"Working," he said with a shrug. "Same old." He cocked his head. "No, I mean it. There's something really different about you." He reached out and wound a coil of my hair around his finger, stretched it out and let it go.

I leaned back slightly and cleared my throat. "Yeah, I guess we all know what that is. My dark fishy side."

Sean smiled, stepped closer and put his hands on my waist. "I wanted to see you tonight, Delia. I've been thinking about something for a while, trying to decide. And the other night I decided. So I'm feeling better about things."

I tried to back away, uncomfortable with this sudden intimate touch, but Sean pressed closer.

"Sean." I gently moved his hands away. "Are you okay?"

"I feel great," Sean whispered. "I've just been wanting to do this, before it's too late."

He pulled me close and kissed me. His mouth was warm and hungry and it felt like every muscle in his body was coiled like a spring. I could feel the pounding of his heart against my own chest.

I pushed him away from me, breathing hard. "Sean, hold on a minute."

He straightened up. He didn't look flustered or put off by my resistance and still held my shoulders in a warm, loose grip. He let his hands slide down my arms before releasing me. "Sorry. Guess I just wanted a taste of what I can't have anymore."

"What are you talking about?"

"Revel," said Sean, his voice low and rough. "I saw how Jax looked at you. And how you looked at him. So now I know where I stand. It makes things easier."

Lightning flashed, illuminating his face. The outline of his jaw looked hard and the skin was taut over his cheekbones. There *was* something wrong. He didn't look sick exactly. Just . . . *changed*. As if he'd aged years since I saw him last.

"Sean, what's happened to you?" I whispered.

Thunder rumbled through the house and shook the embroidery frames on the walls. Sean didn't answer, only turned and strode away. I heard him call Buddy to him and the back door slam as he went back out, into the storm.

CHAPTER 27

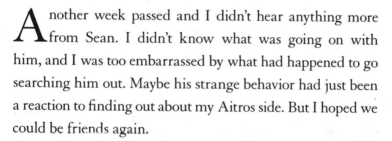

Another week passed and I didn't hear anything more from Sean. I didn't know what was going on with him, and I was too embarrassed by what had happened to go searching him out. Maybe his strange behavior had just been a reaction to finding out about my Aitros side. But I hoped we could be friends again.

To be honest, I had a hard time keeping my mind on anything except the changes I was going through. So many strange, impossible things were happening.

For example, I was wearing a two-piece.

I regarded myself in the mirror. The bikini had belonged to Mom, who'd apparently been more daring than I thought. I'd found it in a trunk with some of her other old clothes in Gran's attic. The skimpy suit of white eyelet fabric with tiny black flowers was a lot more revealing than I was used to. But if I swam in anything that covered my gills, it felt like I was breathing through a mask.

And I had to swim.

At this point even if someone had told me that the Aitros changes would go away if I stayed out of the water, I wouldn't have done it. I couldn't have. I needed to be in the water for at least an hour every day, longer if I could. I felt tired and restless without it.

I think I looked good too. My body was getting stronger with the swimming. Lithe, toned muscles had appeared in my arms and legs and belly. I stood straighter and held myself taller. Unfortunately, I hadn't *grown* taller, at least not that I could tell.

But the first time I stepped from the water and saw the webbing between my fingers, I *did* freak out.

The pearly membranes of tissue were almost see-through. And they were between my toes too. They definitely helped with the swimming, and after I was out of the water for a while, the webbing retracted. So it wasn't so bad. But the thing I feared the most didn't seem to be happening. Not yet. I hadn't developed a fin when I went into the water.

Wouldn't *that* be special.

———

"Come on," Jax said, waving me to join him. He'd been wanting to take me out to see the reef. It would be the farthest I'd swum so far.

I tugged off my T-shirt and dropped it to the sand, then unbuttoned my shorts and slipped them down. When I stepped out of the shorts and used my toe to kick them onto the blanket, I glanced over at Jax. His raised hand dropped slowly into the water and he stared at me with those relentlessly blue eyes as I ambled to the water.

"What is that?" he asked me, his voice sounding strained.

"It's a bathing suit. I can't wear the other one anymore because of these." I passed a hand over my gills.

He opened his mouth and closed it again. Nodded.

Ever since Revel, when he'd learned that I had Aitros blood in my veins and this strange power in my voice, Jax had been different. He was diligent about helping me learn my way around the waters of Trespass, and seemed to enjoy being with me. In fact, when we were together, he never left my side and was as protective as a mother hen with a chick.

But we hadn't spoken about my voice or what happened that night. And Jax hadn't kissed me again or even touched me. Even though sometimes I thought he wanted to. I stepped into the surf. The water sliding over my skin felt like a caress, but rather than thrill me, it only made me yearn more for his touch.

A rising wave lifted me and I felt the answering joyful surge in my belly. I arched down and kicked, slicing deep beneath the water. I came up beside Jax.

"Tell me about sirens," I said.

I'd never seen Jax look unsure or hesitant about anything, but he did now. His brow furrowed and his eyebrows pulled together, making his expression look at once fearsome and, strangely enough, worried. "I thought we were going to swim."

"We will. After you tell me about sirens. Gran says that I can't run away from this thing, that I need to learn how to use it."

"You've never heard of them?" Jax asked, searching my face.

I shrugged. "From what I recall, they're girls with big busts and long hair that used to sit on rocks and sing to sailors, luring them to shore and making them wreck their boats."

Jax rolled his eyes. "As usual, the Landers have twisted the tale beyond any sense." He frowned and stirred the water between us absently with his hand, creating a small whirlpool. "I can't tell you very much, because a siren is a rare thing among our race. There hasn't been one in these waters since the days of my forefathers. Two hundred, perhaps three hundred years." Jax glanced up at me, his mouth curved in a faint smile. "It's no wonder Mikos doesn't have a clue what you did to him. He still seems to think you had some hidden device or trick to injure him so."

He swept the miniature whirlpool away with a careless gesture. "Simply put, a siren is a female demigod of the sea but with the power of her will in her voice."

"What does that mean?"

"Just this," said Jax. "With the power of her voice, a siren can move the minds and the hearts of men. She can persuade armies to battle or bring peaceful resolution to a violent conflict. The most powerful sirens can also kill with their voices." He looked at me steadily. "As you did."

Jax reached out and took my hand in his tanned and sinewy one. The simple touch between us felt electric to me, but his expression was unreadable.

"A siren is the most deadly weapon an Aitros clan can possess," he said in a measured voice.

A *weapon?* As unbelievable as it was, I *had* killed with my voice. I'd seen the Icer's head explode. And I'd hurt Mikos enough to disarm him and escape. But I didn't even know exactly what I'd done to *make* those things happen.

I wasn't so much of a weapon. More like a loose cannon.

"But why are there so few sirens?"

Jax was looking down at my hand and closed it gently inside his own. "Probably because they don't live very long. The stories say that sirens were often killed as children, or even infants."

"You're not serious." I pulled my hand back.

"You think I would joke about that?" His gaze shot to mine.

"No. I don't know," I said in a small voice, sinking down in the water. I realized that this had become a protective posture for me. I felt safer when I was enclosed like this, wrapped in water. "I just need time to understand what's happening to me."

"That's why I told you not to tell anyone," he said. "I

warned you on the night of Revel. I don't think anyone in the clan should know. Not yet."

I frowned, trying to remember his words that night. "I think I might've been passing out then."

"Oh."

"But I haven't told anyone. Only Gran knows."

Jax nodded. "According to the stories, a siren is considered too dangerous to be allowed to live unless she can be controlled. In ancient times the ones that managed to reach adulthood sometimes acted as independent assassins. Mercenaries of the gods."

I shook my head, unwilling to listen to any more.

Jax came closer to me. I could feel the heat radiating from his sun-warmed skin, and I wanted to curl myself inside the safety of his arms. But something in his eyes held me back. He'd put some kind of a distance between us.

"I don't want this," I said. "I never wanted *any* of this. I just wanted a place. A home."

Jax nodded. "Many Landers come to islands looking for a safe haven from the storm."

I nodded, my lips trembling despite my efforts to hold myself together. "Yes."

"There is a problem, *Diabolika,*" Jax whispered. His gaze fell to my mouth and lingered there, his eyes doing what I wished his lips would. "You *are* the storm."

CHAPTER 28

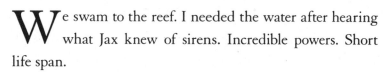

We swam to the reef. I needed the water after hearing what Jax knew of sirens. Incredible powers. Short life span.

Still, the newly discovered thrill of being in the ocean ran down my spine as cool water rushed over me, tugging at my hair. Did Jax feel this way when he swam? Maybe he was so used to it he didn't notice anymore. I felt connected to the water, not just in it. Like my nerve endings didn't stop at the surface of my skin but reached out into the water, sensing the salty minerals dissolved in it, the pressure of the depth and the thrumming vibrations of little fish.

I was learning to swim as the Aitros did. They used not just their bodies, but the water itself. There were currents everywhere, like miniature aquatic jet streams, and if I angled my body the right way, I found myself carried along, lifted and propelled.

Jax shot past me, spiraling through the water. The iridescent dorsal fin curled around him like a brilliant banner, and I smiled. He could be such a show-off. He always stayed close, but he wanted to lead. Whatever it was, I decided, whether he was being overprotective or just plain male, I wasn't going to let him get away with it.

I kicked and felt the cool rush of a fast channel of water sweep over me. I surged forward until Jax and I swam side by side. Glancing over, I saw the answering smile and the gleam in his eye. I couldn't remember ever feeling as happy as I was like this, swimming beside Jax. It was like a combination of joy and adrenaline bubbling inside me.

It was so beautiful here, a new world to discover. And beneath the water, I could see better than ever before. The water must have acted like some kind of superpowered lens, or maybe it was just being part Aitros, but when I was swimming, my vision was 20/20. Or whatever was better than that. Every rock, every ripple of sand, stood out in clear, sharp detail.

I spotted waving tendrils of bright green sea grass fluttering near a column of coral and thought we must be getting close to the reef. I swam down to it and wove my fingers through the delicate strands of undulating grass. It was lovely.

"We call it kettle grass."

I whipped my head up and let out a startled gasp. Bubbles frothed up around my face.

Jax was yards away, watching me with that same amused, sardonic expression he so often wore. But I'd *heard* him speak. Underwater.

"Yes, you can hear me in your head. It's another ability that was left to us by the gods. We can communicate with each other."

It was exactly as if he stood next to me, talking.

"Can you read my mind?" I asked, thinking the question to him.

I noticed that I'd kicked against the water, increasing the distance between us. The idea of Jax knowing all my innermost thoughts made me uneasy. On oh so many levels. I stared at him.

God, I don't want to have to start wrapping my head in tinfoil.

"As attractive as that sounds, it's not necessary," came his reply, complete with sarcasm. "I can sense your mood, but to read an individual thought there has to be an intention, you have to *want* to tell me something. It's like talking, except in our heads. I can't really hear anything you don't want me to."

"Hmm. That's almost comforting," I told him. "I'm not sure I like the idea of you being in my head. Even if it is by invitation only."

"Why?" He swam closer. "Have you been entertaining fantasies about me?"

"Not at all." I hoped my telepathic lying skills were better than my normal ones. "And don't try to plant any either," I added with what I hoped was a mental glare, in addition to the one on my face.

"A pity."

I smiled. I enjoyed this flirtatious bickering between us. But somehow I got the feeling that he was using it to stay away from anything deeper, more serious.

"The reef is a little farther ahead. Are you tired?"

"No. Let's keep going."

I still didn't have the same stamina and speed in the water as the other First Ones. Jax told me that it would take a little time. As he put it, I still had "Lander dust clinging to my toes."

A bright flash of pink caught my eye as a tiny fish darted by. I'd looked up the names and pictures in one of Gran's nature books, and now I knew some of the ones I saw, like the yellow tang that glowed placidly against the coral and the busy parrotfish that pecked at the food hidden within. They didn't seem afraid of me. If I got very close and tried to touch one of them, they'd usually just sidle away. Many of the fish and corals around Trespass weren't usually found in northern waters. They were warm-water species. It was another example of how the strange climate of the island had created sort of an underwater greenhouse.

Ahead I could make out the faint outline of the reef—a huge, irregular formation of coral. From a distance, the pale, twisted shapes of the coral vaguely resembled a line of people, heads upturned, arms reaching.

I churned water with my legs to stop as I saw the reef through the wavering shafts of sunlight from above. A sickening fear gripped me.

The reef didn't resemble people. It *was* people.

Reaching up toward the surface as if yearning to touch sunlight stood the stony, frozen forms of men encased in coral.

The Hundred Hands.

"Don't be afraid," said Jax. I heard his voice in my head, as clearly as if he were talking to me in a quiet room:

"When the first Landers arrived here, it was in a storm. Some say one raised by Poseidon himself. Their ship sank and these men drowned. The stone coral around Trespass absorbed them, entrapped them. Now they guard the island, along with the Glaukos. Here you see the one hundred able hands aboard that first ship. The Hundred Hands."

"Are they alive?" I asked.

"No. They are cursed."

Skull-like faces were still visible, their features blurred beneath the crust of barnacle-covered coral. Clumps of soft-fingered anemones clung to their arms. Bright fish darted in and out of their hollowed eyes.

A shark skimmed by the top of the reef, and one of the stony hands gripped closed.

I jerked back, startled. "They can move."

"There's no need to be afraid. They're only mobile enough to prevent unwelcome visitors from swimming through. If someone or something is unlucky enough to be caught in their grip for too long, it becomes part of the reef as well."

He extended his hand to me. "Come deeper."

I took Jax's hand and turned away, leaving the reef of trapped seamen behind, though I wouldn't be able to forget so easily.

We dove straight down. We were still inside the protective ring of the reef, but Jax led me down into a dark depression. The layers of grassy rocks passed by in shadowy waves of emerald green.

"This is the Hollow. You might find it interesting. The wreckage from the boat of those Landers drifted into this chasm."

"The *Dover*?"

"Yes, I believe that was the name."

The water became cooler. The coral disappeared, giving way to massive dark boulders. I could feel the pressure of the depths around me, but it wasn't unpleasant. It was exciting.

Jax slowed and looked at me, as if to make sure I was okay. His long, muscled form dappled with the shifting shadows of water.

As we paused in our descent I noticed something bright glimmering in a dark niche beside me. Without thinking, I reached for it. Instantly, a sharp pain jabbed my finger, and I let out a yelp.

"What is it?" Jax pulled me to him so quickly that the momentum spun us together and we drifted away from the rocks, bodies entwined.

I clung to him for a moment longer than I needed to. Okay. Maybe a couple of moments.

"I'm fine," I said as I disentangled myself. "Something bit me."

"Let me see." Jax took my hand and examined it. It seemed

strange to see that dark head bent in such an absorbed study of my finger. For one so fierce, he could be surprisingly tender. It was nothing. Only a tiny curl of blood rose from the tip of my finger, dissolving instantly. But I enjoyed watching the way Jax's dark hair rippled in the water and the strongly molded curve of his shoulders. "There are moray eels in some of these crevices," he said. "Very irritable creatures. It doesn't seem to have caused much damage." He released me and swam back to the spot. He peered through the narrow opening.

"But this is something else." He reached in and withdrew a small item.

It was a gleaming golden brooch, inlaid with pearls in the shape of a crescent moon.

"The pin must have stuck you." He smiled and let it fall into my hand.

"It's so beautiful," I said, rolling the delicately styled piece on my palm. "May I keep it?"

"Of course. The sea gave it to you. And extracted its price," he added, taking my hand once more and gently rubbing the pad of my finger. I drifted closer to him.

I tried *not* to think of the words that were drumming impatiently in my head. But he must have heard them, because soon our lips were only inches apart.

What happened next was fast. I sensed something behind me, perhaps from a subtle movement in the water. At the same time I saw the flash of alarm in Jax's eyes.

I whirled around.

The huge, grotesque face of an Icer hung in the water before me.

I gasped, inhaling a mouthful of water, and kicked backward, barreling into Jax's hard chest as the thing lunged toward me. In a flash of movement Jax put himself between me and the creature.

Jax slashed at the Icer with his knife and somersaulted backward over the thing's back, grabbed my hand and somehow propelled me ahead of him as we swam away from the beast. The monster followed, snapping its jaws as it attacked. The long fangs made a metallic noise that scissored through the water around us.

I glanced behind us. Dangling pieces of shaggy algae hung from the Icer's jaws and lips, and the blind staring eyes rolled in its head. Behind the fish head were the bulky torso and tail. Here in the water the Icer moved very differently from the one on the beach; the arms and legs hung almost motionless as it swam. But it was fast, very fast.

Another dark form joined it. Another Icer.

"Jax! There's another one."

"Swim, Delia! Get away from here."

I turned to see Jax stopping in the water. Every muscle in my body was screaming for me to do just as he said, but I hesitated.

Jax coiled up and struck, slamming his heel into the face of the Icer closest to him, sending a cloud of blood churning into the water. His long dagger was out again, slashing furiously.

The next Icer that approached him lost a hand. Then only the slashing, stabbing glint of metal was visible through the murk of slime and body parts.

And through the swirl of violence, I caught glimpses of Jax. His expression remained cool and focused. It was as if this was his element.

I swam in a circle, uncertain what to do.

"Head for the caves!"

The sound of Jax's command in my head was urgent but with a clarity that surprised me and somehow calmed me. Despite the sense of self-preservation that told my body to simply obey, I hesitated. I wasn't going to leave him like this.

There were more Icers now. Three hulking bodies came out of the shadows.

As Jax faced the three Icers he straightened. He looked calm and almost regal as he floated before them, motionless except for the subtle movements of the winged fin on his back. Jax cupped his hands together before him and with a sudden, explosive movement threw his arms forward.

The boom reverberated back and rocked me as a literal cannonball of water screamed toward the Icers. The blast was invisible except for its aftereffects. Two of the creatures were flung backward, bloody gobbets of their flesh flying through the water. The third Icer wasn't hit but swerved away and headed straight for me, its teeth gnashing. It swam with side-to-side movement, its massive upper body lurching. But it was still fast, careening toward me like a derailed train.

I kicked hard, arching backward to swim away. The caves were to the north, I remembered, just past a broad underwater shelf. I might be able to make it.

My arms and legs thrust through the water as my pulse hammered in my ears so hard I couldn't sense anything else. I didn't dare look back.

The plateau of rock came into view and I surged over it. The top of one of my feet whacked against stone in my frenzied kick, and somewhere, dimly, I registered the pain. Maybe someone like Jax could have outmaneuvered this thing in a minute. But I was still a clumsy swimmer in comparison. And panic only made it worse.

Think.

Stopping to try to use my voice was out of the question. I didn't have any idea if that would work again, or how to control it.

I bolted into one of the smaller cave openings, hoping to find some secure place that the Icer wouldn't fit through. All concerns about what was inside the caves flew out of my mind. I didn't care. I'd take a faceful of moray eel any day over the monster behind me. Inside the mouth of the cave was a long, narrow chamber. Small breaks in its ceiling let tiny flecks of light through. I swam along this channel as fast as I could.

There was a surge of pressure behind me, and a faint darkening of the light. The Icer had followed me into the tunnel.

Now the space became a little narrower. I could reach out and pull myself along as I swam, both hands clutching at the sides of the tunnel. Unfortunately, it was still wide enough for the Icer too. I could sense the thing behind me getting closer. The tunnel slanted down, going deeper, but there was no choice. I couldn't turn around now.

Finally I came to a place where I had to squirm through a narrow opening. I found myself in a small, roughly round space, with no exit. A dead end. There was barely room to turn around and face the opening. The walls of stone scraped my skin. I pressed myself back as far as I could against the back of my little hole. Great.

Brilliant plan, Delia.

I felt rather than saw the presence of the monster beyond the opening. It was too big. It couldn't get in here, could it?

I leaned forward and tried screaming at it. "Die!"

Nothing happened. The Icer was moving, trying to fit its jaws into the opening. The stone must have blocked my voice. Or it wasn't the magic word. Or it just wasn't working anymore.

The Icer's ribbonlike tentacle floated into the space. The glowing knob of tissue at its end lit the cramped black hole around me. I cringed back as it dangled there, inches from my face.

Now I couldn't move anywhere and the full truth of my situation hit me: I was trapped in a cave underwater with no escape. I was going to die here. I was going to die in this small, dark place under the water.

The Icer was too big to pass through entirely, but it reached a long arm in and swiped at me, slicing my shin and sending a plume of blood into the water. It sickened me that I could taste it.

The creature peered in, ravenous mouth open. Again the hideous hand came scrabbling toward my face. I couldn't move back any farther. My body was balled up as small as I could make myself. Now it was just a matter of time. It was going to reach in and claw me to death. Slowly. Piece by piece it would get me.

I felt breathless and realized that my tightly coiled position was pressing my legs up too tight against my belly, making it hard to breathe. I straightened slightly, allowing water to rush over the gills. But the movement brought me within range. The Icer's claw snagged my hair, yanking my head forward against a sharp stone. The stab of pain was so intense that for a moment it drove out the fear. My blood tinged the water again. Outside the tiny niche I sensed the Icer's frenzy of excitement, of hunger.

It could taste me too.

It held on to my hair, pulling harder; the top of my head ground forward against the sloping roof of the crevice.

It was trying to drag me out.

Rage at this ugly creature, frustration that I was trapped here like a mouse in a hole, and the throbbing ache in my head all combined. I gripped my hair and yanked it from the clawed grip.

I needed to do something different, now.

I aimed my voice. Not at the small opening, but at the wall of stone in front of me.

"Break!" I screamed.

Nothing happened.

Panic flooded me. It didn't work. *Why didn't it work?*

Desperately I tried to calm my mind. Tried to forget where I was. The thing that was trying to kill me. I gathered my breath and focused my mind on the image of the stone exploding.

"Break!"

The blast was deafening. The wall shot out and away as if I'd detonated a bomb. I clung to the back wall of my now-opened hiding place. Gradually I straightened, waving the floating dust from the water before me, and swam out into a rain of gravel. The Icer lay beneath a pile of rubble, its body mashed into pulp.

Okay, that works.

Jax hurtled toward me through the muddied water and pulled me close. "Are you hurt?"

"Just scratched up a little," I told him. "Are you okay?"

He nodded, and looked distracted as he gazed at the rubble piled around us. "We need to get out of here. I don't know how many more there could be. We'll take a different route back. Stay close to me."

He wasn't going to get any argument. My swimming wasn't graceful or efficient anymore. My muscles screamed with fatigue and I was pushing as hard as I could to simply move.

After we'd been swimming for maybe ten minutes, Jax stopped abruptly. "That's impossible," he said, staring. "Look. There's a break in the reef."

I looked to the right. There was a huge gash through part of the reef there. It was as if some giant wrecking ball had smashed through, leaving a gaping hole about twenty feet wide.

"*This* is how the Icers got through," said Jax. "But why hasn't it been reported?"

"Maybe no one noticed it."

"It's the duty of the Glaukos to patrol this perimeter," Jax said. I could hear the fierce anger in his mind as well as his concern for the safety of the island, of his clan.

He cared a lot more than he wanted anyone to know.

"We need to go back now," he said. "The clan needs to be warned."

CHAPTER 29

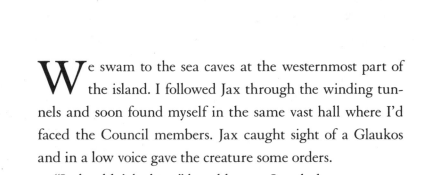

We swam to the sea caves at the westernmost part of the island. I followed Jax through the winding tunnels and soon found myself in the same vast hall where I'd faced the Council members. Jax caught sight of a Glaukos and in a low voice gave the creature some orders.

"It shouldn't be long," he told me as I sank down to rest on a low step.

Soon Xarras appeared at the mouth of one of the tunnels and hurried toward us.

"Jax," he said, raising his arms to embrace his son. "What's so urgent that you need to meet me now? And in secret?"

"The island's in danger," Jax said in a low voice. "The Hundred Hands has been breached. That was how the Icer came through on the night of Revel. Delia and I were attacked by five of them near the wreck in the Hollow less than an hour ago."

"But how?" wondered Xarras aloud. "The reef is indestructible."

"Apparently not," said Jax. "The Glaukos need to be dispatched immediately to guard the break, and to repair it if they can."

"Of course," said Xarras, frowning in contemplation. "I'll tell Lukus of this at once." He glanced at me. "Ah," he said with a courteous smile. "I have the pleasure once more, my dear. I hope you are well?"

"Yes, thank you."

"I understand that there was much excitement over your attendance at Revel. I heard the accounts from Mikos, at some length." He gave Jax a conspiratorial smile. "A very intriguing tale, I must say." His gaze settled on me once more, and I thought I saw a flicker of approval. "I think Mikos owes you an apology, my dear. But to be honest, I do not expect you will receive one."

He turned to Jax. "Thank you for coming, Jax. I know it hasn't been easy for you. Tonight you've done a service to the clan." The two of them clasped arms. "It won't be forgotten."

The usual composure on Jax's dark feature's broke, and I could see how much those words touched him as a spark of pleasure lit his eyes. Then the momentary lapse was gone and he was in command again, nodding courteously to his father.

Xarras looked at me and added, "Take care of her, Jax. She's one of us now."

276

Jax led me through a curving tunnel.

"This isn't the way we came."

Jax looked at me with surprise. "Very good. It is a different path."

"So where are we going now?" I asked as I followed him down narrow steps. I was exhausted and dirty and bloody. This had better be important.

"To see someone who may be able to help you," said Jax. "His name is Kephalos. He's an oracle. It's possible he can tell you something about how to control your voice."

"So I take it you don't approve of the way I dealt with the Icer back there?" I asked archly.

"Oh, I approve," Jax said with an amused curl of his lips. "It's just that in the future a little more finesse may be required."

"Kephalos is a fortune-teller?"

"Nothing so crass. An oracle doesn't accept money for his visions. They're considered gifts bestowed on him by the gods. And it's dangerous to consult him unless you have a good reason."

We walked farther in silence; then, "Here," said Jax. He stopped before a small black opening in the wall. "I have to wait here. You must see him alone."

"Oh," I said, eyeing the entrance doubtfully. I didn't like the idea of going in there all alone. "Really? Okay. What if he's asleep?"

"The oracle doesn't sleep," Jax said impatiently. "Just don't say anything to offend, him. He's touchy about his appearance."

"Right." I crept through the narrow hole, supporting myself with a hand on either side, gripping cool, wet stone. I came out into a dimly lit cave, the floor of which sloped down to a pool in the center.

"Hello?"

Only the drip of water answered, echoing through the chamber.

Then there was a splash and a faint sloshing sound.

I narrowed my eyes, trying to adjust to the dim green glow that came from the pool. There was something in the shadows. Gray tentacles unfurled under the surface of the water, and I felt a chill of revulsion as the rest of the thing crawled from behind a rock. A bald white head appeared. A man's head. For a moment I couldn't register what I was seeing.

The head floated toward me on top of the water. It was attached to the coiling body of an octopus. I reared back so fast I nearly lost my balance on the slick rocks.

It came closer, seeming to skim over the sand at the bottom of the shallow pool. "You've just been born." Kephalos spoke the words with a trace of a lisp from beneath a crooked overbite of large teeth.

It took a moment for me to recover and decipher what it, or rather *he*, had said. Just born?

"No," I said unsteadily, "I—I'm seventeen."

The head lurched slightly, side to side, as the purplish-gray tentacles shifted. It moved closer. Kephalos's bulbous eyes rolled up to regard me.

"I meant the Aitros in you. That was just brought to life, wasn't it?"

I put a hand to my belly, where the gills felt like newly exposed skin. "Oh. Yes."

"Why do you come here? I don't like to be disturbed." Kephalos peered at me expectantly.

Jax hadn't exactly prepared me for this part. What was I supposed to ask?

"I want to know about being a siren," I said. "If I'm meant to stay here on Trespass and what I'm supposed to do."

"Those are three vague and useless questions," Kephalos snapped. Green blotches of color suffused his fleshy arms as they unfurled toward me, matching the mottled colors of the rocks they came in contact with. I was fascinated by the chameleon changes of color and pattern that made Kephalos blend in with his surroundings. At least the octopus part. His head seemed to stay the same pasty white.

"Then I don't know the right question to ask," I said, watching the undulating tentacles.

"Good," remarked Kephalos grudgingly. "The first step in acquiring wisdom is to acknowledge that you lack it. *Actually,* the first step is having an adequate brainpan. And, as you can see, I've been blessed with a capacious cranium." He eyed my head critically. "As for you. Well. We'll do the best we can."

There was a pause. It could have definitely been called an awkward pause, considering the fact that I was waiting to hear what an octopus-man that I'd never seen before was going to tell me about my own life. And he'd just insulted me.

"I told her you would be a siren," Kephalos said softly.

Gooseflesh prickled my skin. "Who?"

"Your mother, when she came to see me. The night after you were conceived. You look remarkably similar," he observed. One of his tentacles reached up and stroked his chin.

"So she did know. Is that why she ran away?"

Kephalos shrugged. At least, I thought that's what the arching at the base of his multiple arms indicated. "I believe so. I told her that her child's only destiny on this island was destruction."

"And what can you tell me now? Has my destiny changed?"

Kephalos blinked up at me. "Yes and no. There are many more options, more dangers. There's only one thing I can see for sure."

"And what's that?"

"Betrayal," said Kephalos.

"By whom?"

"That I cannot tell. But you must learn to use your voice more wisely. Remember that it's a weapon. Always."

"Well, how do I use it?" I asked him. "Do I sing? Or learn special notes, special words? How do I direct it?"

"You can sing if you like, for a more old-school effect. But it really doesn't matter," said Kephalos. "It's your will, your desire, that you manifest with your voice. The more you know yourself, what you want, the more powerful your voice will be. As for control, the only thing that will be affected by your voice is the thing you focus on. It's not about the decibels. It's about what's up here." Kephalos tapped a sucker to his forehead.

That made sense. Especially after the experience I'd just had in the underwater tunnel.

"Can you tell me anything else?" I asked.

"I've told you more than I should have already," said Kephalos, wrinkling his broad white brow. And with that he crawled away.

I couldn't say I was sorry to see him go. I'd appreciated the advice, but Kephalos gave me the creeps.

When I emerged from the oracle's cave, Jax was gone.

I heard a shuffling step from the darkness of the tunnel behind me.

"Jax?" I called.

No answer.

I walked carefully toward where I thought the sound had come from. It seemed curiously silent now. Except for the muffled plink of water, there was no noise.

"Jax!" I called.

"What is it?" his voice answered behind me.

I whirled around, my hand to my chest. "Oh, you scared me."

"Sorry, I wanted to make sure that the Glaukos guards were being sent out. Where were you going?"

I pointed down the passage. "I heard footsteps down that way."

Jax looked around as if he was calculating our position, then strode forward into the passage, disappearing into the blackness for a few moments. When he emerged, he shook his head. "It's as I thought. That passage is blocked off only a few meters in."

"But someone was walking that way," I insisted.

"Perhaps you heard my steps. The echoes can be very deceiving," Jax said. He took my arm. "I'll take you home now. You must be very tired. By the way, you dropped this."

Gently he put the pearl-studded crescent moon in the palm of my hand.

CHAPTER 30

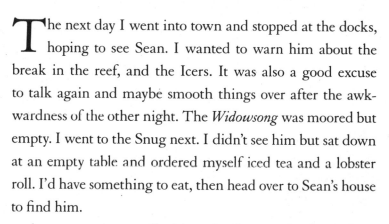

The next day I went into town and stopped at the docks, hoping to see Sean. I wanted to warn him about the break in the reef, and the Icers. It was also a good excuse to talk again and maybe smooth things over after the awkwardness of the other night. The *Widowsong* was moored but empty. I went to the Snug next. I didn't see him but sat down at an empty table and ordered myself iced tea and a lobster roll. I'd have something to eat, then head over to Sean's house to find him.

A young woman walked into the Snug, took a book from the shelf and sat down in a booth. I only glanced at her at first, until I realized it was Zuzu. She looked different somehow.

She was dressed in loose-fitting jeans and a pink button-down cotton shirt and sneakers. Her hair was pulled back into a neat ponytail.

I practically ran across the tavern but stopped short when she looked up at me coldly.

"I don't want to talk," she said in a dull, expressionless tone. "To you," she added. She turned a page of the book.

"That's okay," I said, sitting across from her.

Zuzu's delicate features looked thinner and there were faint purple shadows beneath her eyes. She wasn't even wearing makeup.

"Are you okay?"

Zuzu didn't look up, but her eyes stopped moving across the page. She put a finger at the spot and regarded me. Her green eyes were cold, distant. "You could have told me that you were one of them. You could have trusted me. I thought we were friends."

"We *are* friends. And you're right," I said. "I should have told you. I'm sorry. I just—I didn't want to believe what was happening at first. I hoped it would stop, that I could *make* it stop. I didn't want to be different."

The pages of the book flipped under Zuzu's impatient fingers. "But you *are* different. You're a First One, a demigod."

"I guess so."

Her eyes shot up to me, red-rimmed but dry. "I suppose we're all just petty mortals to you."

That felt like a knife in my belly. "No," I said firmly, "you're not. Why does this have to separate us? Why can't we still be friends? I want to be here for you. I heard about the punishment that the Council ordered for your family and I'm sorry. How can I help?"

"We're fine," said Zuzu, turning a page. "I'm fine."

I didn't believe her. Something was gone from inside Zuzu. She looked pale and sad.

"Has someone hurt you? Darius didn't come after you, did he?" I asked quietly. The thought of him trying to hurt Zuzu made me want to practice my siren-focus thing in a big way.

Zuzu looked down at her book. "No. It's just that Revel wasn't the way I thought it would be."

"I spoiled it, didn't I?"

She shook her head. "No. You were right about it all along; maybe that's the part that makes me mad. I just didn't listen. You were right about the First Ones too—they're cruel and cold. I'm done with all of them. From now on I'll stick to my own kind." She returned to her book. "Maybe you should do the same."

"I can't do that. I care about you, and about Sean and Reilly." I drummed my fingers on the table. "In fact, I need to find Sean. I saw him the other night, during the storm, and he acted . . ." I hesitated. "Different. Do you know what's going on with him?"

Zuzu closed her book and sighed. "Of *course* I know," she said. "Everyone on the island knows. Maybe if you weren't so busy with your own stuff, you'd notice what's happening."

My fingers went quiet and I dropped them to my lap. "I don't understand. Tell me."

285

She shook her head. "He told us not to say anything to you. And I promised him I wouldn't. But now it probably doesn't matter anymore. It's too late to do anything about it."

"Zuzu, you're scaring me. Tell me. If there's anything wrong with Sean, I want to know. I want to help."

Zuzu bit her lips and her green eyes filled with sadness as she looked at me. "He's undergoing the transformation."

"Transformation?" I stared at her. "What transformation?"

"Sean's becoming a Glaukos."

CHAPTER 31

The floor wasn't solid. Neither was the bench I sat on. They both rose up beneath me and fell, making my stomach lurch. And even then Zuzu kept talking, relentlessly, saying words that just couldn't be possible.

"Every few years a boy is chosen to be a defender of Trespass. They go through training, initiation and finally a treatment to transform into a Glaukos."

"No." I closed my eyes tight at the image of the Glaukos creature that had been chained to the rocks. That hideous thing could *never* have been a man. But even as I tried to deny it, small things tugged at me. The misshapen head that did somehow remind me of a human skull, the clawed fingers grasping, looking almost like someone's hand reaching . . .

Was it possible? Was everything on this island a nightmare?

"Sean wouldn't do it," I insisted. "He's happy here. He loves this place."

"That's why he *will* do it," said Zuzu. "And in exchange for his sacrifice, his mother will be cared for by all the islanders and the First Ones. For the rest of her life. It's already begun."

Dazed, I recalled small clues that I probably should have wondered about. The way Sean was treated around here. The "Your money's no good here, Sean" refrain, the pats on the back. Yes. He was treated like a soldier, about to go off to war.

And even the mayor's comment at Revel came back to me. *We're all depending on you.*

Reilly walked in and sat next to Zuzu. She took his hand. "I just told Delia about Sean."

"Why didn't anyone tell me?" I asked. I felt sick to my stomach. Like crying and screaming all at the same time.

"These guys give up their lives for us," said Reilly. "We respect that. It's not anyone's place to go talking about it. We didn't know that you had a relationship with Sean. And even if we did, it should have come from him."

"We don't have a relationship," I said in a quiet voice. "Not like that. But I care about him."

"Sean chose to serve," said Reilly. "He could have said no, and another name would have been picked."

As if Sean would ever do that, I thought. The way people were raised here, it was probably unthinkable. Dishonorable. Never in a million years would he have backed out.

Just like no young woman says no at Revel.

"How is it done?"

"They take trapweed," said Zuzu. "They start during the summer, and by the time winter comes, they're transformed. It's a gradual process. And not easy."

"Then he can stop taking it," I said, sitting forward.

Reilly shook his head. "Nobody stops taking trapweed once they start. Supposedly it's an incredible high. Like a combination of testosterone, cocaine and adrenaline. Increased muscle mass, reflexes, focus, along with sense of well-being, confidence. So basically you feel like Superman," he said. "The only downer is, you turn into a Glauk. Which, uh, pretty much eliminates any recreational use," he finished in a low voice.

"So the creatures out there, all of them were men from Trespass," I said. "And how long can they live . . . like that?"

Reilly shook his head. "Nobody knows for sure, but longer than we do. A hundred years. Two hundred."

"And the names on the monument in the cemetery. Those are *their* names."

Zuzu nodded. "Some were fishermen who died from normal causes, but a lot of them are Glaukos. And we honor all of them."

"A Trespass sailor never dies," said Reilly.

"He's only lost at sea," I finished in a dry whisper.

CHAPTER 32

Sean was at home, sitting hunched over a desk in his room with his back to the door. His clothes were rumpled, as if he'd slept in them, and his unkempt hair lay at odd angles. As I walked in he shut the lid of a wooden box that sat on the desk in front of him.

I came and stood behind him, putting a tentative hand on his shoulder.

"Sean?"

He didn't answer. In fact, he didn't even seem to be aware of me at all. I leaned over him to see his face.

"There's a sugar maple out in the yard there." Sean gazed out the window in front of his desk, his expression trancelike. "It's always really pretty in the fall. It doesn't get cold enough for us to have a lot of color on the trees here, but that one

turns red. I think I see a couple of leaves changed already."
He rubbed at the corners of the carved box in front of him
with the pads of his thumbs. "How are you doing, Delia?"
He glanced at me, his eyes roving. He bounced his legs, tapping his feet on the floor.

I didn't answer.

"Oh, great," he said, looking away. "You know."

"Why, Sean?"

He pinched the inner corners of his eyes and rubbed at
them. "I was chosen by lottery, but I agreed to it. And I was
chosen long before you came to Trespass."

"And you never told me." It was hard to keep the hurt out
of my voice.

Sean slid the wooden box closer to him on the desk, circling it with his arms. The wood was shiny and dark, as if
it was old and had been handled a lot. The box was carved
with symbols. The largest of these was a dagger, circled by
coiling vines.

Just like the tattoo on Sean's arm.

"I didn't tell you because I promised myself there wasn't
going to be anything between us. There couldn't be. And I
didn't want things to get all weird." He glanced at me. "Too
late for that, I guess," he added with a hint of the gentle
humor that was *him*.

"Listen to me. You have to stop."

He shook his head doggedly. "No one can stop the transformation once it's begun."

"The hell you can't," I said in a shaking voice. "Who's doing this to you? Who do we have to talk to? That creepy mayor? The Council? We'll just stop it."

"Nobody's doing it to me, Delia." Sean's laugh was dry. "It's the trapweed. You start eating the trapweed and you start changing. It's part of me now. I couldn't stop even if I wanted to."

"Just slow down," I begged him. I grasped his arm and felt the thick biceps bunch and recoil against me. "I need to understand what's going on. We can figure this out and fix it."

He pulled away from me. "No."

"Are you saying you don't want to?" I said, searching Sean's face. Was it my imagination or had that changed too? It didn't seem so boyish. His skin was deeply tanned and his blond hair didn't look as thick as it had.

Sean sighed. "I'm saying . . ." He threw up his hands. "Hell, I don't know *what* I'm saying. This is my life. This is what it is. I can't change it suddenly, just because you decided to come. This is what I'm supposed to do. Protect this island. And the people I love."

"By turning yourself into a monster."

"Nobody here calls us that"—his eyes were hard and flat as he looked at me—"except you."

"It's just a drug." I paced away from him, looking at the disarray in his room. Dirty clothes and half-eaten food littered the floor. "They get you hooked and then they own you. You're a slave."

Sean's face hardened and his eyes glinted up at me from his slouched position. "You don't understand," he said. "You don't know what it's like to grow up here. It's not the soft life you've had. People out there in your so-called real world? They live like sheep, doing the same old jobs, earning money to buy more stuff. It's different here. There's actual danger here, do you understand?" His voice kept rising as he spoke, and he stood up, pushing the chair away with a jerking motion that nearly toppled it over. I stepped back quickly. "We have to fight to protect what's ours. Haven't you heard? The Icers are coming. Some people even say *you're* bringing them here, Delia." He gave me a calculating look. "That true?"

"Don't be ridiculous, Sean. Have you lost your mind?"

"Maybe," said Sean. "But they're coming. They want this island and they want to kill everyone on it. A war's coming, and I'm going to fight."

Sean's eyes were hard, defiant. The pupils were hugely dilated, the black almost obscuring any color at all. He was breathing hard, his chest expanding and filling his shirt like it would tear the fabric with the next breath. He looked savage, and excited.

"You sound almost happy about it," I said.

"Yeah. Clarity makes me happy. I was confused for a while. About you, about how I felt. Now everything is simple. It's better this way. I'm a soldier, Delia. And you're going to need the Glaukos for this fight. You're going to need *me.*"

Sean's eyes blazed and I thought I saw a flicker of yellow in the brown. For the first time I was truly frightened. I didn't know who this was. But it wasn't Sean.

Maybe he saw the fear in my eyes. He blinked, swallowed and shook his head as if trying to clear it. He looked down at the box and placed a hand over the top. Was it possible that his hands had grown larger? His fingers draped over the edge as he clutched it.

"See, when I take this," he said in a low voice, "I feel like everything is going to be okay. I feel like I can do anything."

The pain in his voice made my heart break. Somewhere inside there was the guy who was so kind and gentle. The guy who took care of everyone else. But he was drowning. And I felt like there was nothing I could do about it.

I took a deep breath. "Everything is going to be okay." I stepped closer and touched his arm gently. Beneath my fingers the overtaxed muscles twitched and pulsed spasmodically. "And you can *do* this."

I reached for the dark box and tried to pull it away from him.

As if he'd anticipated the movement, his arm shot up. He snatched the box from my hands and pushed me.

It happened so fast. The slam of his hand against my shoulder felt like a sledgehammer. I flew backward, striking my head against the edge of the door. For a moment my vision went gray as my knees buckled. There was a trickle of warmth on the back of my head. And blood on the door.

Sean's face was a sickening gray color. "Oh my God. Delia. I didn't—" He let out a low moan and reached out a hand to me.

I ran out the door.

CHAPTER 33

I sat on the sand, watching the sun go down and fingering the smooth piece of blue glass at my throat.

"Jax, I need your help."

Jax sat beside me, elbows resting on his bent knees and his hands clasped loosely together. His face was so still, so composed, that I couldn't tell what he was feeling. "This thing you would ask me to do, you know that it betrays my own people. And yours."

"I'm not asking you to do anything," I said. "Just tell me. What happens if the Glaukos stop taking the trapweed? *Can* they stop? Can the changes be reversed?"

"It's because of him, isn't it?" Jax said in a low voice. "The Lander Gunn who is undergoing the transformation. Are you in love with him?"

I closed my eyes. *I'm in love with* you. *You chowderhead.* We weren't in the water, so I thought it was safe to think it. And to use one of Gran's favorite expressions. But my feelings for Jax, and his for me, weren't the most important thing right now.

"I care about Sean," I told him. "And this is wrong."

Jax nodded. "The Glaukos will suffer if the trapweed is withheld. They'll become violent and unmanageable. But there's no reason to think that it would kill them." He grimaced. "Though they may well kill each other."

"And the changes?"

Jax broke his hands apart in a gesture of uncertainty. "I've never heard of them reversing. Ever."

"That's not very encouraging."

"It wasn't meant to be," said Jax curtly. He rose. "I have to go." Before he had walked two paces toward the water, he stopped and turned. "If this is what you believe to be right, Delia, then do it. I will defend your actions, and you. Always." He raised a hand and touched his chest briefly. *"Kardia mou."*

He was gone before I had the chance to ask him what that meant.

———

I knew what I had to do and I was going to do it before anyone tried to stop me. The next day, I found Ben Deare at the docks and told him what I wanted: gasoline, and lots of it.

"Miss Delia, I've got a bad feeling about this."

"Do you know what I am?" I asked him, searching his face.

Ben nodded. "Ayuh."

"Then you know you don't want to mess with me, right?"

"I'll have you stow that fresh talk, missy," Ben snapped. "Course, I knew from the start. Who do you think helped your poor mother get away from this accursed place? You're a siren. A dangerous piece of work," he said, nodding to himself. "And shouldn't old Captain Deare know it."

"*Captain* Deare," I repeated. I looked at the brown wrinkled face and his keen blue eyes. And suddenly remembered those same eyes twinkling out at me from a picture in a book.

"Ben," I said slowly, "how long have you been here on Trespass?"

"Pshaw," said Ben. He squinted skyward as if calculating. "Let's see. Lost track a few years back. Well . . ." He shrugged. "Ever since the *Dover* sank and tried to take me down with her."

"That was in 1776," I said. I put my head into my hands. I didn't know how much more of this I could take. "You *told* me that you're older than you look. I guess I was thinking years. Not centuries."

"Ayuh," said Ben. "Some folks say Poseidon raised that storm, but it ain't true. 'Twas a siren witch that wrecked the *Dover* that night and took His Majesty King George's gold down to the bottom of Casco Bay. That she-devil cursed us

298

for surviving and trespassing on this island. My crew is out there," he said. "One hundred able sea-hands trapped forever in that reef. As for me, the witch cursed me to scuttle around this island like an old crab until the day the old gods return and allow me to die."

"Then you knew I was a siren and you still wanted me to come here?" I asked.

"No. It wasn't for me to say. The *bones* said you were meant to come here."

"And the monster you told me about in the portents?"

"Well, I'm thinking *you're* the monster, Miss Delia. No offense."

"None taken," I said weakly. "That's what I was thinking too."

"So now you know the lay of the land," said Ben. He handed me the last gasoline can. "Good luck, Miss Delia."

"Thanks, Ben."

That night I went to the gardens and soaked every trap-weed plant I could see, stepped back, struck a match, tossed it in.

At first I didn't think it was going to catch. Then the field exploded into flames with a rushing, crackling hiss. A wall of superheated air pushed me back, and I turned away from the searing heat and covered my nose against the thick, resinous stink of the burning trapweed.

Pungent black clouds roiled away across the hillside and down toward the water.

I thought of the men out there, transformed into mindless beasts that served the First Ones like slaves. And about the curse that kept a sea captain and his men trapped here. About girls giving themselves because *it was tradition*.

I was so angry, the gasoline was probably overkill. My rage could have burned that field to ash.

———

The next morning, the air was bright and clear, and the plot of trapweed was a smoking tangle of scorched, dead vines when Gran came walking fast along the path to the garden. Her heavy chest was bouncing with the effort and her face was bright red. Burning the crop under the cover of darkness had allowed me to work without interference. But I figured Gran would be the first to realize what I'd done.

I leaned on the shovel and waited for her. By this time she would have discovered that I had already destroyed the dry trapweed in the cellar too. My shoulders ached and the lump on the back of my head still throbbed from where I'd struck the door in Sean's room. But the fierce anger that had kept me going was leeching away. I was exhausted and yearned for the cleansing feel of the water.

And to see Jax.

"You shouldn't have walked all this way, Gran."

"What have you done? Have you lost your mind?" Gran cried. She put a hand to her covered eye as she turned, looking at the ruined field. "They'll die without the trapweed! They'll all die."

"It's an addicting drug. It's turned Sean into something awful. And you've been helping."

Gran slapped my face.

I reeled back from the sting of the blow.

"What do you know about love?" she cried. Her face crumpled in red blotches. "He's out there. Charlie's still out there. Counting on me." She wrung her hands together and rocked her upper body back and forth as she paced along the edge of the field. "What'll become of them?"

"You're talking about my grandfather, right?" I held my throbbing cheek and straightened up. "Maybe he's lived like an animal long enough."

"No. Not an animal. He knows me still. Inside. I know he does." Gran put a hand to the scar on her neck. "He just can't control himself."

I took a shaky breath. "I have to save Sean. This is the only way I know how."

"And what about all the others? What gives you the right to kill them?"

"It won't kill them!"

"You don't know that," she said in a grim voice. She strode into the smoking field of trapweed, stamping with her heavy shoes to put out the glowing embers, peering among the blackened vines. She was obviously looking for viable plants.

She bent down near the edge and lifted a leaf. It was still green.

I should have known I wouldn't be able to eradicate all of it. Maybe this had been for nothing.

"You didn't see him, Gran." I broke off, tears blurring my vision like seawater never had. I pressed the balls of my hands to my eyes, trying to make them stop, but they wouldn't. "He's turned into something so ugly. It's not even him anymore."

Gran came to me, holding me tight and rubbing my back as I wept.

CHAPTER 34

The Glauks went crazy.

They still came to the place where they'd been fed. After two days without trapweed the water roiled with their thrashing bodies. They were suffering from withdrawal— lack of trapweed had them tearing at their own flesh with their clawed fingers. It was painful to watch them. Even if I hadn't known that those were human beings, their suffering was horrific.

I prayed for it to be over soon. Somehow.

Gran still went to the bluff every morning. And I made myself go too, partly as punishment for what I'd done, partly in hopes that some miraculous change would occur.

I stayed after Gran left, looking down at the Glaukos. Their eyes were trained on me with pain and pathetic hope that I had the plants their bodies were screaming for. But I had nothing to give them.

It was true that a few frail plants had survived, but it would be weeks before Gran could cultivate enough to provide even a small amount of trapweed.

Down below I saw a black dog standing on some rocks, barking frantically at the water.

It was Buddy.

Sean came out of the water.

He stepped onto the rocks and strode quickly over to the path that climbed up to the bluff. I watched in horror, unable to move from the spot. He'd changed even more dramatically in the days since I'd last seen him. It didn't seem possible but he was taller and much broader across his chest. He moved like a predator. Head forward, heavy muscles of his chest and arms tensed, prepared for conflict. His posture was stooped. Almost as if the massive enlargement of muscles in his torso was dragging him down.

His skin had darkened, and his hair was so thin his scalp showed through in patches of dark, roughened skin. But it wasn't only the changes in his body.

I stared at him, searching for some glimpse of the boy I had met when I'd first come here.

"You stupid girl," he said as he reached me. His voice was like sandpaper and his eyes glittered, unnaturally bright and wide. "Do you have any idea what you've done? You've put everyone here at risk."

"I was trying to save you."

Sean snarled, "Do I look like I need saving?" He struck a closed fist against his chest. "We protect this island. I'm not ashamed of what I am."

"You're sick, Sean. You need help. Maybe we could find a cure for this."

He grinned, and the smile split his face into a leer. "You didn't really want that guy I used to be." He grabbed my arm in a grip that was too much like a wrestling move for comfort. "The nice guy."

I wrenched away.

"Come on," he said, his voice rasping with the increased rate of his breath. "You might like me better now."

"Let go of me."

"The trapweed made me strong. Maybe that's what frightens you," he said.

I was chilled to see the look of wary calculation in his eyes.

"You're afraid that I'll become as powerful as you, or Jax."

He turned and raced away, moving amazingly fast, and dove off the bluff.

He fell, it seemed like forever, before cleaving the water. I lost sight of him.

He was gone, I thought. Off the edge of the world.

———

"There's a break in the reef," Ed Barney said later to the people who had gathered in the village square. The mayor of Trespass spoke with his chin jutting out and a look of satisfied outrage on his face. "Just got word from the Council. A section of the Hundred Hands," he barked, "twenty foot wide, busted right open. That's how these things got through. And more coming. They're swarming here like there's some kind of a signal calling them."

"How'd it happen?" demanded a voice from the crowd.

The mayor scowled. "I'll tell you how. We got a traitor here. It's her fault," he said, looking accusingly at me. "Ever since she came here, there's been trouble. You know what she is? She's a siren. She seduces them with her voice. They can't resist her. As long as she's here, they'll come."

"That's crazy," I said. "I didn't call the Icers. Why would I do that?"

"Why did she destroy all the trapweed?" demanded the mayor, throwing up his hands. He didn't even address the question to me, but to the rest of the people. "It was the only way to control the Glauks. Now they've gone crazy. Even the First Ones won't be able to handle them. They won't be able to defend us, to fight off the Icers."

"When this island needs our Glaukos most, this girl is killing them," someone shouted.

"The Hands were our primary defense," said another man. "If there's a breach, there won't be any stopping the Icers from attacking the island." He turned to Ben Deare and asked, "Ben, have you seen it? Do you know how it happened?"

The old man adjusted his Red Sox cap, and his wrinkled face pleated up as he squinted. "Don't know for sure. It would've taken something mighty powerful to blow up stone coral like that."

"Could a siren's voice do it?" demanded Ed Barney.

Ben glanced at me. "Well, I don't know. Maybe."

"I didn't do it!" I said. But angry faces were turning toward me.

A hand gripped my elbow and pulled me back from the crowd.

"Delia, run," said Gran in a low voice.

I ran.

I went to Wreck Beach, searching for Jax. It was getting dark now and I didn't know where else to go. The villagers were afraid of the Icers, afraid of me; who knew what they would be capable of? I couldn't go back to Gran's house. There was no place to hide on this island where they couldn't find me. The only place was the sea.

Fear slithered between my ribs like a snake, coiled around my heart and squeezed. In my terror there was only one thought that kept me sane, kept me hopeful.

Jax.

I wanted Jax beside me.

"Delia."

I spun around.

"Jax, thank God it's you." I ran into his embrace and felt the warmth and strength seep back into me. I burrowed my face beneath the angle of his jaw. "I don't know where to go. Please help me."

He held me close. "Shh. It's all right. You're safe," he murmured. "I'm going to take her back." I looked up at his face.

He was speaking to someone else. Someone behind me. I twisted in his arms.

"No!" said Jax. He gripped me tighter.

The blow snapped my head forward. The dark exploded in my head, transforming into bright red pain and then finally a gray dimness.

Somewhere in the gray I heard low voices. Only bits and pieces, very distant.

" . . . cannot be controlled . . . must be silenced . . . never be peace on this island while she . . ."

Then one phrase that I heard more clearly:

"You are the true leader of the Aitros, Jax. Now is the time to prove it."

Then nothing.

CHAPTER 35

Consciousness was just out of reach. It came to me slowly, letting in sharp little jabs of pain through a fuzzy cloud. My mouth felt swollen, and it hurt horribly when I tried to swallow.

I was aware of darkness and a cold pressure digging into my shoulder. Pushing up on one elbow, I felt around me. Bare, damp stone met my searching fingers but I couldn't make out anything in the murky black. Where was I?

No, I did remember something. Jax had been there. Holding me. Then something had hit me from behind. His voice had been in my head, whispering in my ear. But after that, nothing. I winced at the pain in my mouth and tasted blood. I must have bitten my lip.

My fingers pressed against the moist rock, sensing the faint vibrations of churning waves. The dank scent of trapped sea-water wafted over me, and I heard the distant whistle of wind through a tunnel. I was somewhere deep underground, in the sea caves.

With a painful effort I tried to sit up but felt a scraping, rattling sound close to my ears, then the pull of something heavy on my wrists. In the darkness I touched them. Metal cuffs. Panic swelled in my chest as I yanked against them, testing the bonds. I was chained to the wall. I wriggled my feet. The same heaviness cut into my ankles.

Gradually, my eyes became accustomed to the dim light. I found a shard of stone on the ground, lifted it in two hands and scraped weakly at the wall. There must have been some glow stone in it; a faint gleam illuminated the space.

It was a dark, square room of stone, maybe ten feet in each dimension. The walls ran with streaks of evaporated salts and green slime. Small puddles of water pooled on the uneven floor.

I was more fully awake now. Something was wrong. My mouth throbbed and again I tasted the coppery tang of blood on my tongue. Heart pounding, I raised my fingers to my mouth. Something was—

"Ah. You're awake." A voice drifted through the darkness. "Good."

I recognized that voice.

I tried to scream. The agonized cry began in my gut and swelled up through my chest, to my throat. Then it stopped.

I couldn't open my lips. There was a tearing, searing agony when I tried to force them apart.

I pulled myself to a shallow puddle of water and saw my reflection.

A thick metal ring had been pushed through my lips, clamping them together.

CHAPTER 36

Pain and fear screamed inside me with no voice.

I twisted against the restraints on my wrists but could barely lift the heavy links of chain that lay in a heap beside me. The faint luminescence from the glow stone was fading; darkness was closing again. I was going to lose my mind.

Eyes wide, I searched for the source of the voice. *Help me.* I tried to form the words but couldn't. A muffled moan was all that emerged from my cracked, swollen lips. Tears ran down my face, stinging the broken skin.

"No, don't try to speak. It will only tear your flesh. The iron ring is a crude measure, but effective. And most necessary, given your abilities."

I spotted a small rectangular hole in the thick stone wall. The voice was coming from there. I kicked my feet against the stone floor and pulled against the chains frantically, trying to communicate in any way I could.

"Please don't struggle so." The softly modulated voice spoke again, this time with a touch of impatience. "I asked Jax to bring you here. So we could speak."

Jax? The words stunned me into immobility.

"Now that I can see the ring is sufficient to silence you, I'll come in and speak with you, if I may."

A grinding noise preceded the movement of the stone wall beside me. I sat up and Xarras entered, bringing a square of light cast from some source outside the cell. Xarras, short and soft-looking, with a balding head and a mild face. He was dressed in the same plain silvery-gray tunic as before.

"Hello, my dear," he said, looking at me intently. He had a hint of a smile on his face as he surveyed me, as though he were visiting some exotic animal in a cage.

I hardly had the strength or will to lift my head. The pain throbbing in my lips was nothing compared to the torture of hearing Xarras's words. And knowing what they meant.

Jax had done this? Had he lied to me all along? Was his desire for control of the clan so strong that he would imprison me, torture me? Maybe kill me? Kephalos had told me to expect betrayal.

I just never imagined it would be Jax.

"I think if you will listen to my proposal, everything will become clear to you and we can be done with this"—Xarras paused and waved a chubby hand at my face—"this unpleasantness. My son Jax thinks he can be ruler of this island someday. On occasion I've led him to believe that I support this notion. I do not."

Xarras stepped over the chain on the floor carefully. "He does not have the will or the cruelty required." He stepped closer and looked into my eyes with deadly calm. "I, on the other hand, have both."

It was unnerving, the way his soft features remained impassive, mild even. He might have been telling me about some unfortunate problem with my dental coverage. And yet I saw the frightening intensity, cold, hard and pitiless, that burned in his eyes. Snake eyes.

How could Jax ever describe this man as weak?

Only something evil could hide behind a façade like this so well. He was a psychopath.

Xarras went on talking in his soft, reasonable way.

"Jax thought my plan was only to hide you to ensure your safety. He really doesn't understand how dangerous you are. I'm afraid he wouldn't approve of the method I've used to subdue you." Xarras lifted a dismissive hand. "Weakness. There you are."

So Jax didn't know what his father had done. The relief flooded through me, bringing a fresh batch of tears streaming over my cheeks.

"I've sent him to lead the battle against the Icers," said Xarras. "He may in fact be dead already. That would expedite matters."

A hot flame of anger shot through me, warming the chill in my bones. For a brief moment it even obscured the torment of the iron that pierced my flesh. If only I could open my mouth, *this* man would be dead.

But the thick ring would be impossible to rip through, and even if I could do it, the pain would most likely make me lose consciousness. It was already excruciating; the only way to bear it was to try to concentrate on something else. I focused on Xarras's voice.

"I've been waiting for you for many years, my dear," he said meditatively. "And Kephalos assured me that your return was foretold. Not that he ever knew the use I planned to make of you. Ever since I learned that a siren had been conceived in these waters, I knew that you would be the key. You see, I mean to be leader of the Aitros and bring about the return of our power."

Xarras removed the cuffs from my ankles but left the ones on my wrists. With a hand on my arm, he helped me to my feet. I hated the fact that I stumbled against him and required support as he led me out of the small stone prison cell and down the narrow passageway.

"It took me years to memorize these passages. I may actually be the only living thing that knows this maze," said Xarras. "There are benefits to being dismissed from people's minds." He glanced at me. "Be sure to stay close, won't you?"

As if I had any choice. He gripped me tightly by the elbow.

Besides, I didn't think I could have even made it back to the cell without support.

"You've been out of the water for some time, haven't you?" Xarras murmured. "It's weakened you."

I tried to keep track of the directions we took, but after endless turns and switchbacks, I got so mixed up it was all I could do to lift my feet and take the next step.

After what seemed like an eternity, Xarras came to a wall. To me, it looked like every other wall in this endless warren of tunnels. But there must have been some subtle marks that only he knew.

"It's behind here," he said, nodding to the wall. "This is it." He pressed his palms together. "Finally. This is the Archelon, my dear. You will open this wall."

There was a sound behind us and I turned.

Jax stood a few yards away. He held a sword in one hand. He was staring at me, and his face took on a look of wild fury.

"By the gods, Father," he whispered. "What have you done?"

A momentary look of anger distorted Xarras's smooth, chubby face. "I *told* you she needed to be silenced, Jax. She needs to be controlled. And we need her to open the Archelon. That's the only way we'll win."

"Win what?" demanded Jax. "What is worth such a cost?"

"Please don't be tiresome, Jax," said Xarras. "Win this battle against the Icers. And thereby win control of the clan."

"How?" Jax demanded.

Xarras sighed. "Do you remember anything from the

316

readings I gave you? From Sun Tzu's *The Art of War*? This was the only way to tip the balance. The Aitros will never accept new leadership unless a crisis demands it."

Disbelief twisted Jax's features. "It was you, wasn't it? You destroyed the reef. *You* brought the Icers here."

"Yes, I created the war—once I knew I had the weapon needed to win it." He glanced at me.

"Delia." Jax looked into my eyes. "Don't be afraid. He's not going to hurt you. I'll take you home."

The strength and calm of Jax's voice had such an effect on me that for an insane moment I thought everything was going to be okay.

His father snorted. "It's a bit late to play the gallant, Jax. Don't pretend that you didn't want to use her."

"Not like this," Jax argued. "I was fool enough to listen to your lies. Encouraging me all these years. Making me think that you would support me. I wanted to lead this clan, to bring it out of darkness." Jax looked at me. "With Delia beside me."

"I'm afraid I won't allow that. Not then. Not now."

"So it's true," said Jax in a quiet voice. "All this time I've tried to put aside my suspicions. Tried not to believe it. It was you who told the clan I was a traitor." He glanced down at the scars on his chest with a frown. Almost as if he needed physical proof, a reminder of his father's betrayal.

"Of course it was," said Xarras gently. "And I was quite surprised by your tenacity in the trenches. You do surprise me sometimes. But really, I don't have time for this, Jax."

"No time?" Jax pointed his sword toward the roof of the

cave. "You have no idea what's going on up there. Many Aitros have died today. You've murdered your own people."

Xarras shook his head. He looked to the wall beside him and laid a reverent hand on it. I could see them now, faint but visible, the Greek symbols I'd seen throughout the island. "Those are not my people. Poseidon, Zeus, Hades, Triton— *these* are the ones that I would align myself with." Xarras's mouth pressed into a grim, cruel line. "All of our ancient powers will be renewed once the Archelon is opened. The Aitros will be true gods once more."

"Father." Jax shook his head wonderingly. "You're insane. This is finished. Delia, come to me." He held out one hand to me. With the other he raised his sword against his father.

Xarras bent his head, snapped his hand forward and somehow, with the lightning speed of a bullet, threw a small dart at Jax. A trickle of blood ran down Jax's throat.

"You should know I would never fight you that way," said Xarras with a contemptuous glance at the sword.

Jax touched his hand to the tiny projectile at his throat and then stared at the smear on his fingers. He staggered and fell to his knees.

"A paralytic agent," commented Xarras as he watched Jax slump to the floor. "Concentrated from the venom of the Rudolpho sea urchin. The urchin injects the poison into its prey, rending it immobile as the creature feeds on its flesh. Power cannot be shared. That is the final lesson I have to teach you, Jax."

Jax lay there motionless, seemingly unconscious.

"Now," said Xarras, turning to me. I let out a moan of agony as he began to loosen some kind of a clamp that held the ring tight on my lips. "You will serve me, Siren."

He pulled the ring from my lips gently, but still the pain made me cry out.

I staggered back from him and went to kneel by Jax, touching his still form. I shook him gently but there was no response.

"Dead?" I whispered through bloody, swollen lips.

"No, not yet, I think," said Xarras, standing over me. "It's a common misconception that the Aitros are difficult to kill. You just have to know how. His breathing seems to have diminished, though. It won't be long."

The man's calm comments about killing his own son were the most malevolent thing I'd ever heard. I tried to speak.

"What was that?" Xarras asked.

"Monster," I said, spitting the word through my own blood.

"Come now." Xarras hauled me to my feet. "It will be easy to open. Childishly easy. You only have to use your voice. I overheard what Kephalos told you. Yes, yes," he said impatiently, "I was there in the tunnel. Well hidden from my son's search."

He dragged me to the Archelon. "Here before you, Siren, is the treasure of Trespass Island. The power of Poseidon lies within. You yourself are the living key to this door."

I raised my eyes to Xarras. "I could kill you now," I rasped.

Xarras smiled gently. "Open the Archelon and I will tell you where to find the antidote for the poison. You can save Jax. If you hurry."

I looked back at Jax. His eyes were closed and I saw no movement of his chest or gills. His skin was a horrible bluish color.

"Stand back." I stared at the wall of symbols to focus my thoughts. But the pain in my mouth was torture. And Jax was lying on the floor. What would happen if Xarras got control of Poseidon's power?

I didn't know. And I couldn't worry about that right now. Everything else shrank beside the fact that Jax was going to die.

Open it, Delia. Concentrate.

"Open."

At first nothing happened. Then the symbols shifted in the stone. Faster now. *Concentrate.*

"Open."

Dust sifted down from the ceiling.

"Open!" I screamed, unleashing my voice. But my voice didn't even sound human anymore. It wasn't my voice. It was some kind of archaic scream that echoed through me from an ancient past. I was only the transmitter.

The Archelon began to open.

CHAPTER 37

With a thunderous crack the walls parted. Xarras came forward, pushed me aside and stood in front of the Archelon, eager for its gift.

This was the treasure, the power of Trespass Island that he'd schemed for. Killed for.

I didn't know what I expected to see inside. Something otherwordly or magical, perhaps. Rays of light emanating from a fantastical realm of the gods. A spill of gold and jewels. Or even Poseidon himself. But it was none of those things.

It was the sea.

When the first fissure in the wall opened, water shot out. A thin stream, pushed with such force and velocity that it cut through the air.

It was a knife of water.

Hiss. A fine blue blade cut Xarras's head from his torso.

A mist of blood rained into the air and Xarras's face flew past me, his mouth open in surprise. I could have sworn he blinked.

The torrent of water, beneath unimaginable pressure, cut into the far wall of the tunnel and gouged into the stone, practically melting it away. Another heartbeat and it surged to a thick column that blasted into Xarras, shooting his still-standing body across the room with the force of a hundred fire hoses.

Seawater. It was nothing but seawater coming through the Archelon. Thundering. Raging. Millions of gallons, and every second flooding the tunnels.

The floor shifted beneath my feet. Clutching the irregular, lurching surfaces, I slipped through the deepening surge of water toward Jax. I still had the cuffs on my wrists, which made my movements awkward. I grabbed on to him, trying not to panic at the feel of his skin. It was cold.

He slumped against me as deadweight. There was no pulse in his neck, no flutter of life in the gills on his abdomen. And as the water washed over him there was no answering change in his body. No fin emerged from the spiny processes on his back.

We had to escape before the entire system of tunnels collapsed. Xarras had been wrong about the Archelon; it didn't contain the power of Poseidon. Or maybe this *was* his power unleashed. The earth-shattering force of the whole ocean itself sweeping through this portal.

Kephalos's words came back to me. My destiny on this island was not only betrayal.

It was destruction.

I pulled Jax's limp body to me. He sagged to one side, his arm weighed down by the sword that he still somehow had in his fingers. Stubborn even now. I pulled the sword away and let it sink in the whirling rush. I was still hampered by the heavy cuffs on my wrists.

I couldn't see Xarras's decapitated body; he was gone, swept away. I wouldn't find the antidote to the poison. And I would never find my way out of these tunnels.

And Jax was going to die. My dark, scarred angel.

For a moment I let myself sink down into the whirling chaos around me. I closed my eyes and tried to block out the roar of the water. It would be all right to just stay with him and hold him. We would stay here together. Until the tunnels collapsed and buried us.

No.

I thought about Gran and longed for her strong, no-nonsense presence. She wouldn't lose her head or panic. Where was she now? What would she tell me?

That I didn't need to be brave. I just needed to keep going.

But I didn't want to. Not without Jax. He was paralyzed. He couldn't breathe on his own.

So why don't you do something about it?

I had to get the cuffs off. Now. I was so desperate to help Jax that my mind became hard and focused on each step that

I needed to do. If only it wasn't too late. I concentrated on the dark metal rings.

The water swirled over our heads now. Probably from the effect of glowstone in the exploded portions of the tunnel, there was the faintest of green lights illuminating the eerie scene around me. But fear put blinders on my vision. All I saw, all I cared about, were those cuffs.

I funneled my thoughts into a single command and let my voice out.

"Break!"

The cuffs shattered like eggshells.

Done.

With my hands free I did the only thing I could think of. I breathed for Jax the way he'd done for me at our first meeting.

I kissed him.

As the water swirled around us I kissed Jax, pressing air into his mouth gently over and over. It seemed like minutes passed with no change. His skin was icy and there was no movement of his chest or the gills on his abdomen.

The green light was nearly extinguished. I felt the water churn around me, pelting us with rocks and debris. I tried to maintain my position, clinging to whatever seemed solid as I puffed air into Jax's mouth. It was dark. So dark. There was nothing in the world for me now except Jax's heavy weight in my arms and my fervent prayer, spoken to him over and over with every bit of will that I could summon.

Breathe.

Until at last I felt him stir. Inhale. Exhale. And he kissed me back.

Between our minds the thoughts passed. And I heard him speak to me.

"Kardia mou," he said. The same thing he'd said to me on the beach. Somehow I didn't need a translator. I knew what it meant now. I could sense the meaning in my mind, in my soul.

My heart.

His hands grasped my shoulders. "My father?"

"He's gone, Jax. We have to get out of here. The tunnels are breaking up!"

When he didn't respond, I knew. We were trapped. If the tunnels had been mazelike before, what condition would they be in now? Blown apart by the force of the Archelon opening, they would be reduced to rubble and dead ends. Impossible to navigate even if I had a clue which way to go. Which I didn't.

But in the darkness a faint glow illuminated Jax's face, and I saw his gaze fixed on something in the water.

"Look."

I turned. I was hallucinating. There were flowers floating in the water around us.

No. Not flowers. It was a multitude of tiny glowing fish, their semitransparent bodies sparkling with neon colors of the rainbow. They flitted past and lit the dark water like tiny beacons.

"Follow them," said Jax.

CHAPTER 38

When Jax and I emerged from the mouth of the caves, the sea was alive with destruction. Fiery pieces of rock and ash rained down into the water, hissing steam as they struck. All over the island, spouts of sulfurous gas spewed into the air, blanketing everything with an eerie yellow haze. And every few moments I could see the ground tremble, rocked by some hidden disturbance.

"I can't believe it. The Archelon was empty?" said Jax, supporting me next to him in the water. The color had returned to his skin and the dorsal fin of his water form fluttered against the rippling surface of the sea. He was still weak from the effects of the poison, and I think the supporting part was actually mutual.

"I think so. Empty except for seawater. Opening the chamber and releasing that pressure only created giant sinkholes to the underground caves."

A booming crack made us turn, just in time to see a wedge of the cliff face tumble into the sea.

"The island is collapsing," said Jax. There was disbelief in his low tone.

If I had ever wondered what it would take to impress a demigod, now I knew. Jax's eyes were filled with horrified wonder at the scene before us. I put my palm against his chest. The island had been his home too.

But the island was still swarming with people. "Could they use the boats?" I asked.

"There won't be enough to get them all off the island," said Jax. "And the Icers will attack anything in the water."

There were Icers on the beach as well. I could see at least three of their hulking forms stalking through the wreckage.

"We have to go help them," I said. "Where are the Aitros warriors?"

"They're out there," said Jax with a toss of his head to the open water. "Trying to defend the breach in the Hands."

"Then find the Glaukos if you can. Bring them here."

"Are you insane?"

"No, I'm just a monster, trying to make things right," I said. Then I gave him a quick soft kiss. It had to be only that:

my lips were still swollen and tender from the iron ring that had torn through them.

I swam for Wreck Beach.

The Glaukos swarmed in the water before me as I stood on the sand. Teeth gnashing, they screamed in fury; the sound was deafening.

"Don't do this," said Gran, standing beside me. I should have known she wouldn't stay home. She'd found a black patch to wear over her injured right eye, and the effect was intimidating. The shotgun she carried by her side helped a bit too. Every so often she would raise the gun, sight coolly along its length with her good eye and fire a shot at an Icer. So far it had been effective in keeping them away so I could approach the Glaukos.

"They'll kill you if you get near them," she said. "They've gone mad with pain."

"That's my fault. I have to try to help them."

My voice is my will.

I stood at the edge of the water. Never in my life had I felt so small or insignificant. What was I, compared to the power and the number of these things?

I was so tired; my lips were still bloody and so swollen they felt tight against my teeth.

It felt like my body might collapse as this island was doing, from the inside out.

"Men of Trespass," I shouted, "listen to me."

The thrashing and screaming continued unabated.

"You've been slaves to the First Ones," I cried out. "They've used you. You've sacrificed your lives for this island. For the people you love."

I might as well have thrown a feather into a hurricane and expected it to fly against the wind. They couldn't hear me. They couldn't hear anything or feel anything except their own pain.

My voice is my will.

Unfortunately, my will had never sounded so weak or insignificant. Between the noise of the Glauks, the underground rumblings of the island and the crash of the surf, I could hardly hear myself think. But I tried again.

"Your families are still here. And they need you now more than ever. But to fight as men, not animals."

They didn't listen. Or couldn't hear me. Either way, it was no use like this.

"You're not monsters!" I shouted. "You're the men of Trespass. The Icers are here. They will take this island or whatever's left of it and leave nothing behind. Not your homes or your families. Do you even remember your families?"

I closed my eyes, trying to recall the names from the granite memorial. The men lost at sea. Only they weren't lost. They were out there somewhere.

"I call Franklin Briggs. I call Mason Tremblay," I yelled. I had no idea if they could hear me. If they did, they gave no sign of it. They made sounds, but not like anything remotely human; it sounded like the screech and chitter of squirrels, only amplified a thousand times. But it was possible the frenzied motion had calmed a little.

"I call my grandfather, Charles McGovern." I looked at Gran. She nodded and came to my side. "I call Simeon Gunn. Simeon Gunn," I cried, "do you want this life for Sean?"

Suddenly, Jax was there beside me.

"What are you doing?"

"Trying to keep you from getting killed," he snarled.

He was in just as much danger as I was. The sight of him seemed to enrage the Glaukos. Jax represented the First Ones who had used them so cruelly. Now that the euphoria of the trapweed was gone, they probably recalled their mistreatment all the more clearly.

He stepped out ahead of me and swept the water before him. "Come out here. The power of your voice is stronger in the water," he shouted.

Jax had created a whirlpool around me, a blue-green wall of water that kept the Glaukos at a safe distance. I stepped deeper into its rushing center and felt the cool strength of it, the endless circle of power that surrounded all life here. The sea. There was calm inside that power. Despite the tempest of savage faces around me, I began to feel stronger.

Bending to immerse myself more fully, I could feel the multitude of disturbances, flutters and cries that vibrated every molecule of water around me. I could hear the Glaukos now. And even though I didn't understand their language, the meaning was clear.

I heard the fear and the hunger and, more than anything else, the pain.

"I'm sorry. I wanted to help you."

The words were so inadequate. There was no reason that they shouldn't kill me.

The whirlpool swirled; through it I could see a parade of monstrous faces that gnashed their teeth at me. Spiked tails flicked in and out, coming ever closer. Jax had once told me the Aitros were immune to the poison of the Glaukos spikes. I hoped I was Aitros enough for that to be true now.

I closed my eyes and raised my face from the center of the swirling eddy.

"Listen to me."

I remembered what Kephalos had said. It wasn't about the decibels. I had to focus my thoughts on what I wanted. I couldn't just scream a command at them. They needed calming. They needed strength. What could I possibly say that would reach them?

Or maybe I could sing. Old school, as Kephalos had called it. But what?

Of course. There was only one. How many times had they heard it in the Snug? They would all know it.

In a low, wavering voice I began:

"From old Long Wharf the Dover *sailed out of Boston town . . ."*

Focus. *My voice is my will.*

I closed my eyes and tried to put into my voice everything that was good about Trespass. The strength and courage, the independence. Everything these men had lost. They had had to rely on the trapweed for strength. Now that was gone.

I had to give them something else.

"With linen, wool and guns and gold for the
    British Crown.
Halifax they'll never see; the Dover's *taken*
    down.
The compass spins from north to south with
    Trespass on the lee,
But a Trespass sailor never drowns; he's only lost
    at sea.
The compass spins from north to south with
    Trespass on the lee,
But a Trespass sailor never drowns; he's only lost
    at sea."

Everything was quiet. I opened my eyes.

The Glaukos stood waist-deep in the water. Line after line of them. There were hundreds. Their black hunched forms were still and the agonized screams in their own strange language had stopped. They stood exhausted, transfixed.

They were listening to me.

Sean stepped forward. He looked so different from the

332

handsome young guy I'd first seen hauling traps onto his boat. His body was darker and bulkier and the bones of his face stood out too starkly. But his eyes were the same warm brown. And they were kind and strong. It was really Sean.

I hugged him close to me.

"Tell me what you want us to do," he said. "I can make them understand now. I'll help."

CHAPTER 39

The Glaukos fought off the Icers, all of them, driving them from the beaches and from the waters around Trespass. They fought beside the First Ones and islanders as the free men they were. The Glaukos responded to my song, *their song,* with honor and courage. By morning they had cleared the beach of the dead bodies of the Icers and all was quiet.

But by morning everything else had changed too. The pretty island of Trespass was gone. Or at least, it was nothing like it had been before. For once, Wreck Beach looked its name. It was covered with debris. Shattered trees, their roots yanked from the earth in massive wedges of soil, rolled in on the surf. The homes that had once lined the cliffs were no more than piles of lumber. The dock and most of the fishing boats had been destroyed. Vast portions of the interior of the island had simply collapsed and were still settling.

And according to reports, the Hundred Hands was gone. The stone coral reef that had entrapped so many sailors over the decades had simply disappeared.

The reef wasn't the only thing that was missing.

No one had seen Ben Deare since the night before.

I had a theory about that. Or a prayer. It was possible that opening the Archelon had somehow broken the curse that held him tied to Trespass Island. Maybe the crew of the *Dover* was resting now, with their faithful captain, Benjamin Deare. I would miss Ben, but I hoped that he'd found peace.

As the weary survivors gathered on Wreck Beach, they were joined by the very beings who had once tried to oppress them. The First Ones gathered here too. Many, including Mikos, had died fighting the Icers, as Lukus told me when he stepped onto the beach. The clan leader looked so different from when I had seen him last. His glittering garments were reduced to bloody rags, and the losses from his people were evident in the lines of pain across his face.

The clan would have to be told of Xarras's betrayal, but not today. And certainly not by me. For now it would be enough to deal with other things. Because with the destruction of the underground sea tunnels and caves, the Aitros were essentially homeless. As were the islanders.

I sat on a fallen pine tree, watching the waves and wondering again at the sea's amazing changes. It was the most beautiful color I'd ever seen. A soft turquoise blue, with diamonds of sunlight on every ripple.

A familiar form ran toward me down the beach and I laughed, then winced at the pain in my lips. It was Buddy. The dog sniffed his way around me and then pushed his head into my armpit until I put my arms around him. "I'm glad to see you too," I murmured into his fur.

Sean stood before me. "Buddy, down."

I didn't want to stare at Sean, but I couldn't help it. His skin was darkly burnished to a coppery brown. He'd lost nearly all of his hair, but his skull was finely molded and still very human-looking. Still he moved with the same ease that he'd always had. And his eyes held none of the stark yellow gleam of the Glaukos.

He was alive. It was enough. But I wondered what changes the trapweed had made inside. And if they were permanent. Would he ever be the same again? Dumb question. None of us would.

"What will you do now?" I asked him.

Sean sat beside me and leaned back, his eyes on the sea. "We'll rebuild. It'll be home again. For all of us. Buddy. Dude. Cut it out," he said, laughing and nearly losing his balance against the canine show of affection.

I smiled at the two of them. It was definitely Sean. The heart of him, anyway.

Reilly and Zuzu appeared, walking down the beach. Reilly's lanky form seemed to dwarf Zuzu's, and he kept a protective arm around her shoulder.

"You're both okay?" I asked anxiously.

Zuzu lifted her chin with a spark of her old sassy attitude. "Of course we're okay. It would take more than a few Icers to mess with Reilly and me. Ouch." She rubbed a bruise on her elbow.

"Easy there, warrior princess," said Reilly in a gently chiding tone. "Why don't you sit down. Take a load off."

My eyes searched the water. I hadn't seen Jax since he'd created the whirlpool to protect me from the Glaukos. Where was he?

I couldn't think about what might have happened. I wouldn't let my mind go there. He had to be okay. In the trauma of the past day's events there had been no time to tell him—

Please. Let him be okay.

Restless, I stood and went to Gran, who sat on a driftwood log nearby. Her braid was disheveled, with gray hair sticking out in all directions, but otherwise she looked remarkably okay. She held a piece of rope in her hand. "Might as well get busy tying a net," she muttered, settling her elbows on her knees and tossing the rope with expert turns. "We could catch some crabs for dinner." She looked around. "Ed Barney," she called out, squinting her good eye at the mayor. "Why don't you make yourself useful and build a fire over there? There's a good man."

"Shouldn't you rest, Gran?" I asked, giving her a hug.

"Nonsense. I never felt better. And there's all these folks to feed."

Maybe my grandmother had some supernatural powers of her own. I nodded. "Just keep going, right?"

"That's right," she said with a smile.

Something made me turn suddenly back to the water. A sense. A knowing.

The moment Jax emerged from the sea I felt my heart contract in one sudden, fierce beat of joy. I leapt up and ran to him.

I splashed through the waves and hugged him so hard that I knocked both of us into the water. He smiled, then held me on his chest as he floated on his back. His blue eyes searched my face soberly.

"You look very happy this morning," he said. "Does causing mass destruction always please you so much?"

"I'm sorry. I had no choice but to open the Archelon. It was the only way—" I broke off.

"To save my life."

"Yes," I said softly. "And it turns out that it was nothing. The legends of some great power source left by the gods were nothing but stories."

"There is power here," said Jax with a thoughtful gaze around us. "More than even my father could have ever imagined. Your own transformation is evidence of it. Will you stay here and help me find it, my siren?"

"Your siren?" I asked, making my expression dubious, even as my insides were humming with pleasure.

"My Lander, then," he murmured, touching his lips gently to mine.

I shook my head. "Sorry. We're going to drop the whole First Ones and Landers thing around here. We're going to live together, work together. One big happy dysfunctional family."

"Then there is only one thing left to call you."

"Not your she-devil." I planted my hands on his chest and pushed, sending him under the surface.

Jax laughed, then shook his head, sending sparkling droplets of the sea from his hair. He stood up and wrapped his arms around me. *"Kardia mou,"* he whispered, kissing the corner of my mouth with a gentle, grazing caress. "My heart." He touched a finger as lightly as a breath to the wounds on my upper and lower lips, and his expression darkened.

"If only I could undo this," he said.

I shook my head. "I wouldn't want you to. The marks will be there to remind me."

"Of what?"

"To never let anyone silence me again."

He touched his forehead to mine. "They would be fools to try."

Maybe it had been a mistake for me to come to Trespass Island. But there was no place in the world I would ever love more. And it would be home again someday. To all of us.

It seemed only natural I would feel salt water on my face as Jax held me close. But it was warm, and it flowed from my eyes.

I was home. No mistake.

ACKNOWLEDGMENTS

Even a labor of love is, well, *a labor*. For this book, however, my labor was made infinitely lighter by the help of many. To my agent, Ted Malawer of the Upstart Crow Literary Agency, many warm thanks for your superb insights, unflagging enthusiasm, and expertise. You're simply a treasure. To my Delacorte Press editor, Michelle Poploff, and her assistant, Rebecca Short, thank you for seeing the story before it was even there, encouraging me to find it and then making it so much better. Also to Trish Parcell, who designed the beautiful cover that brings this story to life in a magical way, thank you. To my wonderful writing friends and critique partners: Angie Frazier, Sonia Gensler, Kim Harrington, and Dawn Metcalf, thank you all for the inspiration, kicks in the butt, advice, and sometimes even brownies. To my long-distance-but-never-forgotten friend of writing and so much more, Marissa Goodell, thank you for allowing me to borrow a name and make up my own little jewel. I'd also like to thank my family. To Ronald and Pat Guibord, my terrific in-laws: you've always been a blessing to me; thank you for everything. Lastly, thanks go to my husband, Ron, and my kids, Luke, Genny and Danielle. Without your support and tolerance of an untidy house and lots of take-out, this book would not exist. I love you all.

ABOUT THE AUTHOR

Maurissa Guibord has been addicted to stories since she read *The Three Musketeers* in seventh grade and fell in love with d'Artagnan. Since then she's been infatuated with lots of fictional characters, and now things have progressed to the point where she's writing about them. Her first book for young adults was *Warped*. Maurissa lives on the coast of Maine with her three children, her husband, and a black cat named Shady. Please visit her website at maurissaguibord.com.